Hometown Prophet

Jeff Fulmer

To Sonja

"Only in his hometown and in his own house is a prophet without honor."

Jesus

PROLOGUE

Young, nubile bodies in swimsuits strained to hold themselves over a slime-filled pool. Clinging to ropes for support, thin torsos twisted and turned this way and that. With a yelp, a young woman slipped and dropped, plopping into waist-high goo.

"Ha!" Ms. Quell cackled. "That was Tiffany. She had it coming."

Peter nodded, half absently. Watching TV with his mom was becoming a nightly ritual. Not a good sign.

"You need to meet a nice girl like Britney," Ms. Quell announced.

It took Peter a moment to realize his mom was referring to a girl on the show—a former model with a heart of gold and a fierce grip on her rope.

"Yeah," Peter agreed. "I'm sure she'd go for a thirty-one-year-old guy who's living at home with his mother."

"Oh, once she got to know you, she would like you," Ms. Quell reassured him.

With a shake of his head, he laughed to keep from crying.

At a commercial break, Ms. Quell motioned to the magazine-strewn coffee table. "There was something in the mail today for you."

Under the day's haul of junk mail was a typed letter with a corporate logo in the left-hand corner. Running a finger along the sealed flap, Peter unfolded the crisp stationary.

Thank you for your interest.... The position you applied for has been filled by someone much better than you.... Something to that effect.

Apparently, Peter's apologetic-sounding cover letter had failed to explain away the gaps in his resume. There had been a decent job or two in his past that, suffice it to say, had not worked out. His last job had been in California with a start-up that had never gotten off the ground. When the money ran out, he had limped back home.

Home was Franklin, Tennessee, a suburb just outside of Nashville. *Home* was also the house he grew up in, where his mother still lived.

"Don't worry," Ms. Quell said, having interpreted her son's defeated slouch. "You'll find something."

Spotting his keys among the magazines and mail, Peter grabbed them and stood up.

"Where are you going?" Ms. Quell asked, alarmed.

"I don't know," Peter answered, making his way to the door.

"Be home early," she called after him, just before the front door shut. "We have church tomorrow."

In the driveway, Peter got into his beat-up VW. Where was he even going? Anywhere but here. Maybe he'd do something crazy, like get a beer. Or really go crazy and sneak a cigarette.

After Peter turned the key, the car sluggishly chugged before essentially rolling over and playing dead. Vigorously pumping the gas pedal as he cranked the ignition only managed to flood the engine.

Another laugh leaked out of Peter, and then a muffled cry—more like a sob.

With a glance around to make sure neighbors weren't watching, Peter wiped at his face, got out of the car, and walked stoically back up the sidewalk.

Back inside the house, only a couple of bodies were hanging from the ropes now.

"That was fast," Ms. Quell commented without looking away from the TV.

"My battery is dead," Peter said, passing in front of the object of his mother's attention.

"Maybe God doesn't want you to go out tonight," Ms. Quell declared. "Sit down." She motioned to the couch. "It's between Britney and Roger."

As tempting as it was to stick around to see if his future wife won the competition, Peter turned to go up the stairs. "I'm going to turn in."

"I want you to go to church with me tomorrow."

A disagreeable sound came from the top of the stairwell.

"I don't have many rules while you are here," Ms. Quell called after him. The upstairs door shut firmly behind Peter, but he could still hear his mother's voice: "But church is one of them!"

Upstairs, Peter flicked on the lamp and surveyed the walls of his room. Red and white ribbons, along with the rare blue, dangled from his dresser mirror as faded reminders of his community swim team mediocrity.

His high school and college diplomas hung next to another framed piece of paper verifying his completion of the "Christian Youth Leadership Conference," a two-week summer workshop he'd attended despite his protests when he was seventeen.

The other side of the room featured a poster of a woman in a form-fitting swimsuit standing statuesque beside a Porsche parked on the beach. That one picture managed to eloquently encapsulate most of his adolescent aspirations. Maybe he had subconsciously followed her to California. And yet, he had ended up as far as humanly possible from that scene.

Imprisoned in his childhood room, Peter was having trouble even imagining a scenario in which his life would improve.

Peter knew in Eastern religions, the ego had to be extinguished in order for one to attain enlightenment. Christ essentially said the same thing with Zen gems like, "The man who loves his life will lose it..."

Peter had always thought he had a basic understanding of these concepts. Only now did he have a true appreciation for the words spoken by another thirty-year-old bachelor who had lived with his mother. Living at home was truly a slow, painful death.

As he traced his past failures to his present predicament, he experienced an almost overwhelming desire to get everything out. Not knowing what else to do, he got out of bed, knelt down, and began to pray.

Unanswered pleas gave way to silent screams, and something that had been building up inside of him burst open and flooded out.

"What am I supposed to do?" Peter cried. "What is it you want me to do? Because I'll do it! Just tell me, or show me. Just give me a chance. Please!"

After the fairly exhausting purge of pent-up emotions, he was hit with a rush of embarrassment. If he had truly been heard by the Creator of the Universe, his plea must have sounded like the petulant demands of a petty child. Still, if nothing else, it had been a cathartic release.

Turning the lamp off and climbing into his twin bed, Peter suddenly felt very sleepy.

That night, he had a dream.

CHAPTER 1

Saturday, July 19
Red round room. Four doors—all locked. Can't get out—scared.
I'm pounding on one of the doors. Finally, it opens—and Pastor Dan is
*there! He's wearing a dress—for the hospital. *Very Real, Intense!*

Propped up in bed, Peter scribbled the cryptic fragment into a red
spiral notebook, worn and crinkled from early morning note-taking
sessions and otherwise known as his "dream journal."

He'd read somewhere that noted psychiatrist Carl Jung had used
a dream journal. Maybe if he kept one, too, over time he could detect
some sort of subconscious pattern, break a code that would tell him
what to do to fix his broken life. Unfortunately, up to this point, all he
had was page after page of weird, random vignettes that added up to an
abstract mess, much like his actual life.

If nothing else, the exercise of faithfully opening his notebook
every morning and straining to catch the last few drops of nocturnal
memories had improved his recall. Now he was usually able to excavate

at least two or three complete artifacts before the delicate strands broke away and the dreams dissolved into dust.

This latest "red room" dream was different, though. There was no way he could forget it. He had woken up immediately after it was over; the ultra-vivid, Technicolor movie had still been reeling in his head. The claustrophobic feeling of being trapped had come back to him—he'd felt this way just before Dr. Dan Cox had made a guest appearance, opening the door and presumably setting him free.

Peter hadn't seen his pastor since he'd been home, and he wondered if the dream was a sign he needed to make an appearance at church. Since he wasn't going back to sleep anyway, he drifted into the shower.

Raising his head, he let warm water douse what was left of his thinning hair. He was just starting to relax when a hard knock sounded through the bathroom door.

"Peter!" Ms. Quell's voice rang out. "Are you in the shower?"

"Yes!" he answered.

"Are you going to church with me?" she asked.

"Yes," he snapped, annoyed by the intrusion. "I'll be down in a minute."

Not sure when church started, he hurriedly lathered, rinsed, and dried off. Making sure the coast was clear, he jogged back to his bedroom where he dressed in casual business attire. Downstairs, he found his mom in the kitchen making her final preparations for departure.

"I'm glad you decided to go," Ms. Quell said, moving to the coffee maker. "I think you'll be glad you did. I know Dan will be glad to see you again."

"Actually, I had a weird dream about him last night," Peter said.

"Dan Cox? What was it about?" she asked, handing him a cup of coffee.

Taking the coffee to the kitchen table, Peter thought back. "It started with me being in this red, round room. When I tried to leave, the doors were locked. So, I was knocking, but no one answered. I kind

2

of got panicky and started pounding on the doors. Finally, one opened, and Dr. Cox was standing there in one of those—What do you call them? The robes they give you at the hospital?"

"Hospital gowns," his mom volunteered.

"That's it," Peter said, taking his first shot of caffeine. "But it was different than a normal dream. I knew I was dreaming and—it just seemed important," he added, not feeling like he was doing the experience justice.

Going back for a second sip, Peter suddenly proclaimed, "Lucid! Lucid dreaming."

Ms. Quell gave a thoughtful *Hmm*, adding, "Maybe you should tell Dan about it."

"I wouldn't know what to say," Peter shrugged. "Besides, I don't know what it means. It probably doesn't mean anything." As he spoke the last words, they seemed to catch in his throat.

"I don't know," his mom said. "Dan is a big believer in prophecy."

"Good for him," Peter managed.

"I'm just saying, Dan would believe you," she said as her gaze rose over her son's head to the hands on the face on the wall. "We need to hurry if we're going to make eleven o' clock."

Peter nodded, not completely thrilled about accompanying his mother to church. Without a running car, he didn't have much of a choice.

The thirty-minute commute to Nashville gave Ms. Quell time to bring her son up to speed on the latest church news, which could sometimes be confused with gossip.

"Some say Dan's message just isn't as strong as it was, and a lot of people have started going to Grace," she said, referring to an upstart church much closer to their home. "They say that Rick—he's the preaching pastor at Grace—has the anointing, and his church has been growing like crazy. A lot of the musicians have started going over there, like Patrick Omega and Jordan Stone."

Ms. Quell emphasized the latter name for Peter's benefit, since he had known Jordan when they were in Trinity's youth group together.

Jordan had always seemed more mature than their two-year-age difference should have led to. Tongue-tied around her, Peter had found it easier to just steer clear. In fact, they had only talked a handful of times in the six years of Sunday mornings and Wednesday nights they had spent together.

On youth retreats or mid-week Bible studies, the self-assured Jordan often broke out a guitar and led worship, occasionally working in her own material. While her songs were all sickly sweet rhyming couplets of devotion, Peter always thought she somehow managed to make them sound sexy. The root of the sin, he knew, was in his own dirty mind.

A year after Peter left for college, Jordan released her debut album that went platinum, and overnight she became Christian music's "Little Miss Sweetheart." And the hits kept coming, along with Dove Awards, music videos, and arena tours.

While Peter would have preferred to avoid all news of Jordan's sky-rocketing career, his mom took it upon herself to keep him posted on her every achievement. So, despite attempts otherwise, he was something of an expert on Jordan Stone, Christian Superstar.

The fact that she no longer attended Trinity was actually a welcome bit of Jordan news. If he had been intimidated by her when they were just two high school kids, he wasn't sure he could handle running into her now that she was as successful as he was not. If he never saw her again, it would be just fine with him.

The faces he passed were friendly, just not familiar, as he followed his mom through the lobby. After they took their seats near the back, Peter looked around and saw that, with a couple of exceptions, Trinity had regenerated itself into a completely different body of believers.

Trinity preached a subtle brand of fundamentalism that he had spent the last decade trying to exorcise. It was also the kind of place where miracles could happen any given Sunday and God had a special purpose for each person—at least as long as you continued to attend Trinity.

Big screens to the sides of the stage projected inspiring nature scenes of waterfalls and sunsets captioned with song lyrics. Following along, Peter mouthed the often-repeated choruses that seemed intent on making absolutely sure God knew everyone really, really loved Him. The worship service went from song to song like an improvisational jam session, sprinkled with the spontaneous chattering of tongues throughout.

"Abbadada Shekonopre…"

Peter had heard it all before. Still, it had been a while, and the halting foreign language seemed more abrasive and abrupt than he remembered. Some of the people who were raising their seemingly incomprehensible voices to God were the same ones raising their hands. Wondering if there was a correlation, he briefly contemplated lifting his own hands just to see what would happen, but he couldn't go through with it.

After the marathon of songs, dancers sprung down the aisle carrying long poles with banners embroidered with words like "Yahweh" and "Hallelujah." As the flag team gathered at the foot of the stage, they twirled and swirled their words of praise, more or less, in unison.

The routine had clearly been choreographed while allowing room for individual interpretation should the Spirit move a particular participant. A couple of overzealous church members jumped up and joined the dancers in the front—badly embarrassing themselves, in Peter's opinion.

The music swelled, signaling the congregation to take it up a notch, which seemed irresponsible and possibly dangerous. On the verge of erupting into anarchy, voices rose, tongues clattered, and arms stretched toward the heavens.

A large woman standing in the front row of the balcony shouted something along the lines of, "Our worship is a perfumed aroma to the foul stench of the world outside." In a moment of ecstasy, she almost fell over the railing.

Gently, the music began to slow and soften, and the congregation

5

settled down. A person who had been "slain in the spirit" and was prostrate in the aisle next to Peter calmly got to his feet and, with a polite smile, smoothed his pants before finding his seat.

A "Thank you, Jesus" or two got in just under the wire as the beaming Dr. Dan Cox bounded out onto the stage in a relatively formal coat and tie. In his sixties now, Dan still seemed amazingly spry. With a full head of thick gray hair and matching wild, woolly eyebrows, he looked like a kindly, absentminded professor or an old country doctor.

Holding a big paw up to God and simultaneously quieting the crowd, the preacher was clearly totally at home in front of his church.

"Good morning, brothers and sisters," he boomed to a smattering of applause. "God is good, isn't He?" More applause of agreement followed as Dan lowered his palm.

"Yes, He is, and we know this not because we can comprehend Him with our intellects. We know this because we feel it in our hearts." His finger tapped at the red tie on his chest. "You know, I had a whole sermon prepared, but my heart is telling me we have something more important to discuss."

Like a captain scouring the horizon, Dan gazed out over the sea of faces. "I feel like we have people here that desperately need to hear from God; they need to turn their hearts to God. Perhaps they've never accepted Jesus, not really. For others, their hearts have turned cold."

Closing his eyes, he held up his hand like it was an antenna receiving a message. "I believe there is a woman suffering a great deal of physical pain in her lower abdomen. She's desperate for relief."

No one immediately responded, which didn't seem to bother Dan in the least. "And there is a man who has lost his family. He did some things to drive them away. Today, he needs redemption. He needs Christ."

Two different men raised their hands.

The list of needs went on with various people responding and prayers being offered. Peter had seen Dan do this many times before.

Taking a tiny pew pencil, he started doodling on his bulletin.

"There a young man who hasn't been here for a long time." Abruptly, Peter put the pencil down. Pacing the stage, Dan looked in his general direction. "Like the prodigal son, he has returned home a broken man."

Shifting in his seat, Peter slumped a little lower.

"This young brother feels lost and trapped," Dan continued. "He is looking for a way out."

Peter flushed as he felt his mom looking over at him. Did everyone know it was him? Should he raise his hand or stand up? Was this his chance to break out of the red room?

Before he could find his feet, Dan had moved on to another hurting soul. While Dan prophesized, questions filled Peter's head. *Did God whisper into Dan's ear about me? Does God really know and care about my circumstances? If so, I have to respond, don't I?*

As he always did, Dan ended the service with an invitation to come forward to receive Christ or, if that base was covered, confess your sins. A tide of parishioners flowed down the aisles while Dan, along with several elders, stood in front of the stage.

Without thinking about it, Peter found himself standing up and sliding past his startled mom. As if he was watching his body from a distance, he found himself halfway down the aisle before he even thought about what he was doing.

The line to see Dan was twice as long as the ones to see the other elders. Planting himself at the end of the row, Peter contemplated what he would say to his pastor. Should he tell him he was the prodigal son who was trapped? Should he confess his sins?

Was there time to confess his sins?

A few people in line in front of him had given up on seeing the preacher and peeled off to see other elders or decided their sins could wait until next Sunday. Peter remained steadfast, slowly making his way down the aisle until he was next in line.

From a few feet away, he watched as his pastor listened intently to the woman ahead of him. As the woman described her appendicitis,

Dan became momentarily distracted and, almost imperceptibly, winced.

It was in that moment that Peter's perspective shifted, and he realized he was looking at his dream backwards. He wasn't here for himself. He was here for Dan.

After a short prayer, the woman took her leave as Dan took a moment to loosen the knot on his tie. Looking up, his eyes crinkled from the warmth of his smile.

"Peter!" his old pastor beamed, motioning him forward. "I didn't know you were back in town. How are you?"

"I'm fine," Peter said, realizing he'd already told a lie. "Not really," he corrected himself. "I'm living at home with Mom."

Dan nodded gravely, understanding his plight.

"That's not why I'm here. Listen, I had a dream last night," Peter continued, leaning in a little closer. "And you were in it."

Dan's eyebrows raised into fuzzy arches as confusion played over his face.

"I dreamed I was in a locked red room, and I couldn't get out. I was knocking on the door, and when it finally opened, you were there in a hospital gown."

Under a furrowed brow, Dan's eyebrows were knitted into a headband of consternation.

"I know this sounds weird, but I just got the feeling that my dream had something to do with your heart, your literal heart. Like, maybe you should get it checked out."

Dan was nodding seriously. "Okay," he half croaked. The bold timbre in his voice had washed away.   Now, he was just a man lost in reflective thought. "Thank you for sharing that."

Then, just as quickly, Dan the Preacher Man was back. With a broad smile, he wrapped an arm around his parishioner in an enthusiastic side hug. "Glad to have you back, Peter! Let's get together soon!"

"Okay," Peter mumbled, grateful to be finished with this strange mission.

As soon as Dan released him, Peter walked briskly up the aisle of the nearly deserted church.

His mom, who had been waiting and watching from her back pew, got up as he hurried passed her on his way to the lobby. "How did it go?" she asked, trying to catch up.

"About as well as telling someone about a dream can go," Peter replied without stopping.

CHAPTER 2

Since moving back in with his mother, Peter had committed himself to getting a job and, more importantly, moving out. This involved a hard half hour of searching through job listings almost every day. The rest of the time, he watched TV and played old video games.

Peter felt himself slipping further into a self-imposed isolation. Besides his mom, and sometimes himself, he rarely talked to anyone. He had lost touch with his few friends from high school and, given his current situation, was too embarrassed to reestablish contact.

His parents had divorced when he was twelve years old, and his dad occasionally called from his new home in New York. A corporate consultant, Mr. Quill liked to offer advice from afar, telling his son what he needed to do with his life (*Get a job, an MBA, a girlfriend*), all the while managing to make him feel even more ashamed than he already did for living at home.

When the phone rang on a Saturday night, Peter ignored it; it couldn't be anyone for him, at least not anyone he wanted to talk to. A moment later, he heard his mom calling up to his bedroom, excitement in her voice, "Dad wants to talk to you!"

"Tell him I'm not here," Peter yelled back down.

There was a pause, followed by the sound of steps being taken in rapid succession. A moment later, his mom appeared in the doorway.

"What's the matter with you?" she asked crossly.

"I just don't want to talk to him," Peter said defiantly.

"I don't care what you want," she said sternly, displaying an unusual amount of loyalty to her ex-husband. "You pick up that phone and talk to your pastor."

"My pastor?" Peter said, realizing the mistake. "I thought you said Dad."

"Dan!" she clarified, louder than necessary at that point.

"Okay!" Peter shot back as he trudged across the room and picked up the receiver. "Dr. Cox?" he answered, shooing his mom out with his free hand, then turning his back to her.

"Peter, I wanted to talk to you about the other day. About your dream," Dan said, dispensing with the small talk. "Well, I had actually been meaning to go to my doctor about some chest pains. I'd just been putting it off. Your dream gave me the push I needed. So they ran me through some tests, and, it turns out, I have a blockage."

"Really?" Peter said, his thoughts flashing back to the locked door in the red room. Lost in thought, he almost forgot to ask, "Are you going to be okay?"

"I'm having emergency surgery in a couple of days," Dan said. "The doctor thinks it will be okay, mainly because I caught it in time. I have you to thank for that."

"I didn't do anything," Peter knew to say, having heard hundreds of humble Christian servants in churches and on football fields say the same thing. "It was God."

"Well, will you thank Him for me?" Dan said with a light chuckle. "I am also very grateful to you. You had to be willing to pass the message along."

With no more modest clichés coming to mind, Peter kept his mouth shut.

11

"Anyway, when I'm back on my feet, I'd like to get together with you," Dan said. "Maybe I could take you to lunch or dinner? It's the least I could do."

"Yeah, sure," Peter said. It was kind of a big deal to have a private audience with the pastor. Maybe Dan could hook him up with a job. He knew a lot of people around town. "Well, I'll be praying for your surgery."

"Thank you," Dan said. "And please let me know if you have any more dreams."

"I will," Peter confirmed before hanging up.

"Well, what did he say?"

Peter turned to find his mom still standing at his open door. She looked so hopeful, he decided to forego the lecture on eavesdropping and just give her the news.

"He said he has some heart trouble, a blockage; he's going to have surgery."

"Praise God!" his mom exclaimed, rushing in to hug him. "Oh, not about Dan's heart. You know what I mean. Just that you knew! It's a miracle!"

Despite being a little repulsed by the outburst of emotion, it felt nice to celebrate something, even if it was open heart surgery. Having her adult son move back home had not been easy on Ms. Quill either. After giving them both a moment, Peter pulled away.

Looking into his mother's eyes, moist with renewed faith, he fought the urge to squelch her enthusiasm. Despite his tendency toward cynicism, he had to admit she was right; it was a miracle of sorts. God had used him to possibly save Dan's life, and he didn't want to diminish or dismiss that.

"Yeah," Peter admitted. "It's pretty amazing."

"Oh, yes!" she said, bopping around his room.

Stepping back, he felt slightly overwhelmed by it all. "If you don't mind, I need a few minutes," Peter said, moving her toward the door.

Ms. Quill looked a little hurt, although she was too ebullient to stay down for more than a couple of seconds. "If you want to talk about it, I'll be downstairs," she offered, pausing at the door to give him another heartfelt smile and fist pump.

"Okay," Peter said, shutting the door as soon as she crossed the threshold.

Sitting down on the edge of his bed, he tried to slow everything down, thinking through what had just happened. Was it possible he had gotten lucky? No, there had been something special about that dream, and he knew the information had come from somewhere beyond his own understanding.

Bowing his head, he willed a thought of thanks for being able to help find Dan's blockage. Even so, the unyielding question kept bubbling up inside of him.

Why me?

When an answer didn't come, he repeated his "Thanks," stood up, and stripped down to his boxers. After turning off his light, he climbed underneath the covers and, in a few short minutes, was sound asleep.

As curtains closed on a silent stage, the dreamer became aware a new play was about to begin.

"Peter?" Ms. Quill's high voice sounded hopeful through his bedroom door. "Do you want to go to church this morning?"

"No," he mumbled, just loud enough to be heard.

"I just thought since you went last week—"

"I said no thank you," Peter cut in. Rolling over, he listened to the ensuing heavy sigh on the other side of the door, followed by the creak of retreating steps.

Waiting until he heard the garage door cranking up underneath him, he slipped out of bed and went to the window to watch his mom's car turning out of the driveway. Glancing down at the still open spiral notebook, he thought about last night's entry.

July 26, 2:20?

Walking down the street—to Trinity Church. A "hissing" sound.

13

See a missile before it crashes into side of church. A third of building falls away. Dan walks out of the ruble and dust—looks dazed, confused.

Like last week's "heart" dream, this one stood out like a 3D movie on an IMAX screen. And, once again, Peter had no idea what it meant. The time before, he had found the key to unlocking the meaning at church, and since this one was directly related to Trinity, too, church seemed like the logical place to start. Unlike last time, he would go it alone.

The service was well underway when he slipped into the lobby. Knowing his mom would be sitting in her usual spot toward the back of the main level, Peter took the stairs to the balcony where he found a seat near the top.

He'd conveniently missed all of the singing and made a mental note of the time so he would know when to show up in the future. A white-haired man Peter didn't recognize took the stage and cleared his throat.

"As most of you know, Dan is recovering from heart surgery and will not be here today," the man said into the microphone. "I am pleased to report he is doing well and will be back on his feet in no time."

"Praise God!" shouted a voice from the front.

"Yes, praise God indeed!" the elder said as the "Hallelujah" chorus joined in. "Please continue to lift him up with your prayers." He paused, clearly atwitter with excitement about his next announcement.

"This morning, we are very fortunate to have a special guest. He's written several books, as well as a syndicated column for newspapers around the county. I'm a big fan and am thrilled he is available to be with us today. Please join me in welcoming Mark Shelton."

The slight man who took the stage looked to be in his mid-forties, although his tightly cropped beard may have added a few years. As the applause died, he carefully arranged his well-worn Bible on the podium. Meticulous and thoughtful, he seemed to be the anti-Dan.

"Good morning!" Mark proclaimed in a surprisingly powerful voice. A few "Good mornings" echoed back. "It's an honor to speak to you today." Seemingly out of the blue, he asked, "Do you know how to boil a frog, ladies and gentlemen?"

He allowed a pause for what Peter assumed was a rhetorical question.

When no one took the bait, he answered, "If you drop a frog into a pot of boiling water, that frog will jump right back out because it's hot. But if you place a frog in a pot of lukewarm water and *slowly* turn up the heat, that same frog will just sit there and let you boil him alive."

Mark scanned the crowd. "We are in a boiling pot right now, and we think it's a just a hot tub." This elicited a snicker from someone. Mark whipped around at the sound. "Let me put it another way," he continued. "We are in the midst of a war!"

The bombshell left the audience more confused. Were we in a hot tub or a war?

"The truth is, there is a cultural war going on all around us," Mark explained. "It's invisible because it's so pervasive. The enemy has cloaked its attack because if we don't see it, we won't fight against it. And that's exactly what Satan wants!"

As the image of war played through Peter's mind, he could almost hear an ammo belt being fed through a machine gun in the background.

"Christianity is under attack from every side," the man with absolute moral certitude proclaimed. "What passes for primetime entertainment would be pornography to our parents' generation. If you think the sex and violence on TV and video games are not corrupting our kids, you need to wake up."

Mark looked around as if hoping someone would challenge him. No one did.

"We have men joining in holy matrimony with men. We have men and women and even children changing sexes. And we still kill unborn babies in this country. Unborn babies!"

15

Several "Amens" added to the already charged air.

"We are slipping closer and closer to Sodom and Gomorrah, and we don't even know it!"

The substitute pastor stepped back, obviously upset by the wretched state of the affairs. After taking a moment to collect himself, he forged on.

"The federal government is stripping away your rights as free citizens. They have enslaved the poor in a cycle of poverty they call 'welfare.' And, if we allow them, they will enslave everyone else under a burden of taxes and regulations."

The sermon went on to explain how the US-of-A was replacing God with Big Brother. This naturally set the stage for the anti-Christ and Armageddon and other bad things to follow. Finally, the general ended his assault with a call to arms.

"In the lobby, there is a table where I have a few things for sale. Now, you don't need to buy anything. If I was motivated by money, there are a lot of other things I could be doing." He chuckled knowingly, as if Goldman Sachs was holding a partnership for him.

"But if you agree with even part of what I'm saying, just stop by and write down your email or your phone number." Putting some steel back in his friendly voice, he concluded, "If you sense something is wrong with this country—with this world—sign up. Stand up and be counted in the war on Christianity!"

In the lobby, two women worked a cafeteria-table-sized booth stacked with books and CDs and bumper stickers. As they exchanged money and swiped credit cards, Mark stood behind his bunker of promotional items, chatting it up with a man who was nodding vigorously.

A clipboard was passed Peter's way.

"Hey, sign this—and put down your email!" a bald man ordered.

"I don't have email," Peter said before turning away. "It's a government plot."

Pushing through the swinging glass doors, the early afternoon

16

sunshine temporarily blinded Peter. Tired, hungry, and exasperated, he leaned against a brick column and closed his eyes. Feeling like he'd been through a battle, an old habit reasserted itself in the form of a craving for a cigarette.

"Peter?"

Shielding his eyes, Peter tried to get a glimpse of the figure who apparently knew him.

"Peter Quill, is that you?"

"Yeah," Peter said, as the person stepped forward under the eaves and into the shadows. A filled-out version of a face from his youth group days came back to him.

That gaping grin had always reminded Peter of the way a coyote might smile at a sheep.

"Are you visiting?" Tom asked.

"No, I moved back," Peter said vaguely. While Tom waited for more, Peter switched the topic away from himself. "So, you're still going to Trinity?"

"I visit around," Tom said with a shrug. "I heard Mark was preaching here today and wanted to check it out. Pretty powerful stuff, huh?" he added with enthusiasm.

Peter nodded, albeit weakly.

As if on cue, Ms. Quill appeared beside her son.

"Peter? You came to church?" she asked, as if witnessing another miracle. "You should have told me. We could have ridden together."

"Hi, Ms. Quill!" Tom said, all teeth. Turning back to Peter, he added, "I couldn't believe it when I saw this guy."

"Yeah, it's really me," Peter said flatly.

"So where are you living?" Tom asked, clearly having already figured it out and just wanting to hear it out loud.

"I'm staying at home right now," Peter said, looking over at his mom. "I'll probably start looking for a place pretty soon."

"That's cool," Tom said. "I just bought a condo in Green Hills. When you're ready to buy, let me know. I'll give you the name of my realtor. She'll hook you up."

"Yeah," Peter said, anxious to have this conversation concluded. "I'll be sure to do that."

"So, what are you doing, brother?" Tom asked, getting back to the inquisition. "Where are you working?"

"Ah, nowhere at the moment," Peter said, trying to suppress a hard swallow.

"Peter is helping me around the house right now," Ms. Quill graciously offered.

Tom nodded, a smirk still plastered to his face. "He's a good son."

"Okay," Peter said, putting an end to this. "I'll see you around."

"Good seeing you, Tommy," Ms. Quill said as sweetly as humanly possible before starting down the concrete steps with Peter following along. Turning back to her son, she added, not too quietly, "Still a twit, isn't he?"

CHAPTER 3

Between the one-way streets outside and the confusing corridors inside, Peter was beginning to feel like Baptist Hospital was a maze, and he wasn't a very smart mouse. When he finally located room 544, he was so relieved he just gave a cursory knock before going in.

As he entered, five or six well-wishers turned in unison to examine him with blank stares.

"Is this Dan Cox's room?" Peter asked.

"Who goes there?" The question came from the bed in the center of the group. The curtain of visitors parted, revealing a pasty Dan Cox in a supine position. The pastor managed a smile as he struggled to sit up a bit.

"Peter!" the pastor said with effort. "Good to see you."

"Good to see you, too, Dr. Cox," Peter said, keeping a respectful distance. Glancing at the others, he added, "I can come back later."

"No, stay," Dan insisted. "We were just finishing up."

Peter hung back as each visitor took his or her turn to say a blessing or a word of encouragement over their minister. Dan took it all in, telling each person how much he appreciated them coming by; even flat on his back, he could still work a crowd.

When the last person left, Peter moved closer to Dan and noticed he was wearing a hospital gown, just as he had dreamed. The normally robust man of God now seemed frail, his gray hair tussled, his eyes watery.

"How are you feeling?" Peter asked quietly.

"Pretty good, considering," Dan said. "They said it was a successful surgery." Reaching out with his hand that was connected to an IV, he clutched Peter's own hand. "Thank you again."

"I'm just glad you're going to be okay."

"The doc says I need to take it easy," Dan said, a twinkle finding its way into his weary eyes. "Of course, that's not going to be easy for me."

"No," Peter agreed. With concern for his passionate pastor, his attention drifted over to the heart monitor and the vitals.

"You look like you have something on your mind," Dan observed. Half-jokingly, he asked, "You haven't had another dream, have you?"

"Well..." Peter pulled his eyes away from the beeping heart to look tentatively at Dan. "Maybe?"

"That sounds like you did, you just don't want to tell me," Dan astutely observed. His eyes flickered with anticipation; his hand gave Peter's a small squeeze. "Tell me."

Thinking back, Peter took a breath. "Well, okay. I dreamed Trinity was under attack. It seemed like a missile hit it—and about a third of the building went down. You came out looking kind of dazed, but okay."

"What do you think it means?" the pastor asked, looking concerned.

"I went to church on Sunday, hoping to hear something that might help me make sense of it."

"Mark Shelton was preaching," Dan said matter-of-factly.

"Yeah, he kept talking about cultural warfare," Peter said. "And it just came to me—this attack has something to do with him."

Dan's caterpillar-sized eyebrows inched together to form a long worm of worry. "How would he attack us?"

"I'm not sure," Peter admitted. "Do you think he would come out against Trinity? Or you?"

"Oh, I don't think so," Dan said, shaking his head slightly. "If Mark thinks someone isn't doing right, he'll call them out, but I don't think we have any major disagreements."

"I keep thinking, my last dream warned you about something that was going to happen, and you were able to prevent it."

"I don't know what any action of prevention on my end would be," Dan confessed, clearly troubled by the news. It made Peter sorry he had brought up his dream to the man who was still recovering, especially if there was nothing he could do about it.

With neither man having any insights, they both fell silently into their own thoughts. It seemed to Peter that Dan was growing weaker by the minute. He'd just had major surgery, but there was more to it than that. He almost seemed afraid of Mark.

"Well, I appreciate you coming here and sharing this with me," Dan finally concluded, again clasping Peter's forearm with his large hand, the tube jutting out of his vein. "You can be sure I will pray on this."

"Okay," Peter said gently. "Get some rest."

"You know," Dan said, his eyelids growing heavy, "you may have a real gift."

"Oh, no," Peter objected. "I've just had a couple of dreams."

"But that's what prophets do, my boy," Dan said, patting his arm. "They have dreams or visions or hear voices." His eyelids flickered. "Then they pass the messages along to whoever needs to hear them. And that's exactly what you're doing."

"I'm still no prophet," Peter insisted. "Sometimes I'm not even sure I believe in God."

"God doesn't need you to believe in Him," Dan insisted. "He can still use you."

Peter stayed quiet, trying to understand this gift he didn't deserve.

"I'm not trying to talk you into it," Dan continued. "It's not a job any sane person would want. In Matthew 23: 34, Jesus says, 'Therefore, I am sending prophets and wise men and teachers. Some of them you will kill and crucify; others you will flog in your synagogues and pursue them from town to town.'"

"No, thanks," Peter said.

"But if you have a gift, it may not be easy to get out of it," Dan warned with a far-away, medicated smile. "Just ask Jonah." And with that, the older man closed his eyes; the fuzzy caterpillar eyebrows curled up and rested comfortably on his forehead.

Backing away from the bed, Peter tiptoed across the room and closed the heavy door as quietly as he could.

As soon as he got back to the house, Peter went upstairs and straight to his Bible. With concentrated effort, he began flipping through the concordance, looking up scriptures pertaining to prophets.

Dan was right. Being a prophet was the most dismal job description he'd ever read. If you only got flogged and chased out of town, you were having a pretty good day.

Peter hoped the passage was primarily to detour people from that line of work. After all, God wouldn't want a bunch of want-to-be prophets and self-proclaimed wise men running around, telling everyone else what to do.

Maybe he was getting ahead of himself. While Dan was a sweet man, he was an evangelical preacher who threw around words like "prophecy" and "miracles" a little loosely. And Peter was not a Daniel or a Jeremiah or a Jonah. He was just Peter, and he probably would never have another dream.

August 4

A young woman plays the guitar in front of a large crowd. I can't see her face because my POV is behind her, facing the audience. She finishes up, and everyone applauds. She puts the guitar down, bows, and walks off.

I follow her off stage.

It's dark backstage—although there's a door with a bright star on it. As I open it, the woman from the stage is there with her back to me again. There is a baby in her arms. In the background, the crowd calls for an encore—"Jordan! Jordan!"

Looking over the page in his journal, Peter sighed. He wasn't sure what to make of the latest entry. All he knew for sure was it had definitely been one of *those dreams*, only this one featured a new "star," Jordan Stone.

Since he didn't really know her anymore, he wasn't sure what to do with this bit of cryptic information. Even if he knew how to reach her, he would prefer not to see her, especially at this low point in his life.

Still mulling it over, he stumbled downstairs to the kitchen. Coffee was in the pot, and the red light was on, indicating his mom was still in the house. Once she left for work, she would turn off the coffeemaker and every other electronic device that could possibly catch fire.

Pouring a cup, he took a seat at the breakfast table, smelling the aroma and trying to wake up. If he was keeping score, only one of his dreams had actually been fulfilled, which didn't exactly make him a certifiable "prophet." At this point, he was just a dreamer who might have gotten lucky. Yet, he still felt like he owed it to the people in his dreams to let them know what he saw, even if he didn't understand it.

His mom came rushing in, jostling her own cup in her hand. "Oh, good morning," she said upon seeing Peter.

"Good morning," he said, instantly deciding there was no way he could tell her about this latest dream. She was incapable of keeping a secret and had told everyone she knew about the "heart" dream. Anything about Jordan would simply be too much for her to contain. Besides, this one seemed like it might be of a private nature.

Still, there was possibly no better source for finding out about Jordan than his mom. As Ms. Quill transferred the remains of her coffee mug to a travel cup, Peter casually asked, "So, what's the story with Jordan Stone? Is she still married to that producer?"

"Why?" she asked, turning off the burner. "Are you thinking of asking her out?"

It was an attempt at humor, which Peter ignored. "I was just wondering."

"They're still married," his mom said, going back to fixing her to-go cup with milk and sugar. "Of course, there have been rumors for years...."

"What rumors?" Peter plied.

"Just that there's trouble in paradise," she said as if it was common knowledge. "Supposedly they've been separated for a while."

"Huh," Peter said. "And how many kids do they have?"

"Two," his mom said, turning back around to stare at him with a quizzical expression. Peter never asked about Little Miss Perfect; he heard enough about the famous member of his youth group without any provocation.

"I was just curious," Peter said in his defense. Unable to come up with any plausible reason he'd be asking about Jordan's personal life, he left it at that.

"You know, she supposedly goes to Grace Church now," his mom said as she gathered up her steaming thermos and leather satchel for work.

"Yeah, you mentioned that," Peter said. Wanting to keep her talking, he asked, "Why did she leave Trinity?"

"Oh, I don't know. I'm sure she's still close to Dan." She headed toward the back door that led into the garage. "Maybe she just wanted to try something new."

Getting up, Peter opened the door before his mom got there. "Have a good day."

"I want you to mow the lawn today," his mom admonished him. "And apply for a job. Any job."

Peter nodded reassuringly. "I'll get on it right away."

As soon as the door closed, Peter looked around the kitchen and rubbed his empty belly. Going to the pantry, he got out some cereal and, carrying it to the living room, turned on the television and ate out of the box.

On Sunday, Peter decided to give Grace Church a try. He didn't want to run into Jordan; however, if God put her in his path, he would take it as a sign and attempt to tell her about his dream.

Although his car needed new brakes and tires, at least he had a new battery, courtesy of his mom. As he pulled out of the driveway, he couldn't help but notice the foot-high grass and made a mental note to get the mower out when he got home.

After driving around Franklin for fifteen minutes, he found a parking place several blocks away. By the size of the crowd, it was clear Grace was the hot place to worship. According to his mom, the church attracted a lot of the area's musicians and celebrities. With the glitterati sprinkled in the pews, the suburban hip would be sure to follow.

As he joined in the stream of smiling people heading toward the steeple, he worried about running into someone like Tom McAllister and having them ask an embarrassing question like, *Where are you living?* or *How are you doing?*

Breaking with the flow of foot traffic, Peter circled around the back of the building to look for a less crowded entrance. When a side door opened, he took the opportunity to duck inside a darkened hallway.

Now there were two ways to go...farther down the hall or up some stairs. As he contemplated the fork in the road, he thought he heard the sound of a baby crying up above him. Reminded of his dream, he began to climb the narrow stairwell.

At the first landing, he turned a corner and almost stepped into the baptismal suspended over the stage. For someone trying to be as stealthy as possible, a belly-flop into a tank of water in front of the church was probably not the way to go.

Carefully stepping back from the slippery edge, he went the

25

other direction and was confronted with a closed door. From the other side of the door, he distinctly heard the muffled sound of a baby. It was all so similar to his dream he had a feeling of déjà vu, and as he opened the door, he half-expected to find Jordan waiting for him inside.

In the next instant, he was a deer caught in headlights. A woman, not Jordan, was seated in a chair, her blouse unbuttoned and a breast prominently displayed. She also held a baby.

"Excuse me!" the mother said sharply as her baby readjusted his angle and went back in.

"Oh! Sorry," Peter croaked, closing the door behind him.

Anxious to get away, he looked around and saw another flight of stairs behind him. Fleeing to the top of the stairwell, he found one more door. It was already cracked open a few inches, so Peter pushed it inward, peering into the darkness.

Giving his eyes a moment to adjust, he made out a small, ten-by-ten-foot box with six vacant fold-out chairs. The side of the room that overlooked the stage was covered in a mesh material, making it virtually impossible to see in or out.

Pulling a chair up to the screen, he listened to the singing that had just started down below. It sounded nice, and yet he didn't feel compelled to sing along or even mouth the words since no one was there to watch him. He could do anything he wanted in his private box except actually see the service.

Behind him, footsteps stopped short and a surprised, feminine voice whispered, "Oh, hi," just as a child clomped into his sanctuary.

Turning, Peter saw a woman reaching out to rein in a rambunctious boy. Fumbling around for a minute, she managed to get herself and her son seated in the fold-out chairs.

Leaning over, the harried woman asked, "Did we miss much?"

"Just the singing," Peter told her.

Openly staring at her now, Peter could make out sandy, shoulder-length hair and pale luminescent skin that shone in the semi-darkness. He guessed she was probably about his age, and she was pretty.

"He can't sit through the singing anyway," she said, gesturing to the fidgety boy, who was probably around seven years old.

"I have a hard time with that, too," Peter admitted.

The woman's smile cut through the room's gloom, and Peter suddenly wanted to keep the conversation going. Just as he prepared to introduce himself, someone below inconveniently started to pray, and the woman respectfully bowed her head.

While the prayer droned on, Peter used the time to try and think of something witty to say at his next opportunity. By the time the "Amen" came, he still had nothing, and the moment had passed.

Pastor Rick jumped into his sermon about how people are all made for connection—connection with God, with our fellow man and woman, and even with animals and nature. The message was particularly convicting to Peter, who had effectively cut himself off from most, if not all, of the aforementioned living creatures.

Meanwhile, Peter could see why the woman had brought her restless son to a room that was far removed from polite society. Perhaps he had stumbled into the place reserved for the church troublemakers.

A couple of times during the service, Peter stole glances at the woman; her silhouette was framed by the slivers of light around the door. Once she looked over and caught him. Giving him an apologetic smile, she simply said, "I'm sorry," as she nodded to her hyperactive son.

"Oh, he's not bothering me," Peter said.

As final announcements were made down below, the woman stood up and whispered, "Come on, Jacob."

Desperate to heed the message and make a connection with another human being, specifically this one, Peter said, "It's kind of like having your own private church up here."

"I know. Don't tell anyone else," the woman said conspiratorially. "This is Jacob's favorite place at church."

"Your secret is safe with me," Peter half-kidded.

"Well, I'm Marian, by the way," she said, holding out her hand.

"And this is Jacob." The boy came over and extended a smaller hand.

"I'm Peter," he said, shaking both hands simultaneously.

Marian's lyrical little laugh was music to his ears. "Nice meeting you," she said, and then she was gone in the flash of a smile.

It was nice meeting you, too, Peter thought to himself.

CHAPTER 4

His visit to Grace had not yielded an encounter with Jordan, and yet, he had met Marian—and Jacob. Even their small exchange took on magnified implications to a lonely man. Maybe he would revisit the little room at church next Sunday.

What if Marian was there again? Could he ask her out? Even if he could muster up the courage and somehow manage to get a first date, she would end it once she found out his current professional and living situation. Any woman would be wary.

Suddenly, he wanted to change his life overnight—get a job and move into his own place. But he knew he just needed to get back on his feet and take a single step in the right direction, make a little money.

For a while, he had considered teaching, but that required quite a bit more education, so that had been filed away as a future possibility. There were, however, no requirements for substitute teaching that he was aware of other than having a pulse.

Since the school year was getting ready to start, he drove his squealing car to the County Office of Education where he was given a lengthy application form to fill out.

The clerk seemed a little apprehensive when Peter had trouble accounting for the last year of his life. If he couldn't get approved to sub, what did that leave for him? Neighborhood lawn boy? Babysitter?

Finally, after a couple of follow-up calls and submitting Dan Cox as a reference, the county agreed to put him on the list of approved substitutes. It was a victory of sorts. Okay, so maybe it didn't warrant a limo-driven, champagne-popping, all-night celebration, but still, he had a part-time, minimum-wage job, and he was grateful for it.

The first few days at middle school were a little choppy. Wanting to be liked by the kids, he tried to befriend them. This technique proved to be disastrous. It got so bad that a teacher in the next room had to come over, and he instantly regained control of Peter's classroom. Peter was amazed with the real teacher's mastery over his hellions.

At the end of the period, a thirteen-year-old girl came up to him with advice: "You can't start out nice. You have to start out mean and get nice later."

Things got better after that.

It was late afternoon when the home phone rang. Thinking it was probably a teacher in need of a warm body, Peter picked up.

"Hello, Peter." The voice was stronger than the last time he had heard it. "It's Dan."

"Hey," Peter said, encouraged. "You sound better."

"Thanks, I feel better," Dan said, although a note of dejection lingered in his tone. "I just got word that Mark Shelton is starting his own church, and it sounds like he's going to take a significant portion of Trinity with him."

"Oh," Peter said. "I'm sorry."

"You tried to warn me," Dan said. "I never should have let him speak at Trinity. Someone gave him permission to collect emails and phone numbers, and he's been using them to poach our members."

"Oh, wow," Peter mumbled, surprised by the slimy tactic.

"I hear he's been doing the same thing all over town," Dan said bitterly. "He guest speaks and then gets their directory or has them sign a petition or something."

A sneak flank attack, Peter thought. Not able to think of anything constructive to say, he remained silent.

"So, you were right," Dan concluded solemnly. "That makes two for two."

"Actually, I had another dream," Peter said.

"Oh?" Dan asked with a bit of trepidation.

"Yeah, but it's about somebody besides you."

"Thank God," Dan said with a little laugh. "Your dreams haven't exactly been a harbinger of good news for me."

"Yeah," Peter agreed. "Sorry about that."

"Have you talked to this other person about your dream?" Dan asked.

"Not yet," Peter said. "I don't know how to contact them."

"Can you tell me who you're talking about?"

Peter couldn't think of any reason not to tell Dan, except that it was somehow a little embarrassing. "Jordan Stone," he admitted.

"Oh, I have her number," Dan offered without a second thought. "Do you want it?"

"She'd probably think I was crazy if I called her out of the blue and told her I had a dream about her," Peter said.

Not necessarily disagreeing, Dan offered, "Do you want to tell me about it, and I can pass it on?"

"I don't know if I should," Peter said slowly. "It's not that I don't trust you. It's just that, well, it could be kind of personal information."

"No, you're right," Dan said quickly. "How about this, I'll call her and tell her a little about the dreams you've shared with me. I'll mention that you had a dream about her and give her your number. That way she can call if she's interested."

"I guess that works," Peter said, not able to think of a better plan. At least, if she didn't call him, he would be off the hook.

It was Sunday evening when the phone rang, which meant it probably wasn't the school, and that meant Peter had no interest in answering it. If it was his dad, he had nothing to say to him. Substitute teaching did not qualify as the level of success his father had envisioned for his son, and he'd just as soon avoid that depressing conversation.

A moment later, his mom yelled from downstairs, "Peter!" She sounded almost frantic. "You have a call!"

Deciding he had to get it over with at some point, he went to the phone, picked it up, and covering the receiver, yelled back down, "I got it!" Putting the receiver to his ear, he waited for the click on the other end. After a long pause, Peter tried again, "I got it." Finally, the click came, and Peter said, "Hello."

"Hey, Peter, this is Jordan."

The words took him straight back to when he was in seventh grade and he'd first been introduced to Jordan Stone, the *stone*-cold fox ninth grader. Working to calm down, he very coolly replied, "Oh yeah, hey, Jordan," as if they talked every night.

"It's been a while," she commented. "How have you been?"

"Okay, I guess," he lied. Was his voice shaking? "How have you been?"

"Good," she sighed. "Crazy."

"Yeah," Peter said, as if he could relate all too well to the tiresome demands of super stardom.

"So Dan called me," she said, getting on with it. "He said you were having these dreams—and you were dead-on about two things that happened to him...?"

"Yeah," Peter said.

"That is so weird!" she exclaimed, sounding somewhat complimentary. "So, he said you had a dream about me or something?"

32

Did Jordan think he'd had some sort of sexual dream about her and disguised it as a "prophecy"? Or that he'd made up the whole thing in an effort to make contact with her? He couldn't worry about that now.

"I dreamed you were on stage and you played one of your songs—at least, I guess it was one of your songs. Anyway, the crowd applauded, and you went into your dressing room, and you were in there with a baby—your baby. At least, I assume it was your baby."

There was a moment of silence before he remembered to add, "In the background, I could hear the crowd calling for an encore, and you had this baby in your arms, and you looked like you didn't know what to do next."

More silence on the other end of the phone. Finally, Jordan asked, "That's it?"

"That's it." When Jordan still didn't say anything, Peter asked the obvious question: "Do you have a baby?"

"No," Jordan said firmly. "My kids are three and five."

"Well, I don't know what it means then," Peter replied. "Sorry."

"It's okay," Jordan said, now sounding a little annoyed. After a weighty pause, Jordan sighed deeply. "Look, I got to go. My youngest is screaming." Peter couldn't hear anything in the background. "Stay in touch."

Before Peter could respond, he was listening to the harsh sound of a dead line.

As he hung up, he flushed with embarrassment, then flashed to anger. He'd been let down by his dream and by God in front of, of all people, Jordan Stone. He hadn't wanted to talk to her in the first place, and now she thought he was a complete idiot or possibly insane.

Turning around, he found his mom standing in the doorway. She was barely suppressing a giddy, childlike smile. "I just got here," she said by way of an excuse. "Was that really Jordan?" Apparently, she already knew the answer because her next question was, "What did she want?"

Wondering if other prophets had to put up with intrusive mothers, Peter got to his feet and calmly walked to the door.

"I didn't hear anything," she added, as if sensing she might have overstepped her bounds.

Once again, Peter found himself gently closing the door on his mom's expectant face.

On Sunday, Peter went back to Grace Church, finding his way back up to the private box. He took a seat by himself and waited for Marian and her son to reappear. By the time the announcements and the singing were over, he knew no one was coming and he would remain alone.

Maybe it was for the best.

He wasn't ready for a date, much less a relationship. Having the dreams had made him feel special for a little while—until the call with Jordan. That had been a bust, and now he was just a substitute teacher who lived at home with his mother. Nothing more.

The sermon was about an old woman who went to heaven, and when she got there, God showed her a tattered piece of cloth. "This represents your life," God told her. The coarse material was laced with mix-matched colors of zig-zag stitching and thick, tied-off wads of knots; the result was a chaotic, ugly mess of threads.

Then God explained, "This is how *you* saw your life while you were sewing it." As God turned it over, He said, "And this is how I saw your life." On the front side of the cloth was a beautiful, multi-colored tapestry full of wonderful swirls and patterns and intricate designs.

Closing his eyes, Peter couldn't help but think of his own messed-up life, so full of wrong turns and dead ends. Maybe he was just looking at it from the backside of the tapestry. Maybe all the pain and confusion was preparing him for something after all.

CHAPTER 5

August 21

I am in an open field. Other people are sitting around on the ground. Looking closer, I see they are actually sitting on eggs—like they are waiting on them to hatch. One lady keeps checking on her football-sized egg; another man polishes his beach-ball-sized egg.

Then it starts to rain—hard. I look up and realize that coins are dropping out of the sky. People scatter for shelter, leaving their eggs exposed. The coins break the eggs—green slime oozes out of the broken shells.

Then the coins stop. The sun comes back out. People reassemble to evaluate the damage—they seem devastated. The man with the big broken egg sits in a pool of sludge and eggshells, his head in hands, grieving.

Peter looked up from his journal, cutting a sideways glance at the clock. Despite being called to school that morning, he had taken time to carefully write down his latest dream. It was weird and fairly involved, and he hadn't wanted to miss anything that might be important like he must have done with what he now referred to as the "Jordan Stone Fiasco."

As he rushed through his shower, he thought of the coins falling like rain, or more accurately, like hail. Since he assumed money was probably not going to literally fall from the sky, it had to be symbolic. He allowed himself a few moments to drift over possible metaphors, but nothing came to mind except random thoughts of Jordan that weren't particularly relevant or edifying.

Remembering he had to hurry, he rinsed and dried off. In his bedroom while he got dressed, he returned to thoughts of how devastated people were about their precious broken eggs.

The eggs, he thought, were the key to cracking the dream, and he made a mental note to develop that lead as soon as he'd had some coffee. Grabbing his keys and wallet, he bounded down the stairs.

It was quiet in the bottom half of the house, which meant his mom wasn't even up yet. Maybe he would have time to make a pit stop for coffee and breakfast after all. For some reason, scrambled eggs were calling his name.

The dream nagged at him all day. Sunday was still a few days away, so Peter called Trinity Church as soon as he got home from school and asked the church secretary if he could speak to Dan. It seemed like she knew who he was and put him right through.

"How are you, Peter?" the senior pastor asked sincerely.

"I'm okay," Peter said. "I've been substitute teaching."

"Oh," Dan said slowly, probably not sure if congratulations or condolences were in order. "By the way, did Jordan call you?"

"Oh, yeah," Peter said. "I told her about the dream, but I don't think it meant anything to her. So, I guess I missed that one."

"Well, you're still batting a thousand in my book," Dan offered.

"Good," Peter said tentatively, "cause I had another dream."

"Go on," Dan said with genuine interest.

Peter carefully repeated what he remembered, beat by beat, coin by coin, egg by egg.

"Well, it reminds me a little of the 'manna' from heaven," Dan said optimistically. "Perhaps a financial windfall of some kind."

"I don't think so," Peter replied. "The coins were hurting people and breaking their eggs. That can't be good, can it?"

"So, maybe it's a disaster," Dan tried again. "Like the plague on Egypt, the one with hail."

"Maybe something like that," Peter agreed.

"In Revelation, they mention giant hailstones that fall on men, causing them to blaspheme God," Dan suggested. "Those are supposed to be one-hundred pounds each."

"These were *coins*," Peter emphasized, growing a little impatient. "Besides, I don't know if what we're looking for is in the Bible. It felt like some kind of a financial meltdown. But it's like a piece of the puzzle is missing. I think it has to do with those eggs."

They both sat in silence for a few seconds before Dan said, "Well, keep your eyes and ears open. It seems like God shows you the answers when you need them." Peter nodded beside the phone. "Have you prayed for guidance?"

"Not really," Peter admitted, a little embarrassed.

"Would you like to do that now?" Dan asked.

"Sure."

As Dan began to pray, Peter thought that if God was sending him these messages—and he believed He was—then God would also provide the key to unlock their meaning. The next thought that came to Peter was that he needed to be open to receiving answers from anywhere, even unconventional sources.

Having finished praying, Dan asked, "Do you want to pray, Peter?"

"That's okay," Peter said. "I was praying silently."

"If I get an inspiration tonight, I'll give you a call," Dan said. "Otherwise, let's pick this up tomorrow." Before they hung up, he gave Peter his personal cell phone number and told him to call anytime.

After flicking on a small TV he kept in his room, Peter watched the second half of a sitcom rerun and the beginning of a local news program before he heard the garage door motor buzzing below. His mom was home, probably with dinner.

Before going downstairs, he watched the TV for the day's top stories on the national news just to see if there were reports of anything that could be construed as falling coins. The only money mentioned were the crazy sums that were expected to be spent in the upcoming political elections.

The phone rang, which he ignored, except to briefly wonder if it might be Jordan calling to tell him she wanted to have his love child. Somehow that prediction didn't ring true either.

He was still watching the news when his mom called up to him, "Your Dan is on the phone."

"My Dan?" Was she jealous? Perhaps Dan had already cracked the code and had an interpretation.

Picking up the phone, he answered with a hopeful, "Hey!"

"Hey!" the unmistakable voice of his dad repeated back to him. "You sound like you're in a good mood."

"I thought you were someone else," Peter said glumly.

"Oh, well, sorry to disappoint you," Mr. Quell said.

Disappointment seemed to be a common theme in their relationship.

"Well, I just called to touch base," his dad said. "How are you?"

"I'm fine," Peter said. With a note of defensiveness, he added, "I'm doing some substitute teaching."

"So I heard from your mom," his dad said without any discernable disapproval. "What grades are you teaching?"

"Mostly seventh."

"That's a rough age."

Peter agreed, mostly because that was the grade he had been in when his parents had divorced.

"Is teaching something you'd like to do full-time?"

"I don't know," Peter said. "Maybe."

"You don't make very much money, you know."

"Yeah," Peter said defensively. The salary of a full-time teacher

38

actually sounded pretty good to him, even if it would never be enough for his dad.

"So," his father continued, "your mom tells me you're having dreams about the future?"

Peter could almost hear the bemused smile in his father's voice, a bit of merriment at the expense of the religious people and their crazy shenanigans.

"Yeah," Peter said reluctantly. "I've had a couple of dreams that came true."

"Well, that is something," his dad said with what Peter interpreted as subtle mockery. "What kind of things have you foretold?"

The way his dad asked the question made it sound like Peter was some sort of fortune teller. Not wanting to discuss it, he simply said, "Didn't Mom already tell you?"

"She told me you have preachers and Christian singers calling the house to ask for your advice," Mr. Quell said, now obviously openly enjoying himself. When Peter didn't respond, his dad asked with a little laugh, "Can you tell me where the stock market is headed? Now, I would pay good money for that."

"I got to go," Peter said sharply. "I have to get up early tomorrow."

"Oh, okay," his dad said, sounding startled by Peter's abruptness.

"Talk to you later," Peter said, hanging up without waiting for a good-bye.

Peter fumed at the phone. *What is the stock market going to do?* Of course, his dad would ask about money since that was the only thing he cared about. What was ironic was that he actually had dreamed about money, coins falling from the sky....

Falling like the stock market could fall? What if the falling money represented the market crashing? For one thing, it would wipe out peoples' savings—or *nest eggs.*

"Yes," Peter muttered, confirming it to himself. He had it. Having to tell someone, he picked up the phone, turned to the scrap of paper he'd just placed on his dresser, and punched in the numbers.

A moment later, Dan picked up his cell phone. "Hello."

"Hey, it's me," Peter said quickly. "I think the stock market is going to crash."

"Why do think it's the stock market?"

"I was just talking to my dad, and he mentioned something about the stock market, and it kind of clicked," Peter said, talking rapidly now. "The stock market is going to fall, and it's going to wipe out peoples' nest eggs."

Pausing to consider the explanation, Dan cautiously said, "All of your other dreams have been more personal in nature. Are you sure about this one?"

Again, Peter checked himself. Was he reading into things? Was he making up answers? Painting bullseyes around arrows? If he hadn't been right before, he would have probably assumed he was engaging in mystical thinking. However, with the possible exception of Jordan's dream, he had been on target, so he had to go with his instinct this time, too.

"As sure as I was about the others," Peter finally answered.

"What do you think we should do about it?" Dan asked.

"I'm not sure," Peter said, not having thought about doing anything.

"Well, I think it's time you went public with this."

"What do you mean?" Peter asked. "I am going public—with you."

"No, I mean, I think you should step out and make a public announcement."

A chill went down Peter's spine. "If *you* want to announce something—"

"It's not my vision," Dan cut in. "You are getting these messages for a reason, and I think you should be the one to share them with others."

"What others?" Peter asked, a slight tremor creeping into his voice.

"With the church," Dan said. "I'll introduce you and help you along."

Talking to a classroom of kids was one thing. Speaking to hundreds of strangers, of grown-up strangers, was something else entirely. A sickly feeling began to gnaw at the lining in his stomach.

"Peter, it will be okay," Dan said steadily. "Just pray, and God will give you what you need."

"I don't know," Peter mumbled, distracted by the thought of throwing up in front of all those people.

"I don't think God wants you to keep these dreams to yourself, Peter," Dan said.

"Okay," Peter managed with one hand on his aching belly.

By the time they hung up, Peter was obsessing on his dilemma. If he was wrong, it wouldn't just upset one diva. This time, it could affect lots of people. Best-case scenario, he'd be a laughingstock. Worst-case, well, he wasn't sure, but it wasn't good.

As a cloud of doubt welled up over him, he found himself praying again—a desperate plea for courage and peace and anything else God could throw his way. By the time he finished, some of the fear in his heart and the pain in his stomach had subsided, at least temporarily.

"Thank you," he said softly, feeling slightly stronger.

Just then, a thought flashed in his head. The idea didn't seem very godly or Christian, and Peter wondered where it had come from. Maybe it was that little devil that sat on one shoulder. Or maybe God had a sense of humor. Wherever the notion had originated, he couldn't resist the urge to pursue it. Picking up the phone, he punched in a number he still knew from memory.

A couple of rings later, his father's curious voice answered, "Hello?"

"It's going to crash," Peter said and hung up, a self-satisfied smile on his face.

CHAPTER 6

For the next few days, all Peter could think about was the upcoming Sunday service and his starring role in it. The idea of speaking in front of the church was frightening enough. Making a grand pronouncement about the future escalated it to a truly petrifying event.

He had told his mom about the plan, and she was worried, too. If it hadn't been Dan's idea, she would have certainly advised against it.

"Are you sure about this dream?" she'd asked him on more than one occasion.

"I think so," Peter would say, doubting himself a little more each time.

"Should I take my money out of my savings account?"

"You don't have any money in stocks, Mom," Peter explained.

And so it went until the first day of the week rolled around, by which point Peter just wanted to get the whole business over with as quickly as possible. He decided he wanted to go to church by himself, which was fine with his mom, who wasn't sure if she even wanted to go at all. Her confidence in him was not terribly inspiring.

Per Dan's instructions, Peter arrived a little early and found a seat near the front. Watching people slowly wander in, Peter thought it obvious the departure of Mark Shelton's followers had made a sizable dent in the church. At that particular moment, he was selfishly grateful to Mark. The fewer people he had to face, the better.

Spotting his mom slink in, he watched as she found a place in the very back row, presumably in case she had to make a fast exit. Just then, Dan came striding down the aisle, giving Peter's arm a squeeze as he passed. Having lost a few pounds in the ordeal, the pastor actually looked healthier than he had pre-surgery, in Peter's opinion.

"It will be fine," Dan whispered, seemingly without a care in the world.

The singing started, and Peter tried to join in just to take his mind off the inevitable. Of course, the "praise and worship" went on for so long that he had plenty of time to dwell on the fact that he would soon be front and center. When the nervous chatter in his mind got louder than the singing, he made a mad dash to the bathroom.

As he splashed cold water on his face, he seriously considered taking off. No one would know except God and Dan and his mom and, of course, himself. Facing the mirror, he knew the look of disappointment that would follow him if he chickened out now.

By the time he made it back into the auditorium, Trinity was still chewing on the last chorus of the same song. Dan shot him a relieved look as Peter sat back down in his seat and closed his eyes, as if deep in prayer, which he mostly was.

"Let this cup pass."

When the singing finally petered out, Dan bolted up onto the stage. "I believe in the gift of prophecy," he boldly boomed.

"Do you know the one gift Paul specifically mentions in all three books that discuss gifts of the Spirit?" Dan stopped to look around at his somewhat diminished audience. Before a preacher's pet could shout out the fairly obvious answer, Dan beat them to it: "Prophecy!"

"Now, some say that the days of these spiritual gifts have long since passed. But we know better, don't we?" There was some knowing laughter and applause. "Critics say we were given these gifts in the infancy of the church to nurture the early Christian's faith and to bolster them through times of persecution.

"But," Dan held out a finger for emphasis. "Nowhere does Paul or Jesus or anyone say these gifts are temporary. In fact, in the end times, we are told that our young men will see visions, and our old men will dream dreams. Now, I don't know if we are in the 'end times.' All I know for sure is that the gifts of the Spirit are alive and well in Nashville, Tennessee. Can I get an 'Amen'?"

He got several of them, then patiently waited for the response to die down.

"About a month ago, after a church service, a young brother told me he had a dream and he thought it meant I should have my heart checked out. So, you know what I did?" He nodded knowingly. "I got my heart checked out. And as most of you know, they found a blockage. In fact, my doctor said that if they hadn't caught it when they did, I could have had a massive heart attack."

There was a hearty "Praise God!" from the crowd for the miraculous early detection.

"A couple of weeks ago, while I was recovering from my surgery, this same brother came to me in the hospital and told me he dreamed this church was under attack and we would lose a third of our members."

The two-thirds that were left were now sitting in rapt attention.

"And we know how that turned out," Dan said, looking around. "So, when he called me last week and said he had another dream, I told him I thought he ought to share it with the whole congregation.

"Now, I can tell you, I know this young brother is trying to obey God with his gift." Turning directly to Peter, he said, "I also know he is nervous about doing this, so let's give him our support. Come on up, Peter."

The crowd clapped as bodies rose in their seats and necks craned to get a better look at the supposed prophet.

Slowly, Peter got to his feet and shuffled the short distance to the stage. Dan graciously came down the stairs to meet him on the floor. Putting one steadying arm around him, Dan held the wireless microphone out with his other hand.

"Just tell us what you dreamed," he instructed.

"Okay, well, it's kind of strange," Peter warned before retelling his dream in a stilting cadence with a slightly trembling voice. "I was outside, and I saw people sitting on these eggs. It was kind of like they were waiting for them to hatch or something."

His little chuckle, which was intended to lighten the mood, only came out awkward and strained. Clearing his throat, Peter plowed ahead. "Anyway, some of the eggs were bigger than others. No matter what the size, everyone seemed to love whatever egg they had."

As Peter tried to swallow, his Adam's apple got stuck in his suddenly very dry throat. With a little gasp, he got over the hump and staggered on.

"Then it started to rain, but it was raining coins—you know, money. People were running to get out of the way of the coins because they hurt. And when the coins hit the eggs, they broke. Everyone was in a panic because their eggs were cracking, and this green goo was coming out. Then, the coins stopped falling."

Peter could have used an "Amen" right about then. No one said a word except Dan.

"Now, as we all know, a tongue or a prophecy is useless unless there is an interpretation," the preacher interjected. "Go ahead, Peter, tell us what you believe the dream means."

"Well, I think the eggs represent our money, or our nest eggs. And we all—or a lot of us, anyway—are too preoccupied with our money. It's become an idol we love more than God. Even if you're like me and don't have an egg, or any money, you can still make an idol out of wanting it. I know I do that."

Peter stopped for a second to collect his chaotic thoughts and dampen his mouth with another hard-fought swallow. "Anyway,

I think the money that was coming down represents the stock market. I think it's going to crash."

Murmurs began to rise up from the congregation.

"It's going to hurt a lot of people financially," Peter continued. "But I also think it will be a chance to focus on what's really important. You know, like, God." Wanting to end the long, painful silence that followed, he added, "Well, that's it."

A man stood up in the center of the congregation. "I have a question." Both Peter and Dan were a little taken aback by the man's boldness as he asked, "Are you saying we should take our money out of mutual funds or anything that is invested in the stock market?"

"We are not advising or recommending for you to do anything one way or the other," Dan quickly said. "All we are doing is sharing a dream this brother had. What you choose to do with that information is entirely your own decision."

The man did not seem satisfied with that disclaimer. "It sounds to me like he," he pointed to Peter, "is telling me to pull my money out of my 401k."

Gently, Peter moved closer to the mike held in Dan's tight grip. "I don't think the dream was as much about keeping your money as it was about not being so attached to it."

A woman was on her feet now. "I'm sixty-eight years old, and I need my savings to retire on!"

Dan nodded, trying to keep a lid on things, yet appearing a bit flustered at the outbursts.

A third man near the front demanded, "What are you going to do? Are you selling your stocks?"

With Dan momentarily flummoxed by the questions, Peter leaned in again. "As I said, I don't have any stocks or money. But if I did, I think I would take it out of the stock market."

The noise level rose again. People were talking openly among themselves; their voices sounded agitated, even angry. More than one person yelled questions, and Peter's thoughts flashed back to his first day as a substitute teacher when he gave his class five minutes of free time, and riot police had nearly been called in.

The questions were still coming fast and furious from the main floor and the balcony. "Does this only affect stocks?" "What about bonds?" "What about real estate?" "Is it just the US stock market?" "Are you sure about this?" "How sure?"

Peter recalled the little girl who'd informed him he had started out too nice after he lost control of his class.

Peeling the microphone out of Dan's hand, Peter shouted, "Please!" Surprisingly, he succeeded in lowering the decibel level. Looking over the anxious faces, he repeated, "Please! Everyone be quiet and sit down."

Most of the people who were standing slowly found their pew seats.

"I've already told you everything I know. If it were up to me, I wouldn't have said anything at all." He cut an accusing glance toward Dan, who had abandoned his side and was standing a few feet behind him.

"Do what you want about your investments," Peter continued. "If you are this worried about the stock market, then you've made my point. We're not trusting God the way we should."

Having momentarily shamed the crowd into submission, Peter held the mike out for Dan, who had returned and was now flipping through a Bible in his hand. When he found his place, the preacher took the microphone back.

"'People who want to get rich fall into temptation and a trap and into many foolish and harmful desires that plunge men into ruin and destruction.'" Dan glanced up with a wary eye at his audience before looking back down.

"'For *the love of money is a root of all kinds of evil*. Some people, eager for money, have wandered from the faith and pierced themselves with many griefs.' First Timothy 6:9-10."

Dan slapped his Bible shut with authority. "Let's pray!" he nearly shouted, bowing his head.

By the time Dan uttered "Amen" and re-opened his eyes, his young prophet had vanished.

With the church in mid-prayer, Peter had slipped out the side door and jogged to his car. Feeling like he was fleeing a crime scene, he sped out of the parking lot, not looking back until he was safely down the road.

Before he hit the interstate, he pulled over, cut his motor, and sat perfectly still as he tried to steady his breathing and calm his racing mind.

How had things spiraled so horribly out of control? When he had moved home, all he had wanted to do was lay low until he got back on his feet. Instead, he had just stood up in front of a church and predicted the collapse of the stock market. That was not "laying low."

And for the one thousandth time, he asked himself, *What if I am wrong?*

The initial assurance he felt when he deciphered a dream always tended to fade a bit, especially after he'd told someone. This time, he'd told hundreds of people, and his confidence was eroding away under a mountain of expectation. While he'd never experienced a nervous breakdown, he felt like he might be on the verge.

As cars rushed by, scurrying to the hundreds of churches, Peter lowered his forehead till it rested against the steering wheel. What followed was an incoherent, muddled plea. It was also desperate and heartfelt.

When he reopened his damp eyes, the world seemed darker, the sky cloudier. Just then, big, fat droplets of rain began to splatter against his dirty windshield. It was just a short shower—without a coin or egg in sight.

Was there a message in the summer storm? He wanted to see a confirmation of his dream, and yet, he feared he was becoming susceptible to self-delusion.

Too tired to think any more, he exhaled, restarted his car, and pointed it toward home.

CHAPTER 7

The last thing Peter wanted to do was sit around waiting for the Dow to go down. As soon as he got home from church, he declared himself on a "media fast," which entailed staying away from all computers, newspapers, TVs, and radios. This, he quickly learned, was not as easy as it sounded since media was virtually everywhere.

Even harder to avoid were the phone calls from "concerned" church members who wanted to know how to best pray for him, followed by not-so-subtle attempts to dig a little deeper into his track record at prophesying. Most of the calls came from people he didn't know, many of whom hadn't even been to the now-infamous church service.

Peter didn't call any of them back.

Instead, he did what he had been doing. On Monday morning, he went to school, this time to sub for Ms. Truman. Try as he might to concentrate on class, his thoughts kept bending back to the Sunday morning spectacle.

Whenever doubts about his prediction came up, as they inevitably did, he found comfort in the knowledge that this too would pass. Even if stocks soared for the next decade, it wouldn't be the end of the world. All of his mistakes would be washed away and forgotten eventually.

Ms. Truman took another personal day on Tuesday, so Peter readily agreed to keep her class again. There was solace in being around semi-innocent children whose main concerns were being accepted by their classmates and getting the hang of pre-algebra. Peter could relate on both fronts. All the while, thoughts of the stock market ticked away in the back of his brain like a bomb waiting to go off.

Once again, he felt the lure of a nasty habit he'd all but kicked. After he moved home, his mom had made it clear that smoking was one vice she would not tolerate. He had still tried to sneak a smoke or two, but he'd had to engage in such elaborate cover-ups it became easier just to quit. Not wanting to go back to those dark, clandestine days, he did his best to resist the nervous cravings.

When Peter got home from school, there were two messages waiting for him on the answering machine, both from people who wanted to know about the impending crash. Only two calls meant that things might be settling down. Not wanting to wait around for the next one, Peter opted for a long jog around the neighborhood to beat the excess energy and nicotine urges out of his body.

That night, he sat down for dinner with his mom on the one condition that they would not talk about the prophecy. That proved to be difficult since it was really the only thing on either of their minds. After attempting to make idle chitchat, Peter finally gave in and suspended the moratorium.

"The stock market went up again today," his mom said, clearly worried. "Several people from church called to ask if you had any new updates...?"

"No, Mom," Peter said. "I'll be sure to let you know if God sends me a hot stock tip."

"I'm not asking for that!" she parried. "People just want to know what to do."

"They don't have to do anything," Peter said with a shake of his head.

"Well, I hope it happens soon," she muttered in a moment of unvarnished honesty.

"You know, an economic collapse isn't a good thing," Peter reminded her.

Ms. Quell looked up. "Well, of course not. But if it's God's will...."

"If it's God's will, then we don't need to worry about it," Peter finished; he said it for his benefit as much as his mom's. Whether he liked it or not, they both had a lot riding on this.

He watched his admonished mom peck at her food in silence and felt compassion for her. Her son might not be a doctor or a lawyer, but if this dream came true, she would be the mother of a hand-picked messenger of God. That would show the neighbors.

Wednesday morning, Peter was awoken by the school. A PE teacher had fallen off his roof while trying to adjust a satellite dish and broken his leg. Grateful for another day filled with rambunctious distractions, he hurried to school before the first-period bell sounded.

While shooting baskets with the kids in the gym, Peter could hear rain drumming the aluminum roof and the occasional crack of thunder. There was electricity in the air, and it struck him with a feeling that something was going down in the larger world. Swatting the inkling away, he continued to pretend he was merely the indomitable seven-foot center to his pre-teen competition.

At lunch, he thought he observed a charged conversation at the teacher's table in the cafeteria. Steering clear, he carried his tray back to the gym. Logically, he knew the lively discussion could have been about anything; so why did he assume it had anything to do with the stock market? As he ate his meal on the bleachers, he wondered if his imagination was finally starting to get the better of him.

And yet the clues, or perceived clues, kept coming. During an afternoon dodgeball game, he overheard a kid on the sidelines joking about his "college fund."

On the drive home, he allowed himself some music and stumbled across an oldie, "You Dropped a Bomb on Me." When the Gap Band finished, the DJ mentioned it was "a good choice for today." Resuming his media fast, Peter snapped off the station and completed the short drive home in silence.

After he got home, he continued his avoidance by deliberately not checking the answering machine. It was almost as if he didn't want to know, as if he wanted to keep things as simple and uncomplicated as possible for as long as possible. Secretly, maybe, he was also taking some perverse thrill in stretching out the suspense.

Call after call continued to pour in, and while he didn't actually listen to the messages, the sheer volume told him something had definitely happened. By four thirty, he knew he was hiding from the truth and merely postponing the inevitable.

His mom was the first to officially break the news. Rushing in from the garage, she found her son in the kitchen putting a bag of popcorn into the microwave. Staring at him with wild eyes, she exclaimed, "Well, it happened! It really happened!"

"Really?" Peter said, trying to sound surprised.

"You don't even know?" she asked, her voice a shrill falsetto.

"Well, not for sure."

His mom glanced at the clock on the wall, then ran into the den. Turning on the TV, she announced, "It's time for the news," just as Peter got into the room.

"It was dropping all day, then it really fell toward the end. Whooosh! I don't remember the exact numbers. Someone said it was the largest drop ever in one day."

"Huh," Peter muttered.

The national news anchor was talking almost as excitedly as his mom about the crash. Peter heard something about "flash trading" and "a free fall" and "trading suspended." All the while, his racing mind came back to the one conclusion: *It actually happened.*

As the ringing telephone blended with the popping corn, Peter knew he'd passed some invisible point of no return, and his simple life would never be the same.

When he reported to gym class on Friday, it seemed like everyone knew who he was and what he had done. It turned out the city newspaper, along with a couple of local blogs, had mentioned him by name. All it took was one pre-teen to put it together, and word traveled fast in the age of instant messaging and social media.

"OMG! Mr. Q is stock-market prophet guy!"

Peter welcomed the inquisitive kids that openly asked questions about his prediction. His stock answer was simply, "I had a dream, and it came true." However, most kids and teachers preferred to whisper and gawk from a safe distance. In one day, he had gone from mild-mannered substitute to super-duper religious freak.

By the end of the day, Peter was called to the office where an assistant principal carefully avoided any mention of "prophecy" while she informed him that he'd become "something of a distraction." It was hard for Peter to disagree with that assessment, so he didn't even try to argue when she said, "We're not going to be calling you for a few days, just until things die down."

On the short drive home, Peter felt the old, ugly nicotine itch reassert itself. Naively, he thought the stress would magically melt away once he knew the outcome of his prophecy. Instead, all the attention, good and bad, just added more pressure.

When he stopped for gas, he made sure no one was around before slipping inside the mini market to obtain his illicit contraband.

That afternoon, behind the house, Peter lit his cigarette. Just as he tried to enjoy the initial inhalation, Donna Oakley, the next-door neighbor, hurried outside, ushering her three kids to the car. Squinting at Ms. Quell's strange son, she gave a cautionary wave.

Peter reciprocated while trying to hide the smoke curling out of his hand.

Feeling about sixteen, Peter gave up and went back inside to begin the cover-up process. After flushing what was left of the cigarette, brushing his teeth, and applying his cologne—*Scent of a Man*—he decided to face the phone messages that had been building up over the last few days.

There were the good calls: "I just want to thank you," a creaky older voice enthused. "I told my son-in-law, who thinks he's a big-shot stockbroker, to move my pension out of the equity funds he put me in. He thought I was crazy for listening to you, but he doesn't think I'm crazy anymore. God bless you, young man."

There were the scary ones: "I heard about what you did," a country voice drawled out of the machine. "If you knew something, or had some kind of *insider information*, you should have said something to everyone, not just that one church. The way I figure it, you owe me money."

There were the annoying messages: "Hey, man, Tom McAllister here. It was great seeing you at Trinity. Great call on the stock market, by the way. So, listen, I've been meaning to see when we can get together and hang. Give me a call, brother."

"Can we hang out at your condo?" Peter muttered before deleting the message.

And, of course, there were the callers looking to cash in, one way or another: a divinity professor who asked him to speak to his class, a financial planner who had a business proposition, and a morning radio DJ who wanted to make fun of him.

Almost all the local media outlets had made contact, including the cute reporter, Cindy from Channel 7, whose body of work he had admired in the past.

Then there was the one message he enjoyed so much he replayed it three times before finally erasing it.

"Well, I'll admit that was a pretty good call. I knew the market was overvalued, but I didn't see that one coming." His dad's voice was friendly, albeit a bit flustered. "If you have any other premonitions, you be sure to let me know. I'll pay more attention next time. Okay, call me when you have a chance."

Premonitions, Peter thought to himself. His dad could never admit that God could figure into the equation. If there was a God, that might mean his dad had some things to answer for, like leaving his mother and him.

The final message had been left by Dan, who simply asked him to call back. Peter called the pastor's cell phone, which was answered before the second ring.

"Hey, Peter," Dan said upon answering. "How are you holding up?"

"I'm okay," Peter said, surmising from the pastor's immediate addressment of him that either Dan had gotten the gift of prophecy himself, or Peter had risen to the rank of being programmed into the pastor's phone. "They don't want me to substitute at school for a while. They say I'm a distraction."

"They can't do that," Dan said, suddenly indignant. "That's discrimination on religious grounds!"

"It's okay," Peter said calmly. "I *am* a distraction. Besides, it's just subbing."

"Well, you should be putting your energy behind your gift right now, anyway," Dan agreed. "You haven't talked to anyone in the press, have you?"

"No," Peter said, "and I'm not planning to either."

"Good, good," Dan said, half to himself. "We need to talk. Can I come over tonight?"

"This is getting out of control," Dan calmly observed. The Trinity pastor was sitting in the Quell living room, a cup of decaf in his hand. "Our church website crashed with all the people trying to listen to last Sunday's service. I've personally gotten about two dozen calls over the last two days, including *The Tennessean* and Channel Seven."

Ms. Quell beamed with pride.

"What do they want?" Peter asked, alarmed by the mention of local media.

"They want a quote about the service," Dan said, as if it was fairly obvious. "Haven't they called you?"

"I don't know," Peter said. "I haven't been listening to the messages. I've been trying to avoid the whole thing."

"Oh, they called," Peter's mom, who had assumed the role of Peter's personal assistant, affirmed.

"Well, you can't avoid them forever," Dan said. "This thing has taken on a life of its own."

"What should we do?" Ms. Quell asked furtively.

"We can't just pretend this didn't happen," Dan stressed. "I'm going to address it in church on Sunday."

"What are you going to say?" Peter asked.

"That prophecy and the gifts of the Holy Spirit are alive and well," Dan answered matter-of-factly. "I'm also going to talk about how we make idols of money, and that cuts us off from the love of God and His miracles."

"Okay," Peter said, nodding. "I just don't want you to talk about me."

"You need to be there, Peter," Dan said, as if that was a given.

"No," Peter said quickly. "I don't think so."

"Look, Peter, it's too late to put the genie back in the bottle," Dan said with some force. "People already know your name." He held out his arms to gesticulate the magnitude of it all. "You called 'Red Wednesday' three days before it happened. That's a big deal."

Peter tried to shrug but couldn't quite pull it off.

"What you did was verifiable prophecy, Old-Testament style," Dan was saying. "Christians, non-Christians, they all want to know what's coming next."

"I don't know if anything is coming next," Peter objected. "I mean, I don't know what I'll dream, or if I'll dream anything else."

"Don't worry about that," Dan said reassuringly, trying to

56

get back on track. "And don't worry about the media. Your first appearance should be at the church," he continued. "I can control the format, and it just makes sense. It's where you made your announcement."

Ms. Quell nodded in wholehearted agreement.

"Honestly, I don't see what the point would be," Peter cut in. "I don't have anything else to say."

There was a pause while Dan readjusted his strategy. "You wouldn't necessarily have to say anything," he tried more softly. "Just showing up would reassure people."

Peter wasn't exactly sure why people needed reassuring, or what his presence would do for anyone, except possibly Dan. He couldn't totally blame his old pastor. Trinity had just lost a significant chunk of its membership (and contributions), and this was going to pack the pews (and offering plates) again.

"Dan is right," his mom spoke up. "No one would even know about this dream if it weren't for him." She turned to her pastor. "Don't worry. Peter will be there."

That was the wrong thing to say. Having been dragged to church every Sunday until he left for college, Peter was not about to be forced now. "No, Mom, I won't," he said firmly. Looking to Dan, he added, "I'm sorry."

His mom looked from her son to her pastor with baffled embarrassment.

"Well, sometimes we have to do things we don't want to do," Ms. Quell started, but then Dan held up his authoritative hand.

"No, it's okay," the pastor said. "Peter needs to do what he feels led to do—or not do."

Although the words were nice, Dan was obviously disappointed. As the pastor put his coffee cup down and got up to go, Peter felt a wave of guilt. Was he being selfish?

"If you change your mind, feel free to show up," Dan said a little pitifully.

"Okay," Peter said, resisting the urge to second-guess himself.

"Stay for some dessert," Ms. Quell called after Dan as she scowled at her son. When his mother followed the pastor out of the room and through the front door, Peter took the opportunity to climb the stairs. He shut his room door behind him.

CHAPTER 8

When Peter awoke on Sunday, he took a moment to scan his mind for any sign of a vivid dream. It had been a couple of weeks since he'd dreamed of coins falling from the sky. Coming up dry, he wondered with nostalgia if his days as a prophet were already behind him.

Maybe it was a desire to feel that closeness to God again that prompted him to go to church that morning. He remembered the anonymous upstairs room he'd discovered at Grace Church and chose it over the spotlight waiting for him at Trinity.

A parking space came easily, and the crowd making their way to the church building seemed a little lighter than usual. Peter wondered if Mark Shelton had poached part of Grace's congregation, too, until he remembered the Titans would be kicking off their home opener in a couple of hours. Over football season, pews would lose seats to tailgates and stadium chairs.

Following his usual route, he circumvented the lobby and snuck through the back door. Taking the flight of stairs, he skipped the baptismal and the nursing room and went straight to the safety of his private box seat.

Two heads turned in unison as he sat down in a chair. It was her—Marian—and her son, Jacob. She seemed to remember him, too, giving him a friendly nod and a slight wave.

A good sign.

Like a soundtrack to a romantic movie, uplifting and hopeful music wafted up from below. Playing on the floor, Jacob pushed a toy dump truck in his direction, unloading a shredded bulletin. Peter rolled the truck back.

Another good sign.

Pastor Rick spoke eloquently about "not selling God short" (an interesting phrase given that the only people who had made money in the stock market were "short sellers"). "He has a plan for your life, and it's bigger than anything you can dream."

The message provided a buffet of food for thought. As he chewed on the implications, Peter also kept thinking about what he should say to Marian. By the time the service ended, he still had no idea.

Getting to his feet, he waited for the only other occupants in their private church to pass.

"Marian—and Jacob, right?"

"Yeah, good memory," Marian said.

"I'm Peter," he offered.

"Yes," Marian nodded pleasantly. "Peter, right."

"Good service," Peter said, motioning to the mesh screen.

"Yeah," Marian agreed again, although her mind seemed elsewhere. "Well, we have to go."

"Going to get some lunch?" Peter stammered. "Because there are some good places around here."

Marian looked a little confused by the overly helpful stranger before seeming to finally realize he was probably angling for an invitation.

"Oh, no, we don't have time to eat," she said quickly. "I have to get Jacob to a soccer game."

"I have to eat!" Jacob protested.

"Yes, well, we'll go through a drive-through or something." Looking back up at Peter, she laughed lightly.

Downplaying the lingering weirdness, Peter turned to Jacob. "So you're a soccer player, huh?"

"Yeah," Jacob said. "A winger."

"Cool," Peter said. "I used to be a defender."

"I have more goals than anyone on my team."

"Wow. Good for you," Peter said with a smile. He looked back at Marian, who was staring down at Jacob.

"Well, I hope you get one today," Peter offered.

"I probably will," Jacob announced.

Wishing he had the kid's confidence, Peter stepped a little farther back, letting them freely pass.

"Have a good week," Peter said to Marian.

"You, too," Marian said as she went by with a friendly, non-flirtatious smile.

Not wanting to give off a stalker vibe, Peter hung back, letting them get ahead of him.

At the door, Marian stopped and turned back around. "I went through a divorce about a year ago," she said. "I need to be careful—for Jacob. And myself."

Peter nodded, appreciating her honesty. "I totally understand," he said with a soft smile.

"Thank you," she said genuinely.

They lingered there for a second before a woman's yell was heard coming from the nursing station room. Marian turned and hurried after her son.

By the time he got home, his mom had still not returned from Trinity. With the place to himself, Peter fixed some lunch and settled on the couch to watch the game. As the scoreless teams traded punts in a battle for field position, his mind kept returning to Marian.

Drifting off to sleep, he was awakened when his mom came

bustling into the house. The game was suddenly in the fourth quarter, and the score was twenty-four to twenty-seven.

"How was church?" Peter asked.

"I went to lunch with Dan and Jenny and a few others," his mom said, exuberant to be included in the Trinity in-crowd. "You should have seen it! There were more people at church than before the split! Everyone was asking about you. You really should have been there!"

"Yeah," Peter said. "They want to know where to put their money now."

"Oh, it's not like that," his mom said dismissively. "They're just excited. If you had come, you would know that."

Before Peter could make another smart remark, the phone rang.

"I'll see who it is," Ms. Quell said, jogging to the answering machine.

"If it's for me, I'm not here," he called. "I want to see the end of this game."

Several seconds after the ringing stopped, a squeal came from the other room, followed by a frantic, "Peter, pick up! Pick up!"

Curious as to who had elicited that kind of response, Peter got up and shuffled to the nearest phone in the kitchen. "Hello?"

"Hey, Peter," a honey-combed voice warbled. "It's Jordan."

"Oh, hey," he said, surprised, but not as nervous as he had been their last conversation. After waiting for the click from the third phone, he called out "Mom?" When he finally heard a reluctant hang up, he asked Jordan, "So what's going on?"

"I wanted to talk, you know, about that dream you had about me."

"Okay."

"Can you meet for coffee at the Mercantile around seven tonight?"

"I guess so," Peter said, recognizing the name of a funky Franklin coffee shop with a loyal Christian following.

"See you then," she said sweetly—or was it seductively? It was always hard for him to tell with her.

The Mercantile looked like an eclectic aunt's living room with kitschy knickknacks and bric-a-brac scattered around old tables, antique chairs, and a couple of art deco sofas. Other than one table of youngish hipsters, the place was basically deserted.

A kid at the counter took Peter's money and pointed him in the direction of canisters where he got to fill up his own cup. Deciding to skip the tip jar, Peter picked a table in the rear for the rendezvous and took a seat with his back to the exposed brick wall.

Sipping his coffee, he studied the twenty-year-olds at the other table. With bracelets and cell phone cases that carried coded religious messages, they had the practiced look of subtle Christian cool.

By his second cup, Peter was rehearsing the speech he was going to give the prima donna princess for making him wait, if she ever graced him with her presence. When the door finally opened and a little bell announced her arrival, he knew he'd never say a word of it.

Flipping her blond mane, she glanced around and, spotting him, bestowed a radiant smile of recognition. The kids who had glanced up at the chime were now openly gaping as the high priestess of Christian Pop made her way to the bean counter.

Whatever she ordered required being specially made by the barista. After putting some green in the tip jar, she glided past the gawking table of kids, tossing them a charitable smile without breaking stride.

After rising to his feet, Peter received a friendly embrace for old time's sake.

"People are talking about you," she stage-whispered as she sat down across from him, a mischievous glint in her eyes. For a second, Peter thought she was talking about the other patrons who were still staring, one aiming a cell phone at them. "Did you really call the stock-market crash?"

"Yeah, I guess I did," Peter said. "I mean, I just repeated what I dreamed."

"Here you go, Ms. Stone," the bowing barista said, offering up an elaborate coffee concoction.

"Thank you!" she said, taking the cup of froth.

As the barista faded, Jordan peeked out from behind her golden ringlets and long lashes. Blue eyes studied Peter. The last ten years had been good to her, accenting her already fine features.

"Well, I wished you would have told me about *that* dream," she said slyly. "My manager says I lost a fortune."

Peter pulled on his coffee, not feeling too sorry for her.

"So, how does it work?" she asked, as if it was all a nifty parlor trick. "You just dream it, or what?"

He nodded.

"I hardly even remember my dreams," she said, her tongue playfully dabbing at the whipped cream on top of her smoking hot drink. "Aren't you afraid you'll forget them or something?"

"These are different; they're memorable," Peter said. "Plus, I wake right up after I have one."

"Have you had a lot of these dreams?"

"Not really," he said. "A couple about Dan, one about you, and the one about the stock market."

"Wow, I guess I'm pretty special," she said, as if she was kidding, although Peter suspected she wasn't. "So, I've been thinking about that dream." She leaned in closer. "What do you think it means?"

"I don't know," Peter said. "I told you everything I know."

"Take a wild guess," she said, waiting out his answer.

"If I had to guess, I would say you are going to have a baby," Peter answered.

"I've already had two babies," Jordan replied flatly.

Peter shrugged. "Maybe you're going to have another one."

There was a long pause as Jordan seemed to be trying to make a decision. "Can I trust you?" she asked. Before he could answer, she did so for him. "I guess if God is telling you everything anyway, I have to trust you, right?"

Glancing behind her, she leaned into the table and mouthed the words, *I'm pregnant.*

"Congratulations," Peter said, not exactly surprised.

"I didn't even know I was, you know—" she glanced down below the table, presumably to her womb "—when you told me about your dream. I had a feeling, maybe. I just had to make sure." She shook her curled swirls of hair and pouted. "I honestly don't know what to do about it either."

"What's the problem?" Peter asked.

Just as Jordan started to speak, she became aware of a presence: the chief hipster from the other table was coming their way. Matted black hair and a soul patch set off a t-shirt with a filigree design under the word "Redeemed" in gothic lettering. A girl with dyed blond hair was tagging along, shyly staying back a few feet.

"Excuse me," Soul Patch said. "I'm sorry to bother you, Jordan. I'm Tucker Hobson. I just wanted to say hello."

As Jordan turned her face upward, she seemed to flip a switch, instantly turning on a mega-watt smile. "Hello, Tucker."

"I'm an engineer for Jack Ham at Salt Mine Studios."

"Oh sure," she said, brimming with feigned interest. Turning to Peter, she added, "I recorded *Hearts on Fire* at Salt Mine."

"Ah," Peter uttered, clueless.

"So how is Jack?" Jordan asked.

"Still a slave-driver," Tucker said with a nervous chortle.

Jordan joined him with a sympathetic smile. "I guess that's why it's called the Salt Mine."

"No doubt!" Tucker said with a big laugh, enjoying himself way too much.

"Well, tell Jack I said hi."

"Sure," Tucker said as his timid friend finally inched up to the table. "Oh, and this is Dana."

"Hi, Dana," Jordan said cheerily.

"I have listened to you since I was a little girl," Dana blurted out.

If the statement bothered the over thirty-year-old songstress, Jordan didn't let it show. "Thank you. That means so much," she cooed as if they shared a special bond. "Thank you both for coming over and saying hi."

"Can I take a quick pic?" Dana asked.

"Sure," Jordan said. As if having anticipated the question, she automatically gave her hair a toss, letting it fall into perfect photogenic place.

Dana and Tucker instantly dropped into their positions behind her.

It occurred to Peter to offer to take the picture, but Dana seemed more than capable of extending her phone out. All three smiled like long-lost friends reuniting.

Picture taken, the twosome almost skipped back to their table, anxious to post their experience for the world to see.

"Where were we?" Jordan asked, then remembered. "Oh, yeah." Checking to make sure her fans were out of earshot, she turned to Peter and said in a low, breathy voice, "You know I'm separated from Danny, right?"

Remembering Danny, a producer, was her husband, Peter muttered, "I heard something about that."

"We haven't really been together for over a year," she explained. "If it was any normal situation, we'd already be divorced."

Trying not to judge, Peter unclasped his pursed lips. Seeming to know how to read her audience, she added, "Danny's been seeing someone else, too."

"So, who is the father?" Peter asked, then immediately regretted it. It wasn't his business.

"I shouldn't say," she said. "No one you know." Giving her hair a shake of despair, she went on. "If Danny and I had just gotten a divorce, this wouldn't be such a big deal. But now, I'm stuck." Her eyes seemed to beg for help, which he would gladly have given her if he could. "I haven't even told the father I'm pregnant."

"Have you told Danny?" Peter asked.

"God, no," she said. "No one knows except my best friend and you—and God, I guess."

Contemplating her situation, Peter asked, "So what choice do you really have?"

"Oh, I have choices, and I've thought about all of them," she said coldly. Lowering her voice barely above a whisper, she added, "I just can't go through with *it*. I don't think it would be right. And if it ever got out...I mean, I could get forgiveness for murdering my parents with an ax, but a baby?" she shook her head. "In this business, that's the unforgivable sin."

They were silent for a minute.

Finally, Peter said, "All I can tell you is, in the dream, it seemed like you shouldn't hide your baby away."

"If it came out that I'd had a 'love child' with a man who isn't my husband, my so-called fans," Jordan shot a glance at Tucker's table, "would desert me. My label would drop me. Maybe if I begged for forgiveness, the Christian Broadcasting Network would let me come on."

"I'm sure you'd take a hit," Peter said, perhaps a little too casually for Jordan's taste. "But you've made your money. I mean, it's not like you're going to starve."

The star's inviting eyes suddenly glazed over with a hard outer covering. "No offense," she said, a razor's edge in her voice, "but it's pretty easy not to give a shit when you don't have anything to lose."

Peter returned her icy stare with one of his own.

As if deciding she might not want to insult the one person who knew her deepest, darkest secret, she added, "I don't think you fully appreciate the pressure I'm under. I mean, I have people depending on me."

"Oh, so this is about your entourage?" Peter asked, still smarting from the "not having anything to lose" comment.

"I have two kids already," she snapped back. "And I do have people who work for me that I care about, including my sister and my best friend."

Glancing around, she settled back in her chair. "And yes, I do care what people think. After ten years of singing and touring and being nice to every Tom, Dick, and *Tucker*, I don't want to be remembered as some slut."

"Maybe some people would think that, but most wouldn't. I

59

wouldn't," Peter persisted. "Think of it this way—there are probably a lot of people who aren't thrilled with the Little Miss Perfect image. Who knows, this could introduce you to a whole new audience."

"I think I know my audience pretty well," she said through a fake smile. "So excuse me if I don't take career advice from you." And with that, she enjoyed a long deep drink of her fancy latte.

Putting her cup down, she found Peter smiling back at her. "What's so funny?" she snarled.

"Can I be honest with you?"

She glared back, waiting impatiently.

"You have a glob of whipped cream on your nose," he said, holding out a napkin.

Blushing, she snatched the paper napkin. While she wiped the white dollop from the end of her upturned nose, Peter enjoyed the last laugh at the expense of Little Miss Perfect.

CHAPTER 9

An old black man pushes a grocery cart in front of a brick building with stained glass windows. (I'm thinking a church—then I recognize the Ryman.) He takes a corner, goes down a dark alleyway.

In the alley, two men from the shadows come toward the homeless man. Circling, the men attack. The black man falls down and rolls over as the men kick at him.

After the beating is over, the two attackers run off into the night, leaving the victim on the ground—not moving.

Peter studied the new entry in his notebook, trying to find a hidden layer of significance.

It seemed like his dreams might be escalating in importance, from his pastor, to his church, to a famous singer, to the stock market crash. If his theory held up, his next prophetic dream might signal a really big event, perhaps even global in scope. This one, however, seemed relatively minor, unless you were the guy getting beaten up.

The assault reminded him a little of the parable of the Good

Samaritan, the story Jesus told about a traveler who is robbed and left on the side of the road to die. The "righteous" people passed by the poor guy, too busy or fearful to get involved. Finally, a samaritan helps the man to a motel and even pays his hospital bills.

Unlike his other dreams, Peter didn't know the transient's identity, so he had no way of warning him. He did, however, have one critical piece of information: the Ryman Auditorium.

Knowing the location meant he could conceivably interject himself into the story, possibly even play the part of the Good Samaritan. Actually, there was a chance he could prevent the beating, making him the Great Samaritan.

While that sounded heroic, the reality entailed driving downtown to hang out in an alleyway. From his dream, he knew the attack happened at night, and since he didn't have to get up early anymore, there wasn't a good reason why he couldn't do it. Knowing he had to at least try, Peter waited until the sun set before getting ready to leave the house.

"I'm going out for a while," Peter announced as he passed between his mom and the TV.

"Where are you going?"

It felt ridiculous for a thirty-year-old man to have to explain his comings and goings to his mother—almost as ridiculous as a thirty-year-old man living at home.

"I'm doing research for a dream I had." Before she could question him further, he quickly added, "I can't tell you about it, so don't even ask. And don't wait up. I might be home late."

His mom let him go with a mysterious little smile that perplexed Peter. It wasn't until he was halfway to Nashville that he wondered if his mom thought he was rendezvousing with Jordan Stone. She would be so disappointed if she knew the truth.

The Ryman Auditorium had been built as an actual church before a radio station started using it for their live show, the *Grand Ole Opry*. While the *Opry's* popularity eventually outgrew the Ryman, the old tabernacle continued to be a venue for artists looking for a more intimate setting with perfect acoustics and loads of tradition. On that night, however, the mother church of country music sat dark and empty.

Not knowing if the attack would even happen that evening, Peter began to slowly walk the city block that encircled the old brick building. As he walked, he prayed for protection and that if this thing had to happen, it would happen soon. Selfishly, he was not keen on hanging around all night, or having to explain his comings-and-goings to his mom.

After a few round trips, he had become pretty familiar with the terrain. He decided the only place for a decent mugging was a wide alley that ran the length of the auditorium and backed up to the honkytonks and bars facing Broadway.

Behind Tootsie's Orchid Lounge, Peter found a wooden crate next to a dumpster to sit for a spell. Legend had it that performers at the *Opry* would sneak across the alley to Tootsie's to grab a cocktail between sets. Because of stories like that, "World Famous" Tootsie's had become an institution that still did a bang-up tourist business every night of the week.

Live music and crowd noise mingled and spilled out the back doors and into the desolated alleyway. Peter momentarily entertained the idea of going in for a beer and just as quickly dismissed the notion. The last thing he wanted to do was miss the whole purpose of his mission because he was having a cold one during "Family Tradition."

If he was going to smoke, this seemed like the place to do it. Lighting up, he listened to the raucous music and thought about the strange places his dreams had already taken him. Just a few nights ago he had been sipping coffee with Jordan Stone. Tonight, he was squatting in a spot where George Jones could have puked.

Grinding out the cigarette stub, he heard a rattling noise approaching from Fifth Street. Hearing the jangling sound of thin metal rods and one bad wheel scraping the pavement, he instantly knew what was coming.

Like a mirage, the shopping cart came into view, pushed by a shabby figure. Peter couldn't make out much about the man except that he looked destitute; the shopping cart was the giveaway.

Once again, he heard them before he saw them. To his left, a couple of boisterous drunks turned into the alley from Sixth Street. They were young, maybe twenty or so, and lean and rangy with wild swaggers.

With a *whoop*, one of the two hooligans smashed a beer bottle on the brick wall, then stepped back to examine his work like a budding Jackson Pollock. His partner, wearing a cowboy hat and boots, went to the glistening wall and lowered his jeans to complete the masterpiece with a signature.

"Hey, look what we have here!" Beer Bottle Kid said, spotting the lost shopper coming their way. "There's a bum!" he yelled at his buddy, who was running low on ink. As quick as he could, Cowboy Hat zipped up and clicked over to check out the urban attraction.

This is it, Peter thought, *the moment I dreamed. Now what?* Focused on finding the attack, he hadn't given much consideration to how he would actually intervene. He'd vaguely thought he could scare them off just by showing up. Now he realized that if he stepped in, he might become a victim, too.

"You got anything in here?" Beer Bottle Kid asked as he began rummaging through the shopping cart.

"Nothing of yours," the older black man said defiantly.

"Just a bunch of junk," Beer Bottle Kid commented, rifling through the odds and ends. In frustration of not finding gold bullion, or at least a case of beer, he pushed the cart over, sending the man's meager possessions scattering over the alleyway.

"I guess all you're good for is a shit kicking!" Cowboy Hat said. Like an angry line dancer, he gave a sharp kick, ramming his boot toe into the man's shin. With a slight gasp of air, the old man sunk to one knee, then crumpled to the ground.

"Hey!" Peter called out.

Surprised, both kids whirled to face the man emerging from

beside the dumpster. "Leave him alone," Peter said in his deepest, most ominous voice.

"Who the *%@# are you?" Cowboy Hat asked.

Resisting the urge to say something cool like, *Your worst nightmare,* Peter went with, "Don't worry about me. Just get out of here." Unfortunately, his nervousness had caused his voice to rise, giving the word "here" a little squeak.

Sensing either fear or budding puberty, the two country boys came closer, sizing up the homeless man's mysterious defender. Seeing Peter was not police or a bouncer or anyone who was remotely imposing, Beer Bottle Kid gave a crooked smile. "You want in on this?" he asked in a nasally redneck voice.

Adrenalin surged through Peter's body, and his legs and hands shook with nervous anticipation.

"Let's do it," Cowboy Hat said, moving within kicking range.

Knowing it was now or never, Peter came forward in two large strides and threw a punch with everything he had. The straight right cross caught enough of the left side of the drunk's slack face to send his hat flying into space.

The young man, formally known as Cowboy Hat, folded over, holding his jaw in place. Feeling like his knuckles had burst and his wrist might be broken, Peter put all he had into not screaming out in pain.

Pivoting to face Beer Bottle, Peter put his fists up, doing his best to conceal that his right hand was out of commission. Not so cocky now, Beer Bottle glanced over at his friend, who was sputtering incoherent obscenities.

"You okay, man?"

The question was answered with a string of bloody curses from Former Cowboy Hat.

"Like I said," Peter said, his own pain putting some real gravel into his voice, "get out of here."

Beer Bottle scowled, but there was more doubt than fire in his eyes. Turning from Peter, he went over to check on his wounded buddy.

While Former Cowboy Hat had managed to straighten up, his mouth still hung open like a cage door with a busted latch. To Peter's great relief, the kids picked up the hat and hurried out of the alley.

As soon as they were gone, Peter walked across the alley to the man who had silently watched the whole thing. Without a word, Peter used his left hand to right the grocery cart then bent down to pick up some of the soup and vegetable cans and blankets that had fallen out.

It wasn't that Peter expected tons of gratitude, but a few ounces would have been nice. Instead, what he heard caused his own jaw to drop.

"Did God send you?" the man quietly asked.

Turning to take in the older black man, Peter saw he was probably in his late fifties or early sixties. A scraggly salt-and-pepper beard covered most of his leathery face. Wild eyes looked up from under a worn baseball cap with "Capitol Records" stitched on the front.

"What did you say?" Peter asked, as he glanced down to a nametag stuck to the man's jacket that read, *Hi, My Name is...* Below, in rough handwriting, was scrawled, *Jesse.*

"You heard me," Jesse shot back.

"Did God send me?" Peter repeated. Seeing no reason to be coy with someone who was living on the streets, he answered, "Yes, He did."

Jesse confirmed it with a slight nod. "I thought so."

"How did you know that?" Peter asked anxiously.

"He told me," Jesse said through a wry smile, his eyes shimmering under the bill of his hat. "Cause I'm a prophet, too."

Peter felt the breath leave his body.

Jesse smiled wide now, showing off surprisingly strong and white teeth. Clearly, he was enjoying the effect he was having on the younger man. "You gonna offer me one of those Marlboros?"

As Peter wondered how Jesse knew about the cigarettes, much less the brand, Peter retrieved the pack from his pocket with his reviving right hand. Shaking a couple out, he gave one to Jesse and one to himself. All the while, he tried to figure out the old man.

He had received a little publicity after the stock market prediction, but even if Jesse had happened to see an article or photo, there was no way he could have recognized Peter in the dark. No, this guy was for real, whatever that meant.

"So, what do you mean," Peter asked, after they were both lit, "'You're a prophet, too?'"

"I go where God tells me to go," Jesse said nonchalantly, blowing a little smoke. "Same as you."

"Did He tell you to come here tonight?"

The elder prophet nodded enigmatically through the fog gathering around "Capitol Records."

"Well, you could have been killed," Peter objected.

"But I wasn't," Jesse said, "cause He sent me you."

"What if I hadn't come?" Peter asked.

"But you did," Jesse said, pointing the red tip of his cigarette in Peter's direction to punctuate the word *you*. Taking another leisurely puff, he reflected, "See, you think you were sent here to help me. But I'm thinking the Big Man sent me here to help you."

"Oh yeah?" Peter inquired. "How are you going to help me?"

Jesse took his time answering, seemingly lost in thought while he enjoyed the last few drags. "I think He sent you here to get over your fear," he finally said.

Even though Jesse's cigarette was down to the nub, a tiny yellow light still glowed. "I think He has plans for you. You just have to be willing to go all the way with Him. See, that's the way it works. It's an all-or-nothing proposition."

Since Peter didn't know what to say to that, he settled on, "You have dreams, too?"

"Oh, mine are more like feelings; I just know things," Jesse answered. "Some say I'm crazy, and maybe I am." Finally, he let the filter drop to the pavement and opened his empty hands, palms out. "But here we are."

"What happened to you?" Peter asked after a moment. "Why are you on the streets?"

"What?" The grizzled man grinned. "You afraid you going to end up like me?"

"It's not that," Peter said, then thought better of it. There was no use lying to a prophet. "Maybe."

"See, that's the fear again," Jesse said. "I told you, you gotta get over that. You lose your fear, there's nothing you can't do." He looked around, as if someone might be listening. "I have my own stuff I'm working out, mostly pride. That's why I'm here."

"Okay," Peter relented. "So I have to get over my fear."

"You did all right tonight. You could have come in before I got kicked," Jesse critiqued, giving his shin a rub. "When things get tough, you have to get tougher."

"Things are going to get tough?" Peter clarified with a note of concern.

"They usually do. Doing the Boss's work ain't easy," Jesse said, with the hardscrabble voice of experience. "But it's always worth it. You remember that. It's always worth it."

Peter clung to the older man's words as "I Got Friends in Low Places" echoed through the brick walls; the rowdy crowd joyously slurring the chorus. In spite of their surroundings, the moment in the alley felt holy.

"You will have more dreams. You just have to figure them out," Jesse said, as if he was prophesying on the spot. "And don't let fear hold you back. When the time is right, don't hesitate."

"What should I do to get rid of my fear?"

Jesse's eyes fell to the pack of cigarettes by his side. "You could start by giving me those."

"What does that have to do with anything?" Peter protested.

"Nothing," Jesse admitted. "You should just quit, especially if you're going to be a prophet."

"Yeah, I don't usually smoke anyway," Peter explained.

"Then it will be easy to give them up," he said, motioning with his gnarled hand.

Begrudgingly, Peter relinquished the almost-full pack to the old man.

"Just take it one step at a time," Jesse said, slowly getting to his feet and taking hold of his cart. "God will take care of the rest."

"Okay," Peter said. "I'll try."

"Dream on, young blood," Jesse said, starting to roll back down the alley in the direction from which he'd come. "Dream on."

CHAPTER 10

September 29

I'm driving and lost. On the side of the road is a diner. I pull over. Inside are a few people at tables and a counter. To no one in particular, I ask, "Where am I?"

A Native American man swivels around at the counter and points at me. "You are here."

I sit down at a table, and a waitress comes over with a glass of water—only the water is black. Before I can send it back, she takes off.

Looking around, I notice other people in the restaurant also have toxic-looking water.

Then, the Native American man goes over to a jukebox and makes a selection. An old, scratchy country song comes on, and he starts doing a little jig.

"What's that song?" I ask him.

"E9," he says.

While he is doing his dance, a low rumbling passes through the diner. Everyone runs outside.

In the distance, a low, dark wall heads our way—swelling in size as it comes closer. A moment later, we are all waist deep in black ooze.

That's when I wake up.

Sitting up in bed, Peter stared at the full page of writing in the red notebook, going over his dream again and again, trying to recall anything else he might have forgotten. The little details could be important, and this dream had been filled with them. They might mean nothing, or they could be the key to unlocking everything.

Behind the wall of black ooze is what looks like smoking birthday candles...?

As Peter scribbled the postscript at the bottom, he tried to think of a better way to explain the columns he remembered in the background. They appeared to be sticking up out of the black frosting. The description was close enough; he knew what he meant.

After climbing out of bed, he made his way downstairs, still carrying his tattered journal with him. His mom had already left for work but had graciously left some coffee in the pot. He poured and nuked a cup, thanking his mom in absentia.

Sitting down at the kitchen table, he reread his dream for about the tenth time. Like the one that had turned out to be about the stock market, this one seemed cryptic and to have wider implications than just one person. Other than that, he couldn't draw any conclusions except to avoid the drinking water at roadside diners.

Not knowing what else to do, he reached for the phone. After leaving a message on Dan's cell, he tried the church, and after a brief hold, the man came on the line.

"Hey, Peter!" his confidant said. "How are you?"

"I'm fine," Peter responded.

"We've missed you at church," Dan reminded him.

Let it go, Peter thought. Before Dan could ask him to make a guest appearance at Trinity again, he spoke up. "I had another dream, and I have no idea what it means."

"Go ahead and tell me," Dan said.

71

Peter read the dream straight out of his journal and afterward gave a brief explanation about the birthday candles. When he finished, he waited for Dan's interpretation.

"So, it was like a tidal wave of what—black slime?"

"Pretty much," Peter confirmed. "I think it was the same stuff in our drinking glasses at the diner—only a mountain of it."

"It almost sounds like the parting of the Red Sea," Dan said.

That theory didn't seem to lead anywhere, so the former divinity professor continued, "Well, water is used as a symbol throughout the Bible, probably most often as the Holy Spirit. For example, when Jesus is at the well and he tells the woman he is offering living water that quenches thirst forever."

"This water looked heavily polluted," Peter said.

"So maybe there's an evil influence that has corrupted individual spirits, represented by the water in each drinking glass," Dan said, getting on a roll. "And then there is a huge amount of this same malignant force coming for all of us."

"Yeah," Peter conceded, feeling there had to be a connection between the goo in the drinking glasses and the flood of it. "You could be onto something."

They thought a little more in silence, both coming up empty. "Well, these things take a little time, don't they?" Dan finally said.

"I guess," Peter reluctantly agreed.

"Why don't we get together tonight?" Dan offered. Since Peter didn't have any other pressing engagements, he was about to agree when his pastor continued, "I've been invited to the Wednesday night service at a church in Donelson. They want me to speak on prophecy, and I would love it if you could join me. We could talk afterwards."

Had Dan just tricked him into making a public appearance with him? There was silence on Peter's end as he struggled with feelings of manipulation.

"You wouldn't have to say much," Dan quickly added. "Just say a few words about what it's like to receive a prophetic dream. People are fascinated."

"I don't know," Peter said, not wanting to be trotted out for amusement. It wasn't fair to him, and it didn't seem to honor the dreams either.

"People really want to see you right now, Peter," Dan said. "They are looking for answers—and I know you don't have them all, but it gives people reassurance and hope. You don't want to 'hide your light under a bushel.'"

Could Dan be right? Was he being selfish with his gift? Besides, sometimes the dreams revealed themselves at church services, so maybe he was being called to go. Maybe he'd find the answer to his dream in Donelson, wherever that was.

"Okay," he relented.

"Great!" Dan said and hastily gave Peter directions to the church before he could change his mind. Sounding pleased, the pastor signed off saying, "I'll see you at seven at the church. And thanks for doing this!"

Peter felt good about his decision—for about five minutes. After that, he began to feel resentful of Dan for baiting and switching him. He started envisioning himself in front of a church full of people, awkwardly trying to talk about things he didn't understand himself.

Then there was the inconvenience factor. It turned out Donelson was located across town in an area he didn't know at all.

Following Dan's directions, he exited the interstate near the airport, all the while thinking about what he should say in the service and whether he should mention his latest dream. If he did, someone might have an insight. At the same time, it somehow seemed premature to talk about it to a bunch of strangers, like it wasn't quite ready for public consumption.

Lost in thought, he spotted a sign for the entrance to the interstate, which was interesting because he had just gotten off I-40. Either he'd made a wrong turn, or two, or he'd entered a time warp. Frustrated by his lack of GPS, he pulled over and rummaged around in the glove compartment, coming up with an old paper relic.

Opening the well-worn map, he discovered it covered all of Tennessee, making it useless for finding his specific location. Just before stuffing it back in the box, he scanned the state, his eye drifting to the margins. The letters of the alphabet (A, B, C, etc.) ran across the bottom of the page, while numbers (1, 2, 3, etc.) counted out the horizontal lines.

A few notes from the jukebox drifted back to him. What was the name of the song? The Native American from the diner had just said it was "E9." Intersecting the lines on the grid, he found himself looking at a fairly desolate area in East Tennessee. It wasn't much to look at, at least not on paper.

For a few long minutes, Peter sat in his car on the side of the road, suspended in indecision. His mind spun a variety of reasons why it was crazy to make the drive: it was probably just a coincidence; it was a really long way; he would arrive late at night; he didn't have enough cash for a motel room; he had made an obligation to Dan.

As much logical sense as it made to go on to the church in Donelson and do the dog-and-pony (aka the Dan-and-Peter) show, he couldn't shake a nagging feeling that he needed to find E9 and see for himself what was there.

Just take it one step at a time. God will take care of the rest. Jesse's words came back to him. *Get over your fear.... You just have to be willing to go all the way with Him.*

With a heavy sigh, Peter took his car out of park and drove toward the on-ramp, trying not to second-guess himself. Even so, he ended up second, third, and fourth guessing himself until he was finally cursing his decision during the last hour of the nearly three-hour drive.

Since he didn't own a cell phone, he made a point of pulling over to search for a nearly extinct pay phone. When he finally found one, he left a rambling, apologetic message on Dan's voicemail, promising to call as soon as he was back in town.

Being a dutiful son, he scrounged up some more loose change from his car seats and made another call to his mom. Again, he breathed a sigh of relief when the machine answered. Just as he was launching into his obtuse excuse for not coming home, she picked up.

"Hello? Peter? Is that you?" Ms. Quell said, sounding concerned. He confirmed it was indeed him. "Did I hear you say you aren't coming home tonight? Why? What's the matter?"

"Nothing's the matter," he tried to reassure her as he scrambled for how best to avoid a lengthy Q and A. Once again, he played the prophet card, which also happened to be the truth. "I had another dream, and I'm trying to figure it out."

"Another one?" she asked. "What's it about?"

"I don't want to go into it right now," he said. "I just wanted to let you know I'll be home late, or maybe not till tomorrow."

There was a long pause, followed by, "Are you with Jordan Stone?"

For a moment, he wondered if it might be easier to just say *Yes*, but he couldn't lie, especially about that. "No, Mom."

There was more silence, which Peter wasn't sure whether to interpret as relief or regret.

"And you have to go in the middle of the night?" she asked.

"Yes," Peter replied.

"Can I at least ask where you're going?" she asked pitifully.

"East Tennessee."

"Oh, *East* Tennessee," she said sarcastically. "Well, if I need to get a hold of you in an emergency, that will save me a lot of time. I'll know to start looking in *East* Tennessee."

Peter sighed. "Are you expecting an emergency?"

"No one ever expects an emergency," she explained, as if talking to a child.

"For over ten years, you never knew where I was or what I was doing," Peter said. "Now, I have to report everything to you just because I'm living at home?"

"That's right!" she snapped. "That's the price you pay for living at home. I'm your mother. I worry about you."

"Well, please don't," Peter begged as he hung up the phone.

Interstate 40 curved around where E and 9 intersected on his map. *Should I be looking for the specific crossing, or just in the general E9 vicinity?* At his first opportunity, Peter veered off on a lonely exit and began searching for civilization or a giant wall of mud, whichever came first.

About a mile down the road, a neon light shone in the darkness. As the beacon slowly came into focus, Peter saw it was a sign announcing a diner, still open for business. It seemed so desolate and out of place that for a moment, Peter felt dislodged from time and space, like he was being pulled into his dream.

Maneuvering into the gravel lot, he parked next to the small, very real building, all the while wondering if this was the E9 he was supposed to find. Inside were a couple of people at the counter, along with two tables of patrons. No one looked like a Native American, nor did he see a jukebox or even a dirty glass of water.

"Sit anywhere," he heard an unseen waitress call out.

Peter found a seat at a table by the window. Outside, there didn't appear to be anything at all around them. It was as if the wall of inky blackness had already come and swallowed the diner whole, which made him think of Jonah in the belly of the whale.

"You know what you want?"

Breaking out of his stupor, Peter looked up to see a fairly cute young woman with a red ponytail and a nametag that read "Debbie" standing over him, her pencil poised above a notepad.

"Ah, I'll take a cheeseburger," he said with a cursory glance at a menu on the table.

"That comes with fries," Debbie said, her country accent coming through her smacking gum. "What do you want to drink?"

"How's your water?" he asked.

"Our water?" Debbie repeated. "Ah, it's wet."

"Nothing wrong with it or anything?" Peter asked, pretending to kid.

But it was late, and Debbie wasn't in the mood for fun and games. "What would be wrong with our water?" she asked, her friendly facade falling away.

"I don't know," Peter said, feeling a little foolish. "I'll just have a Coke."

Without another word, Debbie took his order back to the kitchen. While the cook pulled his ticket and started frying his patty, Peter mulled over his situation. If he couldn't crack the code pretty soon, he would need to start thinking about what he was going to do for the night.

Tired and a long way from home, he wasn't entirely sure he, or his car, could make it back, at least not right away. As a last resort, he supposed he could put a hotel room on his credit card and figure out how to pay for it later.

"Is there a motel that's close?" he asked Debbie when she came back with his drink.

"Go east one more exit to Kingston," she said, pointing in the direction.

His waitress was about to head off to her next table when Peter spoke up again, "So, what's there to do around here?"

Clearly assuming the customer was trying to flirt with her, Debbie stopped and cocked a hand on her waist. "Pull for the Vols and burn coal," she said, if as she'd repeated the line a few thousand times.

Peter knew the University of Tennessee (whose team was the Volunteers) was just up the road in Knoxville. The coal reference, however, he didn't get. "So, is there a coal mine or something around here?"

"Coal-fired power plant," Debbie clarified, deciding it was time to give the pesky patron fair warning. "My boyfriend works there."

"Huh," Peter commented, deciding to deduct a dollar from her tip for the needless boyfriend reference.

The hamburger came and went. Having not eaten in hours, Peter wolfed it down so fast he wasn't sure if it was any good or not. The calories did make him feel better, and by the time he settled up with Debbie, he gave her twenty percent anyway.

Heading back to the parking lot, he wondered where to go next. He still had no idea what his dream meant, but he wasn't prepared to drive all the way back to Nashville, at least not yet. Compromising with himself, he decided to check out the nearest town and look around.

Rather than double back to the on-ramp, he kept east, hopefully heading toward Kingston. After a mile or so, he turned onto Swan Pond Road, mainly because the name sounded nice. When he passed back underneath the interstate, he knew he was headed in the right direction.

With railroad tracks on one side and a line of trees buffering the other, the road felt like it might just trail off into the woods. Just as he was about to turn around, an imposing fence stretched out in front of him; a "TVA" sign on the gate informed him he would not be going any farther anyway.

Creeping forward, he aimed his high beams at the smaller print on the sign: "Kingston Fossil Plant." Coming to a complete stop, he stared through his windshield at a row of lit-up smokestacks rising into the night sky. From a distance, they looked a little like candles on a birthday cake.

Once again, he felt like he had fallen into his dream world, only he was awake, and this was real. Not only had he found the diner, he'd discovered E9, and he knew it was going to be the site of some sort of disaster. Now he just had to get home.

CHAPTER 11

Trinity had more than made up for the members that exited with Mark Shelton. From the balcony to the main floor, the service was jam-packed with worshippers squeezed into the pews until they spilled out onto fold-out chairs set up in the aisles and lobby. Three cameras, representing the local TV stations, positioned themselves in the back while reporters waited near the exits.

In a small backstage area, Peter wondered how he had ended up in this situation—again. Being loyal to his pastor, he had called Dan as soon as he had gotten home and told him about the upcoming disaster. And, against his better judgment, Dan had talked him into waiting three days, until Sunday, to make the announcement.

If he had been nervous about announcing the stock market dream, he was petrified now. Not only was it a full house, but whatever he said was going to make the news. There was no going back after this one.

Beyond the door, Peter could hear the keyboard starting a new melody for the next song.

"You about ready?" Dan asked as he came over to join Peter.

"Not really," Peter said, looking up helplessly. "I was just thinking how much easier it would have been to call the newspaper. I could have phoned the whole thing in."

"This will get you a lot more publicity," Dan said. "And that's the point, isn't it? Letting as many people as possible know about the disaster?"

"I don't know," Peter said, fighting the waves of nausea washing over him.

"Why don't I pray for us?" Dan suggested. Peter nodded; that might be a good idea. The pastor closed his eyes and raised his head, "Oh Heavenly Father, we come to you this morning...."

As Dan lifted them up, Peter noticed the singing getting progressively louder. With the eyes of the city on them, Trinity was going to put on a show. Or maybe they thought if they sang loud enough, the prophecy would be a wonderful blessing. Peter wished he had something sexier to work with than a coal-plant disaster, but he didn't write his own material.

"Amen," Dan said, opening his eyes and looking at his young prophet. "You feel better?"

Peter nodded, even though he didn't. For a moment, he contemplated throwing up on Dan's loafers. When the feeling passed, he asked, "What if they don't like what I have to say?"

"The disciples worried about the same thing," Dan replied pleasantly. "Do you remember what Jesus told them?" Not sure where Dan was going, Peter shook his head to save time. "He said if a town doesn't listen to what you have to say, shake the dust from your sandals and go to the next town."

Smiling in his reassuring, fatherly way, Dan added, "Remember, this isn't about how you or I come across. It's about getting God's message out. That's all that matters."

That actually did help a bit, although Peter's stomach still felt tied in knots.

"Come on," Dan said, patting him on the leg. "We'll go out

together. You take a seat in the chair on the stage while I say a few remarks. Then I'll introduce you."

They both stood up, Peter a little shakily. As Dan swung the door open, the music and energy in the sanctuary flooded over him, almost physically knocking him back. A couple of cameras flashed as he came out on stage just as the song hit a crescendo.

Half-blinded, Peter stumbled and groped around before finding an empty chair. As soon as he sat down, he picked a nice spot on the carpet to stare at, trying to avoid eye contact with the crowd. But not seeing them did not make them go away, and he could feel them straining to peek at the freak.

The song came to an end, followed by an extended season of tongues, chants, and general utterances of praise. After a couple of minutes, Dan held out his arms to quiet the scattered cries of "Hallelujah" and "Praise God."

"I believe we have a new face or two this morning," Dan joked as he scanned the full house. "To all of you, welcome to Trinity Church!"

As was his style, Dan began to pace the stage with the microphone in his hand. "In case you haven't heard, we have a prophecy this morning from Peter Quell." When mentioning his name, Dan extended an arm toward Peter, who felt his heart palpitate.

"Two weeks ago, Peter foretold of a stock market crash. If you were here, you remember that Peter made it clear that the message was more about resetting our priorities than preserving our assets. God was calling us to let go of the false perception that money can ever be our security or our savior in this world."

The pacing stopped long enough for a dramatic pause. "As we all know, three days later, on 'Red Wednesday,' the stock market plunged."

Walking from side to side, Dan filled in the back story. "This was not the first prophetic word that Peter had. He personally told me two things that proved to be true. One of them probably saved my life."

Taking a stand again, the pastor looked out over the anxiously awaiting audience. "Today, Peter comes to us with another word."

Holding his ground for a beat, he announced, "Let us open our hearts and minds to a message from the Living God."

With that introduction, he turned to Peter, who swallowed hard and rose with a wobble. Trying to find his stage legs, he came forward to the extended handheld microphone. As soon as he took hold of the mike, it began to tremble. Seeing the quiver, Dan coolly took the mike back and placed it in the stand.

"Go ahead, Peter," the pastor calmly said.

When Peter stepped up to the stand, the silence seemed to expand to fill the entire room like a balloon about to burst. Peter cleared his throat to break the ice-cold, dead air. Letting out a big breath, he leaned in toward the microphone, which amplified his exhale into a rushing whirlwind.

Stepping back, Peter closed his eyes and tried to figure out if he was going to faint or not. In the couple of seconds of quiet darkness, he thought he felt a Presence pass through him.

"Wow, this is pretty scary," he said when he reopened his eyes, getting a couple of friendly laughs in return. "Okay, um, let me just tell you what I dreamed...."

In a series of stops and starts, the story dribbled out. First the dream, followed by an abbreviated version of putting the interpretation together. The whole speech took about two minutes, but it felt like a couple of hours to Peter.

"So, I'm not exactly sure what is going to happen," Peter admitted in conclusion. "I mean, I believe there is going to be a problem with the coal-burning plant, and I think it's going to happen pretty soon." He stared at his audience, waiting for them to start shouting questions like before, but no one said a word.

A few seconds later, a large hand clasped his shoulder. Startled, Peter looked over to find Dan standing beside him.

"Let's pray," the pastor said. "Heavenly Father, we come to you this morning...."

With Dan literally holding onto him, Peter could not escape during the prayer as he had after the stock market announcement.

Instead, he stood under the bright lights, trying to remember what he'd said, wondering if it had made any sense at all.

Finally, Dan proclaimed "Amen" and squeezed Peter's shoulder so hard it actually hurt. With a gentle shove, he directed the prophet back to the chair on the stage.

"I want to say a few words about what we've heard," Dan said. "God uses prophecies in different ways. Sometimes, God uses prophecy to admonish His church, warning us to shape up in some area. But the ultimate purpose of prophecy is always to build up faith. God wants us to know we are not alone, and when prophecy is fulfilled, we know He is watching over us."

There was the usual slew of "Amens."

"You know, when we hear the word 'prophet,' we think of old men in the Old Testament. Even if we believe in modern-day prophecy, we consider it an extremely rare gift that is only given to a few, like Peter here."

Turning back, he gestured to where his prophet was supposed to be sitting. The chair, however, was empty.

Having slipped through the door behind the stage, Peter could hear Dan force a chuckle—or was it a grumble? Relieved to be out of the limelight, Peter stayed put, listening from the wings to his pastor carry on.

"But I'm here to tell you, prophecy should not be thought of as a rare occurrence. We are clearly called to prophecy, just as we are encouraged to speak in tongues, and heal the sick, and support one another."

Peeking back out to the stage, Peter saw Dan dramatically pointing at the congregation and proclaiming, "Brothers and sisters, the gifts of the Spirit are ours for the taking," his big hand closed, grasping the air, "if only we have the faith to take them!"

Despite his powerful words, the news cameras were being snapped off their tripods, and reporters were slipping out the back. The main event was over.

Peter would have to hurry to beat them out.

Sneaking through a side door, he scurried down a corridor, hoping he wouldn't run into anyone. Without incident, he found the exit that led out near the church entrance.

As soon as he hit sunlight, a scrum of bodies pressed in close, some brandishing microphones. The scent of hairspray wafted in from the reporters, backed up by the sweaty musk of sturdy cameramen. A quick, frenzied look around revealed he was penned in.

"Peter! When is this accident going to happen?"

"Have you notified the coal plant?"

"Why do you think God has chosen you for these visions?"

"Is it true you shorted the stock market and made millions?"

The inquisitors kept coming at him even as Peter pushed ahead. A gap opened, and the throng followed, moving with him down the front steps of the church toward the sidewalk.

"Do you have any other messages from God?" one of them called after him.

Once he hit the sidewalk, Peter quickened his pace to an easy jog. If they were going to hound him, he was going to make them work for it.

"Is it true you are romantically involved with Jordan Stone?"

That one made him glance back. The reporter closest on his heels was the brunette from Channel 7, Cindy Sizemore. She thrust her microphone out at him like a baton in a relay race.

"No," he managed to sputter before heading up the street in an all-out wind sprint, leaving Cindy and the rest of the action news teams in the proverbial dust from his sandals.

Watching himself on TV was like having an out-of-body experience, Peter thought. A body he did not necessarily want to inhabit anymore. Images of him stammering and stuttering on stage at church repulsed him, yet it was impossible to look away.

Peter had made all three local channels, and the stories were all billed as some variation of "Local Prophet Predicts Disaster at Coal Plant." The clever minds at Channel 3 were referring to him as "Peter the Prophet." Channel 7 devoted twenty of their twenty-three-minute broadcast to him, including long unedited shots of him rambling about birthday candles and a wall of goo. And, of course, there was the obligatory chase scene.

"Why were you running away?" his mom asked. "You look like you just robbed a bank."

Peter merely shook his head in disgust.

"Why did she ask about Jordan?" his mom asked, her interest piqued again.

"I don't know," Peter said. "I guess someone saw us having coffee together."

"But there's nothing going on, right?" she asked, clearly still holding out hope he was hiding a secret liaison.

"No, Mom." Exhausted, he stood up and announced, "I'm going to bed."

"I'm going to stay up for the ten o' clock news," his mom said. "Do you want me to record it?"

"Please don't," he said, trudging up the stairs.

After shutting the upstairs door behind him, he brushed his teeth and fell into bed. As tired as he was, sleep was elusive. Images of crowds and reporters demanding answers and refusing to let him get away kept whirling by him.

Getting out of bed, he knelt. "Okay, God, I think you're sending me these dreams. And that's really cool. It's just, I'm just not sure you have the right guy because all this attention—it's too much."

For some reason, Jesse came to mind, an image of him pushing a grocery cart down a dark alleyway.

"I know, I know, I need to get over my fear. So I'll do my best. I'm trying. I'm just saying, if you don't send me any more dreams, it will be okay. It might even be for the best." He paused. "Your will be done."

Afterwards, he stayed silent for a long time before getting back in bed, where he found sleep waiting for him.

By morning, Peter felt slightly better. He lay in bed, realizing the school would not be calling him to substitute—ever. It was depressing not to have a job or any other good reason to get up, so he resolved to stay in bed all day. Twenty minutes later, he couldn't take the boredom and went in search of stale coffee.

With a warmed-up cup, he padded into the den, plopped on the couch, and turned on the TV, where the hosts of a network morning show breezily chatted in their mock living room. Just as Peter reached for the remote to search for something a little less cheery, the program cut to their news desk for the day's top stories.

"At a coal-burning plant in East Tennessee, a dam at a retention pond has burst, releasing hundreds of acres of coal ash," the news woman said over the aerial video of a rough rural landscape caked in dark sludge.

"This 'coal ash' is a byproduct of coal burning and contains high levels of lead, mercury, and other heavy metals. While there have been no reported fatalities, there is concern it could contaminate nearby rivers—a primary source for drinking water in the region."

And then the news anchor was onto a story about civil unrest in the Middle East.

For a while, Peter simply stared at the TV as thoughts raced through his head, his overriding one being, *My God—it happened!*

Among the other secondary questions that flitted through his head were, *What is coal ash again? What does this mean for the people in that area? Why did I wait till Sunday to make my announcement? If I had said something sooner, could more have been done to prevent this?*

The phone rang, startling him out of his shame spiral. He popped up, sprinted to listen to the message, and immediately recognized Dan's voice asking, "Are you there?"

Snatching up the receiver, Peter answered, "Yeah, I just heard."

"Has anyone called you for a comment yet?"

"Not yet."

"They will," Dan assured him. "I have a feeling this could go national. Maybe we should have a press conference."

"I don't want to call any more attention to me," Peter said, still trying to process the latest developments. "I should have done more, made an announcement sooner, or at least talked to the coal plant people when I was there."

"You really think they would have taken you seriously?" Dan asked incredulously.

"Well, I did predict the stock market crash," Peter replied, a little defensively.

"Most people don't know about that," Dan said. "And not everybody that knows about it is convinced you really did it."

"But there's audio—"

"That can be forged," Dan said. "Most people, especially non-believers, assume we're cooking the books somehow." His voice lowered with conviction. "This time, we have reporters and video—real, verifiable proof."

"Maybe I could have convinced them to do *something*," Peter said weakly, wondering why God would warn him about a disaster if he couldn't help prevent it.

"I guarantee you, coal workers were not going to shut down their plant to do a safety inspection based on the word of a self-proclaimed prophet," Dan insisted.

Right or wrong, Dan was at least making Peter feel a little better.

"That's not to say we shouldn't get out in front of this thing. If you don't talk about it, then everyone else is going to shape the story. Doing a press conference will at least give you a chance to explain yourself."

After a long pause, Peter sighed. "Let me think about it, okay?"

"Think fast," Dan said.

"Yeah, okay," Peter said, growing tired of being pushed around. "I'll call you soon."

"Okay," Dan said, sounding equally put out by the lack of game plan.

As soon as the receiver hit the base, Peter's phone began to ring.

CHAPTER 12

Peter sat by the phone, listening to the messages as they came in. Several were from strangers who were offering their support and prayers. Tom McAllister called to congratulate him, making it sound like Peter had been a big winner on a game show: "You nailed it again! It is awesome the way God is using you, brother!"

Striking a different note, Jordan Stone's accusatory message asked why there were rumors they were dating and demanded he call her to straighten things out.

Mr. Quell called sounding seriously bewildered after having heard that a young man with his last name predicted a coal plant disaster.

Mostly, there were the local reporters, especially the ones that had been at the church service and heard the proclamation firsthand. Only now there was an excited edge to their messages. "You need to call me." "We need a statement." "We are coming over."

When the doorbell first rang, it startled Peter, sending him flying to a window where he could make out a news van parked on the street. Retreating upstairs to his bedroom, he scuttled along the floor like a hermit crab, trying to avoid more windows and prying cameras.

As the phone and the doorbell continued to ring, Peter felt his anxiety level, along with the urge to flee, rising. If he could get to LA or Atlanta, he had friends he could stay with, at least for a while. Of course, that kind of trip would cost money and was a little extreme. All he really needed was a quiet place to get his head together.

Thinking through his options for a temporary escape, he realized he didn't know anyone in his hometown anymore. The only person he'd had any contact with was Jordan Stone, and the idea of staying with her seemed like a stretch. And yet, he was kind of desperate.

It wasn't like it would have to be romantic. Surely, she had enough room to put him up for a day or two. Plus, she had asked him to call her anyway. In between the incoming calls, he picked up the receiver and punched in the number she had left for him.

A couple of rings later, a young woman answered with a brisk, "Yes."

"Jordan?"

"Who's this?" the woman shot back—definitely not Jordan.

"Peter Quell," he said, wondering if he had a wrong number.

"Hold on," the woman said, sounding irritated.

A full three minutes later, Jordan came on the line. "Someone took pictures of us at the Mercantile," she said by way of a salutation. "It's posted on some website. I just saw it. Can you believe that?"

"One of your fans at the next table," Peter said.

"As if I don't have enough to deal with," Jordan moaned. "Can you hold on?" Before he could answer, she was gone.

Glancing outside, Peter noticed a second news van had arrived and wondered if they could somehow tap his phone line. One paranoid thought led to another: *Can the reporters hear me? Can the cameras see me? Am I on TV right now?*

Pulling himself back from edge of paranoia, he realized

he had been on hold for quite a while. Just when he was about to hang up, Jordan announced, "Okay, I'm back!" like it was an encore performance.

"Well, I need to go," he said, if for no other reason than that he didn't like her thinking she could make him wait indefinitely.

"You are seriously blowing up!" she said, ignoring his idle threat. "Everyone is talking about you."

"I've got news vans outside my house right now," Peter said.

"Not doing any interviews is smart," Jordan commented. "It plays into the whole mysterious prophet thing."

"Yeah, that's what I'm going for," he said dryly.

"It's working!" she said seriously. "The more you ignore them, the more they want you, at least while you're hot."

"I'll try to remember that," he said. There was a moment of silence into which Peter threw out his line. "Yeah, I've got to get out of here, or I'll go crazy."

Jordan was either distracted or simply ignoring him. Either way, she wasn't taking the bait.

He cast again. "I need to find a place to lay low." With no nibble, he tried, "What do you do to get away from the media?"

"I shut the front gate."

Giving up on wrangling an invitation to stay at her place, he decided to follow up on the dream he'd had about her in the first place. "So what's going on with you and, you know, *everything*?"

"Nothing. Everything is fine," she shot back, a little too defensively. "Oh! Callie just peed her pants. I got to go. Call me later." And then she was gone, leaving him holding a dead line.

As he placed the phone on the cradle, Peter realized that when the chips were down, the only people you could really count on were family. Unfortunately, he didn't have many relatives in town except his mom and his mom's older sister, Aunt Dorothy.

There was also Uncle John, his dad's younger brother who lived in Gallatin, a suburb northeast of Nashville. As quiet and unassuming as Uncle John was, sometimes it was easy to forget that he lived as close as he did. Going to his address book, Peter looked up the number and called.

While Peter was in the middle of leaving a message, a younger version of his dad's voice picked up. "Well, hey there, Peter!"

"Uncle John," Peter said. "How have you been?"

"Pretty boring compared to you," John quipped. "You've been making news."

"Yeah, that's kind of why I'm calling," Peter confessed. "I hate to ask, but you think I could spend a night or two at your place?"

"Sure," John said, without hesitation. "You remember how to get here?"

"I think so," Peter said, the distant memories of past visits coming back to him.

"I'll see you soon."

And with that, Peter packed a couple of changes of clothes and left a note for his mom, telling her where he would be. From his window, he could see at least two news crews setting up in the front yard. If he went out the back door and circled around, he had a decent shot of making it to his car undetected.

After grabbing his bag, he tip-toed through the kitchen and into the garage. From the small windowpane in the upper part of the door, the coast appeared to be clear, although the tiny window didn't allow much peripheral vision.

Peter took a step of faith into the backyard and closed the locked door behind him. To his right, he could see the front of his car parked to the side of the house. Thirty feet to freedom. Scampering from the grass to the gravel driveway, he heard a voice calling behind him in a hushed, urgent shout, "Peter!"

"What?" Startled, he whirled around to find the Channel 7 action reporter, Cindy Sizemore, on his trail once again.

"Just give me a second," Cindy begged in a low hiss as her cameraman appeared, chugging along behind her through the backyard.

Peter didn't respond; he just kept moving to his car where he unlocked the driver's door.

"Why do you think God is revealing these dreams to you?" she called after him.

"I really don't know," he managed as he got his car door open and tossed his bag inside.

Catching up to him, she lobbed her next question from behind his shoulder. "Do you think you were supposed to help avert these disasters?"

Remembering how foolish he'd looked running away from her at church, he turned around to face his questioner, aware of the camera rolling beside her. The little voice inside his head reminded him that whatever came out of his mouth was going to be on the six o' clock news.

"I don't see how I could have stopped the stock market from crashing," he said. "Besides, I think the dreams are more about calling attention to a problem. Like, why aren't you covering this coal spill?"

"Well, that's not our market," she half-whispered.

"You cover the Vols, don't you?" Peter shot back. "I mean, this sounds like a pretty serious disaster, and everyone just wants to talk about the prophecy."

"Because receiving a dream from God is more unusual than an environmental disaster," Cindy countered. "That's what 'news' is—the unusual. You know, man-bites-dog."

While that exchange would probably be edited out of whatever aired, it was a valid point, and Peter didn't have a ready response.

Cindy morphed back into her news persona, her voice altering as well. "So, Peter, what do you believe we are supposed to learn from the stock market crash and this environmental disaster?"

"In my stock market dream," Peter said slowly, "I felt like money had become an idol. I said that from the beginning. I'm not sure about the ash spill."

As Peter heard his own words, he realized he hadn't bothered to understand the disaster either. He was no better than the media; he still didn't even know what coal ash really was.

As Peter slipped into the driver's seat, Cindy daringly shoved her microphone into the door as it was swinging shut, coming within a hair of getting her forearm crushed before Peter stopped the door from closing.

"Where are you going now?" Cindy asked, undaunted.

"I guess I'm going to try and understand what happened at the coal plant."

With that, Peter gently pushed her mike hand out of harm's way and closed and locked his door. In his rearview mirror, Peter saw the news reporter from Channel 3 who had missed the interview frantically running up the driveway. Starting his car, he put the gear in reverse.

As he backed up, the desperate reporter rapped so hard on the moving windshield with his ring finger that Peter was afraid the glass might actually crack. Giving his car some gas caused Channel 3's "man on the scene" to step back.

Out of the driveway, Peter put the car in drive, veered around the bulky news vans, (Channel 3 half-parked on his mom's lawn), and screeched up the street. All he wanted to do was hide out in Gallatin. As nice as that would be, there was something he had to do first. Like a good reporter, he knew he had to see his story through, and to do that, he had to go to the source.

Already a long state, Tennessee seemed to be stretching out before him today like Gatlinburg taffy, the endless road refusing to let him reach his destination. His only stop had been a late lunch at a Cracker Barrel.

By the last hour of his trip, Peter was getting cramped and crabby in his tin can of a car. He'd been worried about where he should go once he got to Kingston, but it turned out all he had to do was follow the activity to the coal plant.

When he got close enough to the main gate, he parked along the side of the road with the other cars and a news van from Knoxville. Wearing an old baseball cap with the bill pulled down, Peter walked through the throng of bystanders to the closed TVA facility.

Outside the locked chain-link fence were a few concerned and curious locals along with a small scrum of protesters milling about; a few carried signs with pithy sayings such as, "Coal: The Dirtiest 4-Letter Word." A camera crew stood around, not shooting anything at the moment.

Twenty feet or so down the fence-line, Peter noticed a smallish man with a tight tan face that featured high cheekbones, dark eyes, and long black hair pulled back into a ponytail. Something about the man seemed hauntingly familiar. It took Peter a minute of openly staring before it dawned on him that this was the dancing man from the diner in his dreams.

Moving closer, Peter edged up to the man and casually asked, "Are you with the protesters?"

The Native American turned to Peter, carefully examining him without any recognition. Apparently, he had not had the same dream.

"I'm not with anybody," the man stated. "I just wanted to see what one of the worst environmental disasters in history looked like."

"You think it's that bad?" Peter asked.

"Yes," the man said plainly.

"I just got here," Peter explained. "Can you tell me a little more about it?"

"Are you with the media?"

"No," Peter said.

"Too bad," the man said, his large black eyes fully focused on Peter now. He seemed to decide that this interested young man deserved an explanation. "You know they burn coal to make electricity?"

Peter nodded to indicate he was with the man so far.

"When they burn the coal, they take the ash that's left and pile it in retention ponds. These 'ponds' are big. The one that burst was forty acres."

"Sounds more like a lake," Peter commented.

"The dike broke, and the ash flowed out like a mudslide over miles of land and into the rivers," he said. "You understand?"

Peter calmly nodded, which did not seem to satisfy the man.

"Do you know what is in this ash?"

"I heard on the news it was some pretty bad stuff," Peter said. Remembering one phrase, he added, "Heavy metals?"

"Coal ash contains high levels of mercury, which is a neurotoxin. It will kill fish. We don't even know all the effects it has on the human body. This spill will leach into the ground, mix with groundwater, and contaminate drinking water in at least three states. Maybe more."

Peter struggled to think of something intelligent to ask. As if sensing he wasn't going to succeed, the Native American spared him.

"The whole process of producing coal is destructive. First, they blow the top off of mountains to get to it. That's called strip mining. Then they dump their waste near rivers and streams.

"When they burn the coal, it sends carbon dioxide into the atmosphere, polluting and warming the air we breathe. Then they put the waste in these ponds where accidents like this are bound to happen eventually. It's a temporary solution to a permanent problem."

"You should let people know," Peter said sincerely.

The man chuckled. "Yes, I've tried," he said, his smile turning wistful. "No one wants to hear it."

Peter thought for a minute. "What's your name?"

"Victor Birdsong."

"Hey, I'm Peter Quell," Peter said. "Stay right here, okay?"

Victor merely looked confused as the stranger hurried off.

Taking off his cap, Peter walked up to a bulky guy with a video camera dangling by his side. "Where's your producer?"

"Who wants to know?" the big fellow asked.

"Peter Quell." When the name didn't seem to do anything for him, Peter added, "Tell him 'Peter the Prophet' and Victor Birdsong will be having a press conference in one hour."

It was dusk by the time Peter and Victor took their places in front of a once-beautiful vista that now overlooked a river of black sludge. A cable news network had materialized and set up a camera and lights. Piggybacking on them was the Knoxville station, also aiming their cameras at the twosome.

As nervous as he was, Peter had to smile when he saw Cindy Sizemore and her cameraman trudging across the field toward them. Politely, he waited until his local action news team was set up before starting.

"Okay," Peter said. "My name is Peter Quell, and this is Victor Birdsong. As many of you know, I had a dream about this disaster and announced it yesterday at Trinity Church in Nashville. The reason I'm here is to find out more about what actually happened and to learn about the environmental impact. That's why Victor is here—to help explain that to us."

"Thank you, Peter," Victor said, sounding like he sincerely meant it. "I didn't know about Peter's prophecy." He paused for a moment before continuing on. "I don't want to take anything away from his gift, but I could have predicted an environmental disaster. I could not have told you when or where, but it was just a matter of time before something like this happened."

"Almost all our energy comes from outdated and dangerous sources: oil, gas, coal, nuclear material. We've seen disaster after disaster, and yet we don't change our ways. I guess it is human nature not to care—unless the oil spill washes up on your beach, or the nuclear reactor gives you cancer, or the toxic sludge comes through your living room.

"The good news is we now have cleaner technologies that harness natural sources of energy like the wind and the sun and the sea."

"Don't those cost more?" an unseen male voice asked.

Victor scoffed. "For decades the government has helped their old friends in oil and gas and coal get richer and richer. 'Intangible drilling cost deductions, depletion allowances, tax credits.' They have given them every possible advantage. Put new technology on a level playing field, and they'll compete just fine.

"What they don't bother to factor in is the environmental costs." Gesturing behind him, Victor asked, "What is this clean up going to

96

cost? What about the long-term health costs? What about the effects on the climate? Then ask yourself, is coal still such a great bargain?"

As Victor spelled out the dangers of burning coal, Peter nodded along, happy just to be there. When the questions came, most were directed at the "prophet." If they had to do with him or his dreams, Peter answered as succinctly as possible. If they had anything to do with the coal plant or the environment, he deflected to Victor.

Cindy stepped close enough to get her microphone in front of Peter—and possibly to get herself in the shot. "Mr. Quell, do you believe that God is concerned about our polluting the planet?"

"I think so," he said, appreciating the soft ball. "I mean, it makes sense. If He created the planet, it seems like He would want us to take care of it. If we mess it up, I'm not sure He's going to give us another one any time soon."

As Cindy prepared to ask a follow-up, another reporter interjected his own question. "Mr. Quell, is it true you were here in Kingston last week?"

It sounded like the same voice that had asked about the cost of green energy. When Peter looked around, he found it belonged to a man wearing a dark suit and looking more like a funeral director than a reporter. He didn't appear to have a camera with him, only a phone which he now held in Peter's direction.

"Um, yes," Peter said. "I was trying to figure out my dream, and it led me here."

"After you were *led* here, what did you do while you were here?" the man queried.

"Ah, I stopped at the diner. I recommend the hamburgers," Peter replied with a smile, all the while wondering why he was being asked such boring questions. "After that, I found the coal plant, and then I drove home."

"Can anyone verify your actions?" the man asked gravely.

"I was alone except at the diner," Peter said slowly. Now everyone was looking back and forth between the reporter and the interviewee. "What are you getting at?"

"Just that it's not known exactly what caused the dam to break. It can't be ruled out that someone sabotaged it, perhaps with explosives." Peter's eyes widened as the man continued, "And you were here just days before the accident—and your *prophetic* announcement."

Incredulous, Peter tried to wrap his mind around the accusation. "Are you saying that I caused this?" His arm waved behind him. "That I planted explosives?"

"This is outrageous!" Victor cut in, his dark eyes blazing at the accuser in the dark suit. "Who are you with? Do you work for the coal industry?"

"I'm a freelance reporter," the man said calmly.

Turning to the other reporters, Victor implored, "You see, this is the kind of smear campaign they wage against anyone who speaks the truth. They lie about environmental reports that could damage their monopolies, and they paint anyone who stands up to them as radicals and criminals." Victor pointed at the man in the dark suit. "You are the criminal, sir!"

The man scoffed, seemingly amused by Victor's outburst.

"Okay," Peter said, trying to calm his new friend down. "I don't have anything to hide Mr.... What is your name?"

The man hesitated. Still donning a slight smile, he simply turned and disappeared behind the gathering of people.

In the midst of the chattering crowd, Peter felt like he'd lost control of the press conference. Rather than try to bring order to the proceedings, he announced, "Okay, I guess that's it. Thank you for coming."

While reporters scribbled their final notes and cameramen started to break down, a bewildered Peter turned to Victor. "I wasn't ready for that guy."

"It's okay. There is always opposition when you challenge the powers that be," Victor said bitterly. "Some people will hear the truth; some people will choose to hear the lies. At least we got the message out."

"What do we do now?" Peter asked.

"Go get one of those hamburgers," Victor said. "I'm starving."
With that, the Native American led the prophet away from the
cables and lights and the ugly blight in the background.

CHAPTER 13

At least the disaster had been good for the diner's business. Most of the tables and booths were filled with disaster workers, protesters, and the media. It looked like a few locals had separated themselves from the interlopers by congregating around the counter.

Working his way through the dinner crowd, Victor found a recently vacated booth in the back for himself and his new friend. Still feeling the sting of the public ambush, Peter slunk down in his seat with his back to the other patrons, hoping to be left alone.

"I felt like the press conference was going so well up until the end," Peter bemoaned.

"It's okay," Victor reassured him. "That was probably more airtime than the whole story would have gotten without you."

"I'm glad my notoriety is good for something," Peter said, pulling his cap down a little lower.

"I'm sorry I haven't heard of you before," Victor admitted.

"That's okay," Peter said. "I'm pretty new to the job."

"So, you have predicted other events that came true?" Victor asked, clearly fascinated.

"Yeah, I announced the stock market would crash right before it did," Peter said. "I know it sounds crazy—"

"No," Victor cut in. "The Native Americans have had many prophets."

"You know, I dreamed about you," Peter said. "You were in a diner like this one, and you sort of told me where this spill was going to happen."

"I'm glad I could be of assistance," Victor said.

Debbie, his waitress from the previous week, sauntered over, smacking her gum and shaking her head, none too happy to see Peter again. "I saw you on TV," she said as she distributed the stained menus.

"Already?" Peter asked, surprised.

"Your little press conference was live," Debbie said, glancing over her shoulder at a small TV behind the counter.

"Really?" Peter asked, wondering if they would comp their meal for his plug on national TV. "How'd we look?"

"Like a couple of grade-A jackasses," she said with utmost conviction.

"Wow, thanks for your candor," Peter replied.

"I guess it's pretty easy to criticize something you know nothing about," the waitress continued.

"You don't think we should criticize a toxic spill?" Victor asked sincerely.

"Accidents happen," she said. "Sometimes a hamburger falls on the floor back there. That doesn't mean we shut down the kitchen."

"Uh—do you serve the hamburger?" Peter asked.

Debbie hesitated a second too long for Peter's taste. "All I'm saying," the waitress explained, "is you don't complain about the lights, and the oven, and the air conditioning. But the second any little thing goes wrong, you people get all high and mighty."

"This was not a '*little thing*' that went wrong," Victor said patiently. "The effects of this 'dropped hamburger' can be very damaging, especially to people who live the closest. If you have cancer or your child comes down with Pink disease, you won't think it's such a little thing."

"Well, I don't have cancer, and my baby ain't pink," Debbie shot back. "I mean, she's pink, but she's the normal kind of pink."

"Glad to hear it," Victor said. "I just want her to stay that way."

"And I want my boyfriend to have a job," Debbie said, making a quick scan of the other tables in her section. "What do you want to eat?"

"Not a hamburger," Peter said, glancing at the laminated menu. "I'll have the blue plate special and a coffee."

"I'll have the hamburger with everything on it," Victor said, looking straight at Debbie. "And water to drink please. I like to live dangerously."

Without another word, Debbie took off with their orders.

"Get used to that kind of attitude," Victor said. "Any prophet worth his salt is going to catch abuse. Most of the time, the world doesn't want to hear what they have to say."

Looking to lighten the conversation, or at least divert it, Peter asked, "So, tell me about the Native American prophets."

Victor thought for a couple of seconds. "Come to think of it, most of them did not have such a great track record," he admitted. "The most famous was probably Tecumseh, who was actually called 'The Prophet.' In one of his alcoholic stupors, he had a vision and began preaching that white people were the spawn of the Great Serpent. Naturally, he found a following, especially the young warriors.

"He wasn't all bad," Victor went on to explain. "He actually wanted to unite the different tribes and form a strong alliance. He and his brother moved their followers to Tippecanoe and renamed it Prophetstown."

"I've heard of Tippecanoe," Peter said. "Wasn't there a battle there?"

"Oh, yes," Victor said, nodding. "The settlers were concerned about this large hostile Indian village, so they sent the militia to check it out. Well, The Prophet had a vision and said that they needed to attack. He even told the warriors that he had magic powers that would protect them from the bullets of the white man."

"So what happened?" Peter asked.

"His magic did not stop the bullets," Victor said regretfully. "The army killed many warriors and chased the rest back to the village, where they killed another one hundred fifty Natives. The militia lost at least as many men. It was a bloody mess. In the end, the US militia ended up burning Prophetstown to the ground. His followers blamed Tecumseh for the disaster and stripped him of his authority."

"Sounds like he had it coming," Peter said, as Debbie came by, sloshing their drinks on the table before hurrying off.

"That also ended the dream of a Native alliance." Victor held up his glass in a mock toast. "To the victor go the spoils."

But Peter didn't catch the pun or participate in the toast. He was captivated by the small pool of spilled water and coffee muddling together on the Formica table.

"I don't know," Peter said morosely. "With what we're doing to the planet, we may end up doing ourselves in."

"'The earth is defiled by its people; they have disobeyed the laws, violated the statutes, and broken the everlasting covenant,'" Victor quoted, a dark timbre reverberating in his voice. "'Therefore a curse consumes the earth; its people must bear their guilt. Therefore earth's inhabitants are burned up, and very few are left.'"

"Is that a Native American prophecy?" Peter asked, looking up.

"Isaiah," Victor said. "He's one of yours."

Even if the service was subpar, the food tasted decent; Peter could only hope it had not been contaminated by the wrath of Debbie. Their meal was not comped, but Victor insisted on picking up the check, a gesture Peter greatly appreciated on his limited budget.

103

As they walked through the diner, Peter became aware of a few heads turning in his direction and, once again, felt self-conscious about his newfound quasi-fame.

"It was good meeting you," Victor said, extending a hand when they reached the parking lot. "I believe it was Providence."

"I feel the same way," Peter said, taking hold of the man's firm grip. "Let's keep in touch."

Victor nodded with genuine intent.

"Hey, Tree Huggers!" a voice boomed from the door of the diner.

Peter turned to see a couple of young men he recognized from the counter moving swiftly across the parking lot. Before he could respond, the bigger of the two was in his face, giving him a sharp push to the chest that sent him stumbling back.

"Did you have a dream about that?" the angry young man said, giving him a quick left jab to the solar plexus. "Huh? Did you see that one coming?"

With his rumble at the Ryman victory still fresh in his mind, Peter felt a surge of confidence. If God had delivered two bullies to him before, He could do it again.

"Did you see this coming?" Peter asked as he took a swing. This time, the clumsy punch seemed to travel in slow motion in the general direction of the target's face, where it was easily blocked.

The big kid returned the wild haymaker with a short gut shot that doubled Peter over, making him breathless. At this point, Victor bravely stepped into the fray, mostly trying to break the fight up, and was instantly smacked down by the second local kid. With Victor already down, any delusion Peter had of defeating these Goliaths was quickly dissipating.

"You think the coal plant is so bad?" the first young man said. "We work there, so now you have a chance to fight the coal plant." His argument was punctuated with another hard shove, knocking Peter against the open tailgate on a parked pick-up truck.

In that instant, Peter experienced a series of mini revelations.

First, his lower back really hurt. Second, a sensible debate on the merits of green energy was not going to be an effective counter strategy at this point. Third, this guy was a lot stronger than he was, and Victor had as much of a chance against his guy as Tecumseh's warriors had against the US military.

At that moment, as if in answer to a prayer, a couple of men came dashing out from the diner. The momentary relief Peter felt was dashed when he saw one of the "rescuers" hoist a camera to his shoulder. They weren't there to break up the fight; they were there for exclusive video of "Peter the Prophet" getting his ass kicked.

The angry coal plant worker came forward, pushing Peter back into the dirty open bed of the pick-up. Pinning him down with his left hand, the kid cocked his right arm.

"I know who you are," Peter said quietly. "You're Debbie's boyfriend, aren't you?" The lack of response told him he was right. "Look, you don't want to do this. It will just make things worse. The whole thing will be on video."

There was a brief flicker of rational thought behind the scowling eyes—and then that light seemed to go out. "Good," the boyfriend said. "I want everyone to see this."

From that point on, it was mostly a matter of Peter trying to cover up against the repeated blows that rained down from above. Every third or so punch got through, sending shockwaves through his head and torso. While Debbie's boyfriend played Whack-A-Mole on Peter's body, the second kid held Victor back without much effort.

"Hold up," Peter thought he heard someone say from up above. The beating stopped, and despite a ringing in his ears, Peter made out the sound of voices around him.

Slowly, Peter opened his eyes, and being flat on his back, he actually saw stars swirling over his head. Managing to lean up in the truck bed, he caught a blurry blue light. Thankful the authorities were there, he sat up, ready to press charges. As soon as he was semi-vertical, a young uniformed man grabbed him by the shirt.

"Let's go," the deputy said, pulling him out of the truck and marching him over to the patrol car where Peter was pushed into the backseat. Through the dusty side window, Peter glimpsed Victor vigorously talking to another police officer while their attackers stood idly by, seemingly without a care in the world.

The deputy came around to the front, sat down in the driver's seat, and began to wordlessly pull away from the scene.

"What's going on?" Peter cried to the back of the crew-cut head. "Is it against the law to get beaten up?"

"Someone wants to talk to you," was the only reply from the front.

Peter got the feeling he wasn't going to get any more information out of the deputy, and he was too tired to try. Ignoring the lumps of soreness sprouting on his face, he put his head back against the seat and closed his eyes, letting the stress of the last thirty-six hours close in on him.

It was a short drive to the local police station, and Peter wished he had a little longer to rest. Without a word, the deputy escorted him through the front door, down a hall, and into a plain beige room.

"Wait here," he said, closing the door behind him.

Rage, fear, and fatigue were in a three-way race, jockeying back and forth inside of him. It infuriated him that his rights were being violated. At yet, he knew things could get worse.

While he waited to find out his fate, he took a seat in one of the two metal chairs and tried to stay calm. Closing his eyes and slowing his breathing, he silently prayed; not even thinking the words, he simply mustered an emotional plea for help.

A few minutes later, the door opened, and a trim forty-year-old man came into the room carrying a handheld recorder along with a folder and a notebook with a flip pad.

"I'm Agent Russ Myers with the Tennessee Bureau of Investigation," the man stated, all business. "I hear you got in a scrape." Myers made a little show of examining Peter's face, apparently deciding it did not warrant medical attention.

"Yeah, I was assaulted," Peter said. "What's going to happen to the guy that beat me up?"

"That's a local matter," Myers said matter-of-factly as he took a seat across from Peter.

Peter thought about asking if he could press charges; however, fear was getting the lead on anger at the moment, so he simply asked, "Why am I here?"

"TVA called us to look into this dam break," Agent Myers said, putting the recorder on the table and turning it on. "And I had a couple of questions for you."

From detective books and TV shows, Peter knew better than to talk to the police without having an attorney present. And yet, now that he was actually here, all he wanted to do was clear himself and be released as soon as possible. "Go ahead," Peter said.

"How well do you know Victor Birdsong?"

"We just met today."

"You've never talked or exchanged emails or had *any* communications with Mr. Birdsong prior to today?" Myers asked. Peter started to say something, but the agent cut in. "Before you answer, be advised I can subpoena your computer and cell phone records. If I find out you're lying, I'll charge you with obstruction, which would be a felony in this case."

"I don't have a computer or a cell phone," Peter said.

Myers allowed a slightly surprised look before making a notation in his notebook. "Do you have any connection with any environmentalist groups?"

Peter shook his head. "No."

"What about when you were in California?" Myers asked. "Did you know anyone that might be affiliated with some sort of *eco-group*?"

"Not that I know of."

"That's a vague answer."

"Well, it's a vague question," Peter retorted. "I mean, I don't know everything about everyone I ever met."

Agent Myers scribbled something in his notepad, then looked up.

"I understand you were in Kingston last Thursday? Can you walk me through that trip?" the agent asked, although it sounded more like an order than a request.

"I drove here last Wednesday night," Peter said, his eyes drifting toward the ceiling in recall mode. "I ate at the diner. I was served by a waitress named Debbie. Afterwards, I drove around and ended up at the front gate of the coal plant. Then I headed back to Nashville."

"Did you enter the gate or go on TVA property at any time?"

"No," Peter said, shaking his head. "I drove up to the front gate and turned around."

"And what was your purpose for making this trip?"

With a sigh, Peter started in. "I've recently had a few dreams that have told me things, things that were going to happen." The agent stared blankly back at him, and Peter surmised that he knew that much about him. "Anyway, I had a dream about this area, so I drove over to check it out."

There was more writing in the notebook.

"Let me get this straight," Agent Myers said, looking back up. "You had a dream there was going to be a disaster at the coal plant, so you drove all the way over here to look at it, then turned around and went home?"

"Well, I had a dream that *something might* happen here, but I didn't know what. When I saw the coal plant, it matched something I dreamed, and I knew it was all connected." Peter shrugged wearily. "I'm sorry, I can't explain it much better than that."

"Why didn't you tell anyone at the coal plant about this dream?" the agent asked. "Or the local authorities?"

"I didn't think about it," Peter admitted. "Besides, I wasn't sure exactly what was going to happen."

The agent frowned, flipping back to read some previous notes. "You were sure enough to make a big announcement at a church in Nashville."

"At that point, I was pretty sure *something* was going to happen here. I just didn't have the details. You can check what I said at the church." He shook his head. "Besides, the coal plant wouldn't have believed me any more than you believe me right now."

"What makes you think I don't believe you?" the agent asked, straight-faced.

"Just a hunch," Peter said. His fear was slowing, and a new emotion, something resembling defiance, was beginning to make a late surge. "Look, I've had a really, really long day, and I have a long drive home."

The agent nodded thoughtfully. "You're finished when I say you're finished."

"Well, I've told you everything I know," Peter said, surprising himself by suddenly standing up. "And I don't think you can hold me against my will unless you charge me."

"You need to read the Patriot Act, son," Myers said, a crooked smile on his face. "I can hold a terror suspect till hell freezes over."

Peter knew the mention of "terror suspect" was supposed to terrorize him, and normally it would have succeeded spectacularly. But he was so tired and numb he didn't feel anything, except possibly a little nudge to call the agent's bluff.

"I need to call my attorney if this is going to continue," Peter said, even though the only lawyer he could think of was a personal injury attorney who advertised constantly in Nashville.

"I also need to inform my pastor that I'm being held as a terror suspect. I bet the media would be interested in that, too. You'd be surprised how fast I can get a press conference together."

The terror suspect stared at the agent, whose cruel little smile now seemed frozen in a slightly sinister snarl. With mocking politeness, the agent said, "If we have any other questions, we know where to find you."

Relieved, Peter stumbled out of the interrogation room, through the police station, and out into the open night air before realizing his car was still parked at the diner. For a moment, he considered going back inside to ask for a ride, then decided he didn't want to push it. Besides, it wasn't too far.

Putting one foot in front of the other, the exercise and the cool air seemed to reinvigorate him. Anxious to get the hell out of dodge, he gritted his teeth and quickened his pace into a jog. If he could just avoid reporters, angry coal workers, and government agents, he might make it home before daybreak.

CHAPTER 14

As Peter drove west into the night, scenes from the day flashed through his mind like opposing headlights: being grilled on national TV, being beaten up in the back of a pick-up truck, being interrogated by a TBI officer.

After stringing all the incidents together, he was amazed he was still functioning. He figured he had God to thank for that. To be fair, he guessed he also had God to thank for putting him through the ordeal in the first place.

Jesse had said he'd have to face his fears, and he was certainly doing that. Peter also recalled Jesus' warning about prophets being persecuted and run out of town. Was this what he had to look forward to from here on out? Beatings, interrogations, and possibly prison cells? If so, he wondered if he could take the next exit ramp.

Trying to find something to listen to besides the negative voices in his head, Peter scanned the radio dial for signs of life. Out of the solitary darkness, a bombastic baritone calling itself "Ed Pressman" crackled through the speakers. The voice, as well as the rhetoric, was stronger than black coffee, and it seemed the perfect companion to keep Peter awake on his journey home.

In Ed's political theater, the world was replete with conspiracies where villains loomed around every bend. Since Peter didn't consider himself particularly "political," he found the diatribe somewhat entertaining. He was also curious whether Ed would mention the coal plant disaster until he realized the show had been pre-recorded.

A rant about "the hordes of criminal aliens invading our country" caused Peter to wonder if America was under attack from interplanetary enemies. When it was revealed he was talking about illegal immigrants, Peter smiled at the thought of an invading force armed with lawnmowers and cleaning supplies.

"These criminals need to be rounded up like cattle and driven back across the border," Ed proclaimed, sounding like a corrupt sheriff in a bad Western. As the diatribe went on, it became less humorous. In fact, it was scary that, judging from the callers, people actually took Ed seriously.

Flipping off the radio, Peter tried to rub his two remaining brain cells together to spark an idea on what his next step should be in the real world. He didn't think any reporters would be waiting for him at his mom's house at this hour—although he wasn't sure about the intrepid Cindy Sizemore.

What he really needed was a place to rest for a few hours, if not days. Then he remembered he had been planning to go to Uncle John's before he decided to make a run to East Tennessee. Better late than never.

It was almost 3:00 a.m. when he was finally approaching Nashville. Before getting all the way into the city, he took the exit for Gallatin and concentrated on getting to his uncle's house. Through bleary eyes, he drove around until he recognized a landmark getting ever closer.

Finally, he found the mailbox with a Commodore logo on the side. After pulling into the driveway, Peter sat in the car and looked at the dark home. This was it. Not wanting to disturb his uncle at this unseemly hour, he put his car seat back and tried to grab a few winks.

In the blink of an eye, a rap on his window startled him awake. A smattering of light in the sky backlit a figure by his window. Peter squinted up at a bearded, middle-aged man wearing a bathrobe and holding a coffee cup.

Peter rolled down the window.

"How long have you been out here?" John asked, looking like he wasn't fully awake either.

"I don't know," Peter said. "It was so late; I didn't want to wake you up."

"I thought you were coming yesterday," he said.

"I know, I'm sorry," Peter said. "I got sidetracked."

"Yeah, I saw you on CNN." Stepping away from the car, John motioned him toward the house. "Well, come on in."

Grabbing the overnight bag he had packed the day before, Peter followed his uncle inside. A college professor who had never married, John seemed to have a nice life. Easygoing and contemplative, in many ways, he was the opposite of his older brother, Peter's father.

The living room looked like a disorderly library, overflowing with books in shelves and stacked on the floor. And beyond the windows and sliding glass door was the vast darkness of the lake.

"I have to say, you look terrible," John said as he assessed his nephew in the light. "Were you in a fight?"

"Sort of," Peter said, touching a bump on his face.

"Do you want some ice?" his concerned uncle asked.

"That's okay," Peter said, waving off the concern.

"Coffee?" John asked, holding up his coffee cup with a gold *V* for Vanderbilt on it. "Something to eat?"

"I don't think so," Peter said. "I think I just need some real sleep."

"Of course," John said, pointing him in the direction of the spare bedroom. "We can catch up later."

"Thanks," Peter said, already moving down the hall with his bag.

Shutting the bedroom door behind him, Peter dropped the bag, stripped down to his boxers, and fell into the bed. Sleep came within seconds of his head hitting the pillow. Dream followed dream, round after round, deep into the morning.... A blur of forgettable images and scenes came and went without meaning or purpose.

And then, Peter dreamed something new.

Oct 6?
Sliver of moon and a star in night sky.
2 men come out of the woods carrying something. They go to a church building w/ dome on top? Break window—crawl inside. Flames leap out of building as the 2 guys run out.
FIRE!

As soon as Peter jotted down the scene, he closed his notebook and went right back to sleep until late in the afternoon. Even after he woke, he lay in bed, resisting the urge to reread his dream. Instead, he rested and took inventory of his pain; the beating from the day had dissolved into a dull, overall body ache.

Despite the soreness and the lingering dream, Peter relished the comfort of the bed, the view of the lake, and most of all, the idea that no one knew where he was. For the first time in a while, he felt completely anonymous and safely tucked away from the rest of the world.

When he finally got up, he went straight to the bathroom to assess the damage: a swollen lip, a couple of discolored lumps on his cheek, and bruising on his chest seemed to be the extent of it. If he squinted, he almost looked like a tough guy.

After a long warm shower and a change of clothes, he felt ready to face the day.

Searching for his host, he wandered into the living room where a curtain swayed in the breeze, revealing an open sliding glass door

114

behind it. Peter stepped out onto a deck with an expanse of water just beyond.

"Hey, good afternoon," John said, looking up from a book. "You sleep well, I trust?"

Peter nodded, semi-transfixed by the shimmer coming off the water.

"How about something to eat?" his host offered.

Realizing he hadn't eaten a real meal since the diner, Peter suddenly felt very empty. "That would be great."

Over sandwiches and soup on the back deck, Peter told John everything—from his very first "heart dream" to the one he'd had only a few hours earlier.

John sat back, taking it in. "So, you had one of your dreams last night?" he clarified. "Here?"

Peter nodded.

"And it was definitely one of *those* dreams?" John asked, almost reverentially.

"Yep," Peter said, dipping the crust of his bread into the soup to sop up the broth.

Turning back to the lake, John remained quiet for a moment before commenting, "Hmm, well, it seems to be literal more than allegorical."

Peter looked up at his professorial uncle, who was busily dissecting the dream.

"Two men walk into a building and set it on fire; that's pretty straightforward," John said. "And that building with the dome, it sounds like a mosque."

"Yeah," Peter agreed, making the connection. "That seems right."

"You mentioned a crescent moon and star in the sky," John said.

"Yeah," Peter said, chewing. He hadn't thought much about it.

"That's an interesting detail," John went on. "It was associated with the Ottoman Empire and became an Islamic symbol."

"So that would connect with the mosque idea," Peter added as he pushed his empty plate and bowl away.

John was nodding along. "Do you think it could have to do with violence in the Middle East?"

"I don't think so," Peter said. "All the dreams have been pretty local. East Tennessee is as far away as one has been." He thought about it some more. "The dreams could be widening in scope, but that feels too far."

John shrugged. "Well, I don't know how many, but there are certainly mosques in the area."

Without a word, John got up and walked inside, leaving Peter to contemplate Old Hickory Lake. He wondered if there could be a more polar-opposite picture to the river of toxic sludge he had witnessed yesterday.

A moment later, his uncle came back out with an open laptop. "Okay, there are only five mosques in the Nashville area," John announced. "They're all right here." He put the screen down in front of his nephew.

"Do you think we should call them?" Peter asked reluctantly.

"I don't know," John said. "You said you wished you had tried to contact the coal company before the accident. This could be your chance to get in front of this dream."

"What would I even say?" Peter asked, putting an imaginary phone to his ear. "Hi, I had a dream your mosque is going to be burned down. Have a nice day."

"Maybe if you tell them who you are," John tried. "If they've heard of you, they might be more receptive."

Peter felt doubtful. Still, he knew he had a responsibility. This time, he wasn't going to wait around till Sunday to make a pronouncement from the pulpit. This time, he was going straight to the people.

With the moral support of his uncle, Peter made contact with all five mosques in Nashville. Not too surprisingly, Muslims could be quite suspicious of strangers, especially strangers that were calling about impending attacks.

116

No matter how sincere Peter tried to sound, he had trouble getting his message across. The first mosque was convinced he was pulling some sort of mean practical joke on them.

The second mosque assumed he was crazy and hung up on him, twice. The third thought he was making a threat and informed him they were calling the police. He could not get a live person at the fourth mosque, so he left a message and hoped for the best.

Finally, at the fifth and final mosque, he was put through to the "Imam," which John explained loosely translated to "the lead pastor."

A man with a slight accent who introduced himself as "Abbas" came on the line. "Is this really Peter Quell—the one who has been having the dreams?"

"Ah, yes," Peter said, taken back to be recognized by a Muslim.

"I have been following you with interest, Mr. Quell," Abbas said with genuine enthusiasm. "What can I do for you?"

"Well, unfortunately, I had a dream about a mosque being burned down."

"I haven't heard of anything like that," Abbas said, concerned. Then, catching himself, he added, "Of course, it hasn't happened yet, has it?"

"No, I don't think so," Peter said. "That's why I'm calling. To try and warn you."

"You think it will be a mosque in Nashville?"

"I'm not sure, but I'm starting here," Peter said. "I'm assuming it's fairly close."

"Have you called any other mosques in town?"

"I tried calling four others," Peter said. "But I'm not sure any of them understood or believed me."

"Yes, I can imagine," Abbas said with a dry chuckle. "If you like, I can make a few calls on your behalf and pass along your message."

"That would be great," Peter said. "And please tell them I was not threatening anyone." After giving Abbas his uncle's and mom's phone numbers, Peter asked, "Would you keep me updated, especially if anything does happen?"

"I will keep you informed," Abbas reassured him.

"Thank you."

"No, thank you," Abbas countered. "Many people would not feel so compelled to warn us."

"Well?" John asked as soon as Peter hung up.

"He seems to know my work," Peter said. "And he said he'd pass the message along to the other mosques."

"Hey, that's great," John said, clearly relieved. "It seems like you've done all you can do for the moment."

"I guess," Peter agreed, taking his time to consider any missing possibilities.

"Do you need to get back home, or can you spend a little more time with your old uncle?"

"I'm not in a hurry," Peter said quickly.

"Great," John said.

"I should probably call my mom."

"I called her while you were asleep and let her know you were okay," John said. "She told me to have you call her as soon as you got up."

Peter was already shaking his head.

"She's worried about you," John said. "And she has a right to be, especially with everything going on."

Peter relented. "Do you mind if I use your phone again?"

Uncle John waved his hand. "While you're at it, you should call your dad, too. I know he'd like to hear from you."

"I don't know," Peter said. "The last time we tried to talk, he pretty much made fun of me."

"Well, this prophecy business is a stretch for your dad," John said, a slight smile creasing his lips. "He doesn't know how to show it, but he *is* proud of you. Baffled, but proud."

"I'll try," Peter relented.

"Take your time," John said, going inside and sliding the glass door closed behind him to give Peter privacy.

Peter called the local number first. As usual, his mom let the machine pick up before she heard his voice.

"Are you still at John's place?" she broke in.

"Yes," Peter said. "I just called to let you know I'm going to be here for a while, maybe even a day or two."

"Oh, I thought you might have another press conference," his mom said, making it sound like an accusation.

"Did you see it?"

"Everyone saw it!" she cried. "Some of the commentators thought you were using the disaster to push an environmental agenda." Her words sounded like they had come verbatim out of a talking head's mouth on one of the cable news shows.

"So what if I was pushing an environmental agenda?" Peter asked.

"But taking advantage of the disaster...," his mom said sadly.

"I don't know," Peter chuckled. "It seemed like a good time to talk about the environment with a river of toxic sludge in the background."

His mom made a disapproving sound.

"Well, I got to go," Peter said. "You know where to reach me. I love you."

"I love you, too," she said.

Taking advantage of the disaster, Peter repeated in his head. People could find fault with anything. And that was supposed to be the easier call. He was not looking forward to talking to his dad, but similar to how he'd felt about calling the mosques, he felt obligated to do it.

With a heavy sigh, he punched in the ten dreaded digits. The phone rang for a while before his dad answered, "John?"

"No, it's me," Peter said.

"Hey, Peter," his dad said, his voice perking up a bit. "I saw you on the news."

"Oh, yeah?" Peter said, preparing for his critique.

"It's good you're calling attention to the environmental concerns with coal," his dad said. "People need to know more about that."

Checking the sarcasm meter, he was surprised not to pick up any readings. "Thanks," Peter said cautiously.

"And you looked good doing it," his dad continued. "Cool and confident."

"That last reporter kind of got to me," Peter admitted.

"That guy came off looking like a slime ball," Mr. Quell stated. "Your partner, Birdcall, kind of lost it at the end. But you were as cool as a cucumber."

"Birdsong," Peter corrected. "But thanks." A foreign feeling passed through him. Despite the coolness of the air, he felt a warmth. Looking across the water, he noticed a few leaves were beginning to change color.

"I had another dream last night," Peter began.

"Oh, yeah?" his dad asked, sounding genuinely interested. "Can you tell me about it?"

CHAPTER 15

After extending his stay in Gallatin for a couple of days, Peter did not make it home till Thursday evening. It had been a pleasant reprieve to get away from the day-to-day grind of being a prophet, and he actually felt more relaxed than he had in weeks. That peaceful feeling was fleeting.

As soon as he walked into the house, his mom scurried into the kitchen to meet him. "I saw your fight on TV!" Stopping short to examine his face, she exclaimed, "And just look at you! Beaten to a pulp!"

Peter had hoped his bruises would have healed enough not to be noticeable. Not that it mattered. Of course someone had recorded his beating, and now it was public record.

His mom was poking at the still-sensitive knot on his cheek, causing Peter to flinch. "This was because of that press conference, wasn't it?"

Putting down his bag, Peter tried to sidestep his mom on the way to the refrigerator.

"I knew that was a bad idea," she said.

"Please drop it," Peter said, looking for a snack.

Ms. Quell sat down at the table. Sighing heavily at her stubborn son, she thumbed through a thicket of sticky notes.

"Well, there were the usual messages," she said, squinting at the first few, then deciding to discard them without sharing them. Peter, who had moved his exploration north to the freezer, came away with a container of ice cream.

"Dan called," his mom said. "He was concerned about that press conference, too."

Without responding, Peter turned his attention to a drawer where he rummaged for a spoon.

"There were the usual reporters," his mother said, flipping a few more notes. "That Cindy Sizemore sure is persistent, isn't she?"

With a slight smile, Peter began to scoop vanilla, chocolate, and strawberry ice cream with impartiality from the box of Neapolitan.

"Here it is," she said, coming across a particular Post-It. "A producer from *Good Morning America* offered to fly you and a guest to New York for a televised interview." Ms. Quell glanced at her son, who was busy sampling some chocolate. "I'll just put that one to the side for you to think about."

"I'm not doing any interviews," Peter said.

"But you can do a press conference?" his mother mumbled before going on to the next one. "Tom McAllister called again. He's a persistent one, too." Peter shook his head, and his mom nodded as she wadded up the yellow slip. "Let's see, Abu or something called."

Peter looked up from his bowl. "Wait, do you mean Abbas?"

"I don't know, maybe," his mom said, already having moved on to the next yellow slip. "He had a funny accent."

"What did he say?" Peter asked.

Going back to decipher her note, she said, "Something about a mosque." She turned the Post-It every which way. "And check the news, I think."

"When did he call?" Peter asked fervently.

"That was today."

Snatching the yellow square of paper out of her hand, Peter left the table and the bowl of ice cream.

"Are you going to waste that ice cream?" she called after him.

Already in the den, Peter opened up his mom's laptop and did a quick search of local news sites. When he saw the word "mosque," he clicked on the link to a video from a Channel 7 report.

"What are you looking for?" his mom said, following him into the den, eating his ice cream. "They're already off that coal thing."

"Shhh," Peter said, backing onto a seat on the couch.

"Last night, a mosque in Columbia, Tennessee, was the victim of an arson attack," Phil, the reliable longtime anchor, announced. "Our own Brian Benton is on the scene."

Fear flashed through Peter, followed by a rumble of worry that he'd blown his assignment. The town of Columbia was two counties removed from Nashville, farther out than any of the mosques he had tried to contact.

Meanwhile, Benton was mentioning "interior damage" as he stood in front of a domed structure, which seemed unscathed except for a broken window. "Because both men have known associations with white supremacy groups, they could also be charged with hate crimes."

From the studio, the anchor asked, "Brian, how were police able to apprehend these suspects so quickly?"

The reporter was nodding in anticipation of the question. "A spokesman for the mosque said they received a tip earlier in the week, so they were keeping an eye out for suspicious activity. When two men were spotted breaking into this facility, the authorities were immediately called to the scene."

A rush of relief passed over Peter as he realized Abbas must have gotten the word to them.

"It was the fast response time of local police and fire departments that made the difference," Brian was saying. "In fact, the fire chief told me that if they had arrived ten minutes later, this building would have most likely burned to the ground."

"Thanks, Brian," Phil said as the clip ended.

"Thank God," Peter said, lowering the laptop.

"Okay, what's going on?" his mom, who had taken a position beside him on the couch, demanded. "Did you have a dream about that, too?"

"Yes," Peter said, feeling energized.

"Did you tell Dan about it?" his mom questioned as she scraped the empty bowl with her spoon.

"Not yet," Peter said, suddenly having a desire to see the mosque personally. Like with the ash spill, there were several good reasons not to go. While it was a lot closer than Kingston, it was still a forty-or-so-minute drive. He also didn't want anyone to suspect his motives or accuse him of being involved with the attack. Yet something inside of him wanted to get closer to the dream.

"You need to call Dan," his mom insisted.

"I will. Later," Peter said. "Right now, I got to go."

It was dark when Peter turned off the road and began bumping along an unlit gravel driveway. He had gotten lost a couple of times and was beginning to wonder if he was in the right neck of the woods.

Any concern vanished when an illuminated white plaster palace came into view. With curved sides and two gold domes, the mosque was an exotic building by any standard. In Columbia, Tennessee, it looked like the alien mothership had landed.

Slowly getting out of his car, Peter walked toward the place of worship. Floodlights bathed the building, revealing a boarded-up window. As far as Peter could see, that was the only sign there had even been damage.

Thirty feet off to the side was the distinctive crunch of loose gravel. Startled, Peter turned to see a man hurrying toward him, waving something in the air.

"Wait!" the man shouted. "Please stop!"

"I just came to look," Peter said, holding his hands up,

surrendering to the guard carrying what turned out to be a walkie-talkie. "My name is Peter Quell."

His name seemed to register, and although he was clearly still cautious, the man's apprehension seemed mingled with curiosity. The walkie-talkie crackled with foreign-sounding words that reminded Peter of tongues he'd heard at Trinity.

While keeping an eye on the trespasser, the security man spoke back in Arabic. During the rapid exchange, Peter caught two words he understood: *Peter Quell*. Lowering his walkie-talkie, the guard said in English, "Would you like to come inside?"

"Sure," Peter said. He was motioned through the ornate, arched entrance.

Passing into the large hall, he immediately saw the damage was far more severe than he'd been able to tell from the news report. Most of the interior was charred to the studs.

Underneath a crudely spray-painted swastika on a remaining wall, a man and woman were sweeping up blackened bits of debris. The man, in his fifties, dropped his dustpan and stepped forward.

"You are Peter Quell?" he asked. "The one who spoke with Abbas?"

"Yes," Peter said, noticing the other half of the walkie-talkie pair clipped to his belt.

"I'm Hassin," the man said, offering his hand. "The Imam here."

"Nice to meet you," Peter said, shaking his hand. Looking around, he tried to reconstruct the scene, unable to avoid the ugly symbol of hate glaring out in red paint. "So, is this where they started the fire?"

"Yes," the Imam said, pointing to a blasted-out section in the middle of the room. "They lit a gas can here in the prayer hall."

Looking at the malicious damage, Peter couldn't help but feel ashamed.

"When Abbas warned us something like this might happen, we posted sentries to keep watch during the night." Gesturing to the man who had escorted him in, he said, "Mo was the one who saw the men break in through the front window."

Mo shrugged humbly. "I just called 911."

"Yes, the two men were caught by the deputies just as they were coming out," Hassin said. The Imam hesitated for a moment before asking, "So, you had a dream about this?"

"Yes," Peter confirmed.

When Peter did not expand on the subject, Hassin said, "Well, I'm certainly glad you did. If you had not, we would all be standing in a pile of ashes right now."

Not knowing what to say, Peter just nodded.

"You know," Hassin continued, "you remind me of the Good Samaritan."

Peter thought of his attempts to be the Good Samaritan with Jesse, and how he had been the one who had been blessed by that encounter. In this case, he had done even less. "No," he said dismissively. "I didn't do anything, just made a few calls."

"You went out of your way to help a neighbor," Hassin said with complete assurance. "A neighbor that is different than you. That makes you a Good Samaritan."

Driving back on the two-lane county road from Columbia, Peter found himself thinking about the parable that seemed to keep coming back to him. This time, it had come from someone who didn't even read the Bible, at least as far as he knew.

Regardless of what Hassin thought, Peter did not consider himself worthy of the comparison. After the attack, the original Samaritan had gone the extra mile for his fellow man, helping him get back on his feet, even paying his medical expenses.

When Peter passed through Thompson Station, an idea began to germinate. By the time he pulled back into the driveway, he had formulated a loose plan of action. Checking the time, he realized it was too late to call Dan to discuss it, so he spent some time reading Luke 10 before falling asleep.

First thing in the morning, he called his pastor, leaving messages at Trinity and on Dan's cell phone asking him to call back as soon as possible. While he waited, he rang Abbas, who seemed cheered to hear from him.

"Hey, you were right, my friend!" the leader of the large mosque in Nashville exuded.

"Yeah," Peter acknowledged. "Listen, I visited the mosque in Columbia last night, and it gave me an idea.

What would you say if some of the churches in the area had a special service to show support, maybe even raised a little money to help fix it up?"

It took Abbas a couple of seconds before he responded. "Have you talked to anyone else about this?"

"Not yet," Peter said.

"Well, I think it's a nice idea," Abbas said carefully. "Let me know how it goes."

Peter assured him he would, but by early afternoon, his normally prompt pastor still hadn't returned his calls, so he tried the cell phone again. Just before going to voicemail, it was finally answered.

"Hey, I was just getting ready to call you," Dan said.

"That's okay," Peter said. "Listen, I'm sorry about not meeting you in Donelson last week. I was on my way and...I just felt like I was supposed to go to East Tennessee and see the disaster firsthand."

"No big deal." Although Dan was clearly trying to sound like everything was fine and dandy, he seemed a little distant. "You've been busy lately."

"Yeah," Peter agreed. "Did you hear about the arson fire at the mosque in Columbia?"

"Yeah?"

"Well, I dreamed that, too."

"Yes, your mother mentioned something," Dan said coolly.

Peter proceeded to fill him in on the details of the dream, explaining how he had called the mosques in the area to warn them. After telling him about going to the site the previous night, Peter got around to his real reason for calling.

"So, I was thinking, wouldn't it be cool if the churches in the area had a benefit to show support? Maybe donated money to help them rebuild?"

There was a fairly long pause before Dan finally asked, "Is this benefit idea something you dreamed?"

"No," Peter admitted. "It just feels like the right thing to do."

"What happened to not wanting to call attention to yourself?" Dan asked with a harsh little chuckle.

"This isn't about me," Peter insisted.

"Well, I don't want to prevent you from doing something you want to do, Peter," Dan said, obviously measuring his words. "But I'm not sure I feel called to get involved with that."

"Why not?" Peter shot back. "Just because these people have a different religion doesn't mean they should be persecuted. We're still called to help them, just like the Good Samaritan did."

"A lot of people are persecuted and need help, Peter," Dan said steadily. "We have to pick our battles."

"And I'm picking this one," Peter said defiantly. "Actually, God picked it first."

"Well, this is the first time you've mentioned it to me."

"I didn't think it made sense to make a big announcement at church," Peter said. "It seemed like the kind of information that needed to be passed along quickly and quietly."

"And I think that was exactly the right thing to do," Dan agreed. "You see, you are making my point. I don't think this necessarily needs to involve Trinity. It seems like the kind of thing you should do on your own, like you ended up doing with the coal plant disaster."

"I announced that at your church," Peter reminded him.

"Yes," Dan said, his true feelings rising to the surface, "and the next thing I know, you're having a press conference with some environmental activist."

"You're upset I spoke out against the ash spill?" Peter clarified.

"No," Dan insisted, even though his louder-than-usual voice said otherwise. "You are free to do whatever you think God, and your conscience, are telling you to do. I just may not hear the same voice."

"You didn't seem to have a problem with my prophecies when I was telling you about your heart problem. Or when I got you out of the stock market before it crashed," Peter said, his own emotions welling up. "Or is it you just don't want to be associated with environmentalists? Or Muslims?"

There was lofty scoff on the other end of the line, which further inflamed Peter.

"You told me to be true to my dreams, and that's exactly what I'm trying to do." When Dan didn't readily respond, Peter pushed on. "Or maybe when you feel left out, or it gets a little controversial, you're not as into that."

"Peter—" Dan began in a paternal voice, but he couldn't get in another word. With pent-up anger from coal-plant bullies to TBI agents, Peter's emotions erupted.

"You know, you're all about speaking in tongues, and prancing around with flags. When it comes to doing the real work—the hard work, the unpopular work—you're nowhere to be found!"

Full of righteous indignation, Peter hung up on the man that had been his pastor for most of his life. For a moment, he felt embarrassed by his outburst, but some of those things needed to be said—or so he told himself. Sweeping sentimentalities aside, Peter was more determined than ever to have a benefit, if for no other reason than to show Dan.

Having a church involved would give the event an air of legitimacy, and the only other church he'd visited since he'd been back in Tennessee was Grace Church.

The more he thought about it, the more Grace seemed like a good fit. Young and growing, they liked to think of themselves as unconventional free thinkers who were willing to try new things.

Calling the church's main number, he left a message with the senior pastor's personal assistant. Within an hour, the highly-sought-after pastor was on the line.

"Is this the Peter Quell who's been having these dreams I've been hearing so much about?" the friendly voice Peter had heard below his private box asked.

"That's me," Peter said. "In fact, that's one of the reasons I'd like to talk to you. I have an idea I thought you might be interested in."

"I'd love to hear it," Rick said with genuine interest. "I hate meeting in my office. How about getting together for coffee?"

"Yeah, okay," Peter said, glad to have the opportunity to talk in person.

"I'm booked solid tomorrow, and, of course, I'm pretty tied up on Sunday," Rick said. "Can it wait till Monday morning?"

"Sure," Peter said.

"I like to jog in the mornings," Rick explained, and for a moment, Peter was afraid he was going to ask him to join him. "After my run, I could meet you at eight-thirty at the Mercantile?"

"Sure," Peter said, his thoughts flashing back to his meeting with Jordan at the same spot. "I'll see you then."

CHAPTER 16

Once again, Peter found himself sitting in the back of the café, sipping coffee and waiting for one of the cool kids in the Christian world to bestow a visit on him. Even if Rick wasn't in the same league as Jordan Stone, being the minister at a mega-church in the buckle of the Bible belt was about as close as it got to being a rock star.

In a sweater vest and hiking boots, Rick looked like he'd stepped out of an L. L. Bean catalogue. Stopping to shake hands at the table nearest the door, he shared a laugh before continuing to the counter where he exchanged a good-natured back-and-forth with the clerk.

With a steeping cup of tea in one hand, he still managed to glad-hand and back-slap his way through the morning crowd, seemingly knowing everyone in the place. When he finally worked his way back to Peter, he introduced himself with a firm handshake and a smile that fell a few watts short of an atomic blast.

Having only seen Rick from a distance, and often through a mesh screen, Peter had thought the pastor was only a few years older than himself. Up close, he saw Rick was more squarely centered in middle age, although he was clearly fighting it. His trim physique had to be the result of careful diet and rigorous exercise, and his hair was clearly professionally dyed.

Adjusting his wireframe glasses, Rick was also checking out his present company, the so-called prophet. "It's good to finally meet you," he said. "I have to admit, I've been curious about you and your gift."

It was hard to tell if Rick was a believer in his "gift" or not. Peter detected something in his demeanor that seemed dubious, although Rick was clearly intrigued.

"Well, there are some things you probably haven't heard," Peter began. "In fact, I've only told a handful of people about my most recent dream. Would you like to hear about it?"

"Sure," Rick said, crossing his corduroyed legs as he took a sip of tea.

With Rick listening intently, Peter launched into the story, starting from the fiery dream that had led him to call Abbas, who had then alerted Hassin. He informed Rick that while Hassin's mosque had been saved, it had also been badly damaged.

"On my way home, I kept thinking about the parable of the Good Samaritan, and how we, the Christian community, should do something to help. So I was thinking of having a benefit of some kind, maybe raising a little money, but mostly just taking a stand. You know, show we care about *all* of our neighbors."

When he finished, Rick nodded thoughtfully and took another, longer drink of his cooling tea before asking, "Why didn't you take this to Dan Cox?"

"I did," Peter confessed. "He didn't feel *led* to do anything about it."

A knowing smile crept up from the corners of the minister's mouth.

"What?" Peter asked.

"The after-effects of 9/11 and the Iraq War will be with us for a long time." Rick shook his head as if saddened by the whole affair. "People are fearful of Islam. It's not right; it's not fair, but there it is."

"Yeah," Peter agreed. "It will definitely take some courage to do this kind of thing."

Rick looked almost amused by the push from Peter. "What do you want me to do, exactly?" he asked. "Make an announcement in church, or...?"

"Host the benefit at Grace Church," Peter said, getting right to the point.

Letting out a little laugh, Rick looked at Peter, who stared back unapologetically. A few awkward seconds passed until it became painfully obvious that Peter wasn't going to back down.

"And how do you 'envision' this benefit exactly?" Rick finally asked.

"We invite all the churches in the area to a big service, really get the word out. We'll have various speakers. You would say something. I know someone in the Islamic community who would be good." With a heavy sigh, he added, "I could even say something, briefly."

Taking time for a little more tea, Rick finally asked, "Can you give me a couple of days to think and pray on it?"

"Sure," Peter said, encouraged Rick wasn't immediately ruling it out.

Staring into space, Rick seemed deep in ponderous reflection on the matter. "What about music?" he suddenly asked. "You think we could get someone to perform?"

"I don't know," Peter said. "It would be great if we could."

"I've heard the rumors. I don't know if they're true. I don't need to know," Rick said, holding out his hands defensively. Glancing around, he leaned across the table and, in a hushed tone, asked, "Do you think you could get Jordan Stone to play?"

Although no longer shocked at the legs on the persistent story, Peter was a little surprised to hear it coming from Rick. "Doesn't she go to your church?"

"Well, to be honest, no one has seen Jordan for a while," Rick admitted.

"Okay, well, I'm not going out with her," Peter said adamantly.

Rick nodded as if he understood Peter had to deny any romantic involvement. Not wanting to let down the expectant look in Rick's eyes, he said, "If you check on having the benefit, I'll see what I can do."

It took Rick a whole week of prayer, plus a two-hour emergency meeting with the elders, to decide the fate of the benefit. After a heated debate, Grace Church finally agreed to host something called "Understanding Islam," which had morphed into a more informative and less supportive event than Peter had originally envisioned.

The Wednesday-night event was also decidedly downplayed with an almost whispered announcement from the pulpit and a two-sentence blurb in the prior Sunday's bulletin. Not satisfied with the puny amount of publicity they were getting, Peter decided to take it up a notch, calling radio and television stations himself.

A major church in the conservative bastion of Williamson County hosting anything for the Islamic community was newsworthy. Throw in that the normally reclusive "hometown prophet" would be making a personal appearance, and the story had instant buzz.

Within a day, the local coverage that Peter generated for "Understanding Islam" sent a collective shiver through the leadership at Grace Church. While the church turned down all media requests for the event, the damage had already been done. Word was out, and the public was going to come to the service the church had hoped to keep nice and quiet. The only question now was whether the thousand-seat sanctuary could accommodate everyone.

As promised, Peter made an effort get Jordan on board. When he finally got a hold of her and explained the situation, she seemed a tad reluctant.

"Oh God, Peter, I'm going to announce my divorce next week, and I'll be showing by next month. Now you want me to do a benefit for Muslims? Are you trying to put the last nail in my freaking coffin? Because that's a career killer. Why not ask me to do a pro-choice benefit? Don't you have a rally for the Communist Party or the KKK

I could do? Maybe I could club a baby seal while I'm at it!"

Fearing Grace might still pull the plug on the event, Peter avoided Rick, waiting to break the news about Jordan's "scheduling conflict" until the last possible moment. By the night of the event, he figured he was safe.

Peter peeked out from around the corner of the stage and watched the steady stream of people filling the auditorium. Maybe because it felt like it was "his event," he was more excited and a little less nervous than he had been prior to his previous announcements at Trinity. Or maybe he was just getting better at these things.

"Looks like we have a full house," Peter announced to Abbas and the Grace Church worship band. As he turned around, he saw Rick had joined them in the backstage area. The pastor looked haggard; the event had clearly wreaked havoc on the pastor's carefully coiffed appearance, and for a second, Peter almost felt bad for dragging him into it.

"So Jordan isn't coming?" Rick asked, looking for an Islamic miracle.

"Pretty sure," Peter said firmly, dousing the last ember of hope in the pastor's eyes.

Peter's previous guilt dissipated, and he felt a pang of disgust for the needy preacher who seemed so caught up in the trappings of celebrity. But as Rick took off his glasses and rubbed his tired eyes, Peter thought he glimpsed a lonely boy who had always wanted to be popular.

"It's going to be okay," Peter said, giving him a compassionate pat on the back.

After walking around Rick and the five youths that comprised the church's worship band, Peter squatted down next to Abbas. "How are you doing?"

"To be honest, I'm a little nervous. I've never spoken in front of so many Christians," Abbas said. "Actually, I've never spoken in front of so many Muslims either."

"Most Christians are pretty nice," Peter said, trying to reassure Abbas, as well as himself.

"Okay, five minutes," Rick said, mostly to the band, who was supposed to go on first and warm up the crowd.

As the guys and one girl gathered up their instruments, the back door opened, and another young man with a guitar case walked in. Needing a haircut and a shave, the straggler looked a little underdressed in faded jeans and a t-shirt under an old sweater.

What was strange was how the other band members reacted to the guitar player, eagerly gathering around him. Even Pastor Rick came over to shake the kid's hand with a deference Peter couldn't comprehend.

A moment later, the newcomer spotted Peter and, after managing to politely detach himself from his admirers, came over.

"Hey, you're Peter, right?"

"Yeah," Peter confirmed. "Who are you?"

"I'm Nathan," the shaggy young man said, almost shyly. "Jordan mentioned the show tonight, and I'd really like to be a part of it, if it's cool with you?"

"Yeah, it's fine with me," Peter said. "You know Jordan Stone?"

"Yeah," Nathan said, pushing some extra hair out of his eyes and revealing a handsome face. "She called to tell me about it. I guess she knew I'd be into it."

"How do you know Jordan?" Peter asked, still trying to place the increasingly familiar face.

"Oh, we opened for her a few years ago," Nathan said. "If you want, I can do a couple of my own songs. I think the band already knows them," he said softly, glancing back at the excited worship team.

"Okay," Peter said.

"Hello," Abbas said to Nathan. "My name's Abbas."

"Hey, Abbas," the guitar player said. "Nathan."

"Are you a professional musician?" Abbas asked.

"Yeah, I'm in a group called Broken Vessels."

Even Peter, who didn't listen to Christian music, knew Broken

Vessels. Presently the "super group" of the contemporary Christian music world, they had easily surpassed Jordan Stone on the Christian charts. Broken Vessels had performed the miracle of crossing over to the mainstream.

"I'm very sorry," Abbas apologized innocently, "I've not heard of Broken Weasels."

"Ha! That's okay," Nathan managed to say between sputters of genuine laughter.

Grace Church's senior pastor bounded out on stage with a renewed spring in his step. Rick said a few eloquent words about acceptance and standing up to racial and religious bigotry. Then, in an overly zealous introduction that made the singer visibly uncomfortable, he announced, "Nathan Trigg!"

The crowd gave a collective gasp followed by a thunderous applause of appreciation as Nathan shuffled on stage. With a wave his hand, he launched into a stirring first song with his new back-up band. Apparently, it was a big hit because many in the audience, especially the younger ones, stood and clapped and sang along.

After he finished his opening number, Nathan waited for the crowd to quiet down.

Leaning into the microphone, he spoke in a conspiratorial whisper. "I just met a man backstage...and I think he's a Muslim." He looked around suspiciously for a second before breaking into a disarming smile, eliciting a few laughs from the crowd. "He seems like a cool guy, even if he's never heard of my group."

More laughs followed.

"Abbas is his name, and he lives right here in Nashville, and that makes him my neighbor. According to my Lord and Savior, I'm supposed to love my neighbor *as myself*." Turning to face the backstage area, he said, "So, Abbas, this one is for you, my brother."

Then he broke into a melodic song that was written to a long-lost friend about what might have been. Peter recognized it as a number-one song that had been in at least two rom-com movies. Somehow, dedicating it to a stranger made it take on a renewed sense of meaning.

Moved by the music, Abbas spontaneously ran out and embraced the singer as soon as he was finished with the song. Caught off guard by the awkward display of affection, Nathan kind of choked up. The two departed the stage arm-and-arm.

A beaming Rick took the microphone. "Thanks, Nathan! That was fantastic!" Turning to the crowd, he said, "You've already been introduced to Abbas Hassim of the Nashville Islamic Center. Let's welcome him again."

There was polite applause as Abbas timidly came back on stage and moved to the microphone. "I want to thank Nathan again. I think he's going to be very big one day." This elicited a few laughs that Abbas didn't seem to get. "I also want to thank Pastor Rick for inviting me here tonight." He took a moment to gaze out at the faces.

"A couple of weeks ago, Peter Quell contacted me about a dream. In my religion, we are used to prophets. We have one hundred twenty-two thousand of them! They include figures you know, like Adam, Abraham, David, Moses, Elijah, and Jesus Christ, and end with Muhammad. So, while I didn't believe this young man was necessarily a prophet, I listened to what he had to say.

"Because I did, some people who wanted to destroy one of our mosques did not succeed. Now, I know these men who set the fire are not true Christians, just like the terrorists who murder people in the name of Allah are not true Muslims. Nowhere does the Quran condone killing innocents. 'Islam' literally means submission to God and is derived from the word 'peace.'"

"Lie!" Like a stone, the one word thrown from someone in the crowd shattered the serenity of the service. Along with almost everyone else, Abbas was startled by the interruption.

"No, it's true," he stammered. "There are many misconceptions about our religion. For example, I believe we worship the same God. The word Allah is simply the Aramaic word for God. This is the word Jesus used when he prayed in his native tongue. In fact, we revere Jesus as one of God's greatest messengers. Like you, we believe he was conceived by a virgin and will return to earth to restore justice."

"Islam is a cult!" the same male voice shouted back. The protester's argument against Islam was not particularly complex, and yet it was amazingly disruptive.

"Yes, there is an element of Islam that is radical, but it is only a fraction of our religion," Abbas responded. "We are growing because Islamic law protects the minorities and the oppressed, and many poor people in the world respond to this message. Please know our mosques are not here to convert anyone. We simply want the right to worship."

"You're a liar!" This time the slur came in the form of a woman's shrill voice.

The rudeness elicited some blow-back from others in the audience who shouted, "Be quiet!" and "Let him talk!"

Though clearly shaken by the hateful hecklers, Abbas seemed to take courage from the voices of support in the midst of what probably felt like the Spanish Inquisition.

"You set up Christian churches in many Muslim countries and worship side by side with us. I am sure if you heard of Christian churches being attacked or burned, you would be upset. All we are asking for is the same respect in this great country that was founded on religious freedom."

Abbas paused for a second, appearing relieved when no one shouted an insult at him.

"We believe that in the past, God sent messengers to a particular nation or group because there was something He wanted them to understand. Perhaps this is such a time. I want to publicly thank Allah, or God, for allowing me the honor of speaking to you tonight. We have differences, yes. But we have much more in common. And, as Nathan said, we are neighbors. I hope we will also be friends."

In the wake of the applause, Abbas retreated backstage, which was Peter's cue to come out. To his surprise, within the claps was a small but vocal strain of "Boos." He had feared a less-than-welcome reception for Abbas; he just hadn't anticipated it for himself.

"Thanks, Abbas," Peter said as he took his mark and felt the tension in the large, thousand-seat auditorium. He had hoped to lighten the mood by telling the story of how he had called every mosque in the area, and Abbas had been the only one who hadn't thought he was crazy. But before he could utter a word, a woman shrieking, "False prophet! False prophet!"

A few people booed at the screaming Banshee—at least, Peter hoped they were booing at her rather than at him. Still, the damage had been done, and it now seemed impossible to attempt an amusing anecdote in the face of such extreme hostility.

"Look," Peter started sharply. "If you hate me or Muslims, there really isn't any reason for you to be here, so there's the door."

No one made a sound or a move in the direction he was pointing.

"I sure don't want to be here right now," Peter exclaimed, hearing the tremor in his amplified voice. "I hate public speaking. This scares me to death. The only reason I'm here is because I believe this is something I'm supposed to do."

"Liar!" shrilled the woman.

Taking a deep breath, Peter told himself not to let the accusations derail him.

"The parable of the Good Samaritan has come to me a couple of times recently. You know, the Jews and Samaritans didn't get along back then. In fact, they worshipped different Gods, or thought they did. But it was a Samaritan who stopped to help the Jewish guy, not the other respectable Jewish leaders."

Except for the normal rustle of a big crowd, it was fairly quiet. Like Abbas, Peter now appreciated any pause when he wasn't verbally accosted.

"You all know the story. The Samaritan bandaged up the other man's wounds and gave him a ride to an inn on his donkey. Then he left money for the innkeeper to take care of him and promised to reimburse him for any extra expenses."

Pausing, Peter wondered how far to push it. Thinking of Jesse, he decided he wasn't there to win a popularity contest, so he pressed on.

"You know, I wanted to take up a contribution tonight to help the mosque in Columbia fix some of the damage from the fire.

That idea got nixed because that was too...I don't know. Maybe too Samaritan, or too Christlike?"

As soon as he said the words, he regretted them. Even if it was true, he felt like he had insulted his audience as well as his host. Peter glanced at Rick, who was standing to the side of the stage, a wounded expression on his face.

"I'm sorry," Peter said directly to him before turning back to the crowd. "Most churches wouldn't even touch this with a ten-foot pole, and Rick stepped up and fought for it, and I appreciate that."

Shaking his head, Peter went on. "I guess I'm new to church politics because I was blown away that this was even controversial. Everything I'm saying is right there in the scriptures we read every Sunday. I guess it's easier to read when it's Samaritans and Jews and not Christians and Muslims."

While the room was eerily quiet, the air felt charged.

"I don't mean to lecture you," Peter said. "I appreciate you coming to learn something about Islam. We all need to learn more about other people. The more we get to know each other, the more we realize we're not so different. And then it is easier to love our neighbors the way God calls us to."

From the corner of his eye, he spotted Rick coming toward him. The pastor gave him a nod, which Peter recognized as a signal for him to stop while he was not too far behind. It was good timing because he had run out of things to say anyway.

CHAPTER 17

Once again, Peter was embarrassed by his performance. He knew he shouldn't think of it as a "performance," but when you're on stage in front of a thousand people, it's hard not to think of it that way.

While video cameras hadn't been allowed in the sanctuary, more than one person had recorded portions of the service on their cell phone and posted it online. By Thursday night, the local TV news channels were replaying bootleg copies. Peter's invitation for the hecklers to leave the church was a particularly popular clip.

As he scanned the news channels, his mom was there to provide pearls of wisdom like, "When people anger you, they get the best of you," and "The first one to get angry always loses." It took a lot of internal fortitude for Peter not to let his mother "get the best of him" or "win." By the time the ten o' clock newscasts were over, he wanted to go on a media-and-Mom fast.'

Over the next couple of days, he took a few calls from people, such as Uncle John and Victor Birdsong. While there were voices of support, most of the calls came from reporters looking for a quote. A documentary filmmaker wanted to follow him around with a camera crew 24/7, even capturing him sleeping. An agent specializing in Christian artists wanted to represent him.

And then there were the messages that called him a "terrorist," or "terrorist lover," or the ever-popular "false prophet." These calls typically ended with a vaguely threatening comment, like, "You'll get what's coming to you" and "I hear the weather in Hell is hot this time of year."

It might have been almost funny if these weren't the same types who had just tried to burn down a mosque. The callers would be happy to know they kept him up at night worrying about himself and his mom.

Ms. Quell was publicly defiant. "No one is going to run me out of my home, not reporters and certainly not a bunch of yahoos," she told her son and anyone else who would listen. But Peter knew she was scared, and the situation was growing untenable.

What he couldn't understand was where all the hate was coming from. Had the "yahoos" held a secret meeting and decided he was evil? Someone had to be telling them what to think and stirring things up against him. He just hoped they would stop short of stirring up a Molotov cocktail and chucking it through his bedroom window.

By Saturday, he decided it was time to pull his head out of the sand and find out who was saying what about him. Since Peter preferred not to use his mom's computer, he drove to the public library to do a little digging. When he got online and typed his name into the search engine, he watched in amazement as page after page popped up.

The first couple of screens were filled with news stories about him, mostly written just after the ash spill. They usually mentioned his other "reputed" prophecies, especially the stock market crash. In spite of what Peter considered to be insurmountable evidence, the jaded journalists always questioned the legitimacy of his predictions, bringing up every possible human explanation from sheer luck to chicanery.

He saw that the Nashville alternative newspaper had just

published a cover story on him. That paper was often the defender of the city's underdogs, so he'd hoped to be thrown a friendlier bone, but he was disappointed to find an exposé with a skeptical, decidedly secular slant. It didn't help that they kept mentioning he had not returned their phone calls, making it sound like he was dodging them.

The writer of the feature article referenced Ed Pressman, the radio shock jock who had "put Mr. Quell squarely in his on-the-air crosshairs." According to Pressman, Peter was "a fortune-teller selling pap and pabulum to infants." So the man was not a fan, but it was still hard to imagine his words inspiring the kind of vitriol Peter had experienced at the Wednesday night service.

On the third page of his search, Peter came across a website entitled "Peter Quell–False Prophet." The site looked as crudely made as artwork by a child coloring outside the lines, and while it was chock full of information, almost all of it was erroneous.

It was unclear whether the person or people behind the site believed the prophecies were true or an elaborate series of hoaxes. The site claimed that if Peter was able to see the future, it was only because he had made a deal with the devil. This camp was divided as to whether Peter was the anti-Christ or merely the second beast in Revelation 13 who performed "great and marvelous signs."

Ranked just below the hate-site was its antithesis, "Peter Quell–Modern Day Prophet." Clicking it, he was treated to an impressive layout that chronicled all of his public prophecies with more detail than he had even dreamed. This site also allowed comments where theories were floated that he had foreseen every major event in the last decade and had only recently begun to go public. And, of course, it was the general consensus that he was Jordan Stone's secret lover.

On the "Modern Day Prophet" site were also links to YouTube videos. A clip of Peter announcing the coal plant disaster at Trinity had received over five hundred thousand viewings. The press conference in Kingston had to be divided into several parts, the least watched garnering over two hundred thousand hits.

A three-day-old video from the "Understanding Islam" service was already at two hundred seventy-five thousand hits and climbing. Not surprisingly, the big winner was "Prophet Gets Pummeled in Pick-Up" with well over a million viewings.

As he scrolled through the pages, he finally came to a site he had seen before: "Peter Quell, Star Lord." Already aware he shared the same name as a relatively obscure Marvel comic book character, he realized he had reached the end of his own notoriety on the internet.

"Hey," a female voice called from behind him. "Peter?"

Swiveling around, he was on the verge of introducing himself as "Peter Quell, Star Lord" when he found himself looking up at an attractive woman about his age. Her light brown hair and pale skin reminded him of someone...from church. It was Marian from Grace Church, who had politely rejected his feeble attempt to ask her out.

"Hey, Marian," he said.

At that moment, a rambunctious little boy ran up with a DVD in his hand. "I want this one!" he yelled in a voice much too loud for the library.

Glancing at the cover, she said, "No, you can't have *Nightmare on Elm Street*."

"Hey, Jacob," Peter said. "How's it going?"

"Good," the youngster responded enthusiastically.

"Go find something else," Marian said, and the disgruntled boy ran back to the shelves. Looking up to Peter, she said, "I'm protective of him. Maybe too protective."

"No, you need to be," Peter said, wondering if she was talking about horror movies or dating.

Other than a Christian singer and television reporter, he had not met many women since coming home. Peter thought Marian was every bit as pretty as Jordan or Cindy, just in a more understated way—like she wasn't trying so hard or maybe had a different set of priorities.

"I can honestly say," Marian said, "that was the most interesting Wednesday night service I've ever been to."

"Oh, you went to Understanding Islam," Peter said, feeling his face flush with embarrassment.

In a flash, Jacob was back with another movie in his hand. He showed it to his mom, who was already shaking her *No.*

"It was very powerful," she insisted as her son protested his mom's decision. "You got a little upset because some jack—" she paused and glanced toward Jacob, "—*rabbits* were just there to make trouble."

"I still shouldn't have let the *jackrabbits* get to me," Peter said.

"Most people there agreed with what you said." Turning to the pouting Jacob, she ordered a little more sternly, "Go find something nice." As her son ran off toward the shelves again, Marian returned to Peter.

"It's really something," she said. "The dreams, I mean."

"Yeah, I know," Peter agreed. "It's crazy."

It seemed like there was a spark between them, and for a second, Peter thought about trying to ask her out again. Maybe he could just suggest getting together at some vague point in the future and see how she responded.

Just then, the little guy came charging back straight into her leg. With his face buried in her thigh, he held up another video.

"This is fine." Looking at Peter, Marian asked, "Have you ever seen the original *Willy Wonka and the Chocolate Factory*?"

"Of course," Peter said enthusiastically. "I mean, it's been a while."

"Well, Jacob and I will be watching it tonight," she informed him. "If you want, you can join us."

"Ah, sure," Peter managed, taken back by her change of heart, as well as her directness. "Are you sure it's okay?"

"I think so," she said, nodding slowly.

It was an actual date. To Peter, the concept seemed stranger than having a prophetic dream. A date with a real, live woman was up there with the Second Coming. He believed it was possible, but had been beginning to doubt it would happen in his lifetime.

Who, after all, would want to date an unemployed thirty-year-old man who lived at home with his mother? Of course, fame could do wonders, even if it was the same kind of infamy reserved for sideshow freaks.

Leaving a vague note on the kitchen table for his mom, he slipped out and drove to the south side of Franklin.

Marian's modest home was in one of the newer neighborhoods that had cropped up in the last few years. Just the fact that she owned her own place put her light-years ahead of him.

Walking up to the front porch, he straightened himself up and rang the bell. A moment later, the door swung open, and a distracted Marian waved him inside.

"Come on in," she said, looking casual, even a little disheveled. "Have you had dinner?"

"I had a sandwich earlier," he said as he entered the house.

"We have some pizza if you're hungry," she said, gesturing toward the kitchen.

Jacob ran through the den with a slice flopping in his hand, then stopped to evaluate the strange man in his house. "Do you really know what's going to happen?" the little boy asked.

"Sometimes," Peter said.

"Have you had any dreams about me?"

"Nope, but I'll let you know if I do."

"What about my mom?" Jacob asked. "You dream about her?"

"Um, not yet," Peter said, glancing in his mom's direction.

With a light laugh, Marian cut in, "How about that movie?"

The three of them settled in the living room to watch the old film as they passed around a big bowl of popcorn. Peter could identify with Charlie Bucket. They were both pretty hopeless characters who had found golden tickets that granted them entrance to a strange, wonderful, and potentially dangerous world.

By the time the glass elevator burst through the ceiling, Jacob was nodding off. Marian left Peter to watch the credits by himself while she carried her half-asleep son to his bedroom. By the time she came back, Peter was watching the news and picking kernels out of his teeth.

"Did Charlie live happily ever after?" she asked, folding a leg underneath her as she plopped down on the couch beside him.

"Actually, the elevator crashed," Peter affirmed. "It was pretty awful."

Marian laughed. "I'm guessing you don't have children?"

He shook his head.

"Well, you're a good sport about this," Marian said. "This isn't most guys' idea of a fun evening."

"Well, I'm not most guys," Peter responded.

"Yeah, I guess you have a point," she said with an easy laugh. Reaching out, she accidentally—or intentionally—brushed his knee with her hand, withdrawing it just as quickly.

"I don't want to get too personal or make you uncomfortable," she said while Peter fixated on the spot of denim where the physical contact had occurred. "It's just, I'm kind of curious about your... ability."

"Thanks, but I don't really feel like I'm doing anything," Peter said, wondering if he had a prophet groupie on his hands and kind of hoping he did. "I mean, all I do is close my eyes and go to sleep." He shrugged. "Sometimes I have these dreams."

"What are the dreams like?" she asked. "If you don't mind me asking."

"It's okay," he said, as his leg involuntarily moved a little closer to hers. "Um, I have normal dreams, just like everyone else. The ones that are telling me something is going to happen are really vivid and lucid, and I wake up right after I have each one."

"Huh," she uttered. For a moment, a faraway look crossed her face. "When I was about sixteen, I was fascinated with the Oracles of Delphi. You know, they were these girls in ancient Greece who also happened to be about sixteen. Supposedly, they could hear the voices of the gods, so leaders and kings would come from far away to ask their advice about really important matters."

"Weren't they getting high on laurel leaves or gas fumes or something?" Peter asked.

148

"Those are theories," she said with mock defensiveness. "Anyway, I thought it would be so cool to be a prophetess." She reflected on her childhood fantasy for a moment. "I guess that makes sense when you're young and don't feel like anyone is listening to you."

"Well, people definitely don't do what I tell them, even if I ask politely," he said after a moment.

"Maybe that's the problem. You're too nice," she said playfully. "Maybe you should get a little more Old Testament on them. You know, start ordering people around, threaten to smite them with the wrath of God."

"Yeah," Peter said, warming to the idea. "I could end every sentence with—" he switched to his Charlton Heston voice, "—*so Sayeth Peter, so Sayeth the Lord!*"

Marian laughed out loud; then, as if thinking of Jacob, she covered her mouth. "Have you thought about growing a beard?" she giggled through her fingers. "I think people expect their prophets to have some facial hair."

"I don't know if I could grow that great of a beard," Peter admitted. "I'm pretty fair."

"How about a goatee?" she asked, examining his smooth cheeks. "You could at least grow some sideburns or a moustache."

"I think you are confusing a prophet with a porn star," he said, causing her to suppress another little laugh. She had a pretty smile, so he kept riffing away, hoping to see more of it. "What do you think about a staff? Or is that too outdated?"

She crinkled her nose. "It's a little old school." Snapping her fingers, she pointed at him. "Maybe a laser pointer. You could put that red dot right between their eyes."

"Like a laser sight!" Peter said. "Yeah, that would get their attention. Kind of like Moses meets the Terminator."

"That would be so cool!"

When he stopped laughing, she was staring at him with a suddenly serious expression.

"We shouldn't make fun," she said. "You do have a gift."

"It's okay," Peter reassured her. "It feels good to laugh about it."

Gently, she reached out and put a hand on his arm. "Then I'm glad."

He reciprocated by putting a hand on her hand. Sensing the timing was right, he gently pulled her a little closer as he leaned in for a landing on her lips. As they lingered in the kiss, their bodies moved to the middle of the sofa cushions where popcorn and loose change had disappeared.

Marian broke away first, leaning back just far enough to get a good look at him. Vulnerability gave way to a girlish impishness as she gently touched his face with the back of her hand. "On second thought, don't grow that beard," she whispered.

CHAPTER 18

October 24 (Sun)

I'm outside at night looking up at the sky when I see a cross-shaped constellation. One of the stars falls away, then another, and another... Three stars fall in all.

While I'm wondering what it means, I feel a whoosh—like a low-flying jet above me. As the burning ball of light races ahead, I see what looks like a capitol in the distance. In seconds, the meteor explodes into the side of the building. The structure seems okay, minus a small smoking hole.

A second star drops from the sky and zooms by a couple of hundred feet overhead. When I look up, I see a radio tower with a blinking red light in the distance. The light seems to act as a beacon, directing the missile toward it. Sheering off the top of the metal scaffolding, the star rocks the tower but leaves it intact.

As I turn away, I see the skyline of Nashville and the third star falling toward it. Its trajectory takes it hurdling toward the cluster of high-rise buildings downtown. The meteor dive bombs, hitting the top of one of

the taller towers. (I'm not sure which one.) Again, the building remains
stable with only a black cave instead of a shiny tinted window.
Then I wake up.

Peter was in his bedroom, carefully rereading the wild dream he had captured in his red spiral notebook. It had taken him some time to reconstruct it all, editing and rewriting until it felt right. Meticulously matching every detail against his memory, he had to make sure he didn't make a mistake or miss anything.

He had been awakened by the crash of the third meteor in his seventh prophetic dream at approximately 4:30 a.m., so technically it was October 25. Going back, he added the time and correct date at the top of his entry.

It had seemed like his longest dream yet; it was probably his most violent, too, although for some reason, it didn't disturb him as much as some of the others had. On the surface, it resembled a terrorist attack; however, he didn't feel like that was what he'd witnessed. The attack didn't seem to come from man; it came from above.

His mind drifted up to the "cross" constellation where the fallen stars had originated. Could the stars represent Christian saints who had passed on and were looking down from heaven? If so, what were they doing buzzing radio towers and plowing into buildings?

For a moment, he wished he could call Dan and bounce the dream off him, although Dan would probably remind him that in the Book of Revelation, a third of the stars fall from the heavens during the last days. And as with most of Dan's interpretations, Peter didn't see what that had to do with anything.

Frustrated and sleepy, Peter stared up at his ceiling and audibly asked, "Why do I have to go through this? Why can't you just tell me what's going to happen? You could have an angel lay it all out for me. That's the way you did it with Isaiah. Not that I'm comparing myself with him or anything."

There was no voice from heaven, no appearance of an angel.

With a sigh, Peter thought about how he'd figured out his past dreams and realized God always put the right people in his path at the right time. Whether it was Pastor Dan, Uncle John, or a surly waitress at a roadside diner, the one constant was a person who intersected his life when he needed to hear them.

Now, Marian had come along, seemingly out of nowhere. Was that a coincidence, or was it something more? It sure felt like more to him. It had been a couple of days since *Willy Wonka,* and he was looking for an excuse to call her anyway.

The alarm clock read 5:21 a.m. Even after a dream that foretold the future, he was pretty sure he should wait a couple of hours before making the call.

Marian seemed intrigued with the prospect of helping him decipher one of his dreams—just not while she was getting ready for work and getting Jacob dressed for school. So she invited him over for dinner that night, which gave Peter all day to obsess over his dream and read from the books of prophets in the Old Testament.

For some reason, he found himself particularly drawn to Jeremiah, who had always been destined to be a prophet. In Jeremiah 1:5, God says, "Before I formed you in the womb I knew you, before you were born I set you apart; I appointed you as a prophet to the nations."

Peter had often heard the first part of that scripture as the rallying cry of pro-lifers. While he was personally against abortion, he found it a little disingenuous to use half a scripture so broadly when it was clearly specific to one individual.

Primarily a "prophet of doom," Jeremiah wasn't the most popular dude in town. He was threatened, beaten, put in stocks, and thrown into a cistern while being opposed by priests, a false prophet, a king, and even his own brothers. His message was a harsh one regarding Israel, but he was also known as the "weeping prophet" because he so deeply hurt for the very people he was compelled to prophecy against.

Permeated with prophets and prophecies, Peter left the house before he started admonishing the house plants. By the time he arrived

153

at Marian's, he was anxious to get started on deciphering his dream and was a little disappointed to find she didn't share his sense of urgency.

While Marian was welcoming, she made it clear at the front door that they had to keep the conversation on normal topics during dinner for Jacob's sake. So, instead of trying to figure out the possible end of the world, they chatted about Jacob's soccer team and a skin rash he had picked up at school.

After the last strand of spaghetti was sucked up, Jacob challenged Peter to a video racing game. Succumbing to the relentless taunting, Peter went into the den while Marian loaded the dishwasher. The seven-year-old took great relish in lapping his geriatric opponent until he became bored with the lack of competition.

When Peter excused himself from his latest fiery car wreck and slipped into the kitchen, Jacob didn't even look up. As the animated engines roared in the other room, Marian poured two glasses from the bottle of wine Peter had brought and sat down at the table with him.

"Okay," the weary single mother said, "let me hear it."

By now, Peter did not need his notebook. Since he knew the dream by heart, he recounted each star's fall to earth, beat by beat.

"So, basically," Marian said in conclusion, "three stars drop out of the sky and hit three different structures."

"Right," Peter said, taking a sip from his glass. Rather than jumping in with his own theories, he held back, waiting to see what Marian might come up with on her own.

"Well, when I think of a star," she said carefully, "I think of a famous person. That's probably stupid though."

"No, that's good," Peter said. For all his thoughts on constellations, dead saints, and eschatology, he'd missed the most obvious connection. "What about the cross in the sky, though?"

They both sat sipping the cheap Cabernet, listening to the distant roar of the race.

"Maybe they're dead celebs?" Peter said, grasping at answering his own question.

"Why do you think it has to do with dead people?"

"Because they're in heaven," Peter said.

"What if they're just stars, you know, celebrities that come crashing down to earth," she said. "They're high in the sky because they're famous or important or respected or something."

Jacob let out a "YEAH!" as the crowd cheered in the background.

"If it was famous people, that would explain them crashing into things like a radio tower or a government building," Peter said. "Famous people are on the radio and in politics."

"So they're crashing into what they're known for," Marian said, her excitement growing. "So maybe it's someone on the radio, like a singer. For the Capitol, you have someone who holds public office."

"And for the office building," Peter said, jumping on the caboose of her train of thought, "a CEO or some big businessman."

"Or businesswoman," Marian added.

Peter nodded, amazed and a little embarrassed that he had so completely missed that line of logic. It all seemed somewhat obvious, at least in retrospect. Sitting back, he looked at Marian with renewed appreciation just as Jacob came running into the room.

"Can I have some ice cream?" he pleaded, looking a little bleary-eyed from his hard-fought race to victory lane.

"I guess so," Marian said, "then it's off to bed."

"I can take off," Peter offered.

"This should only take a few minutes," she said, motioning for him to stay put.

Not wanting to miss out on a little more private time with Marian, Peter stuck around for dessert. While Jacob was taken to the back of the house to get ready for bed, Peter drifted into the living room to watch the local news.

The top story of the day was a pro football player who had been arrested for drunk driving and having an unlicensed firearm in his car. By all accounts, the All-Pro had been a pillar of the community, actively involved with his church and charities.

When Marian finally came into the room, she was carrying the half empty bottle of wine with a refilled glass. "Do you want some more?"

"I don't think so," Peter said, muting the TV. "I've been thinking about that cross in the sky."

Setting the bottle down on the coffee table, Marian took a seat next to him, listening.

"What if it represents the church?" he asked. "Like Christian celebrities or leaders?"

"Yeah," she said, slowly nodding as she mulled it over. "Maybe they're not really acting like Christians. That's why they're going to take a fall."

"That's good," Peter said, feeling the final piece of the puzzle neatly slipping into place. "I think you solved it."

"You solved it," Marian said modestly. "I just helped a little."

"You did more than that," he insisted, reaching out to take her hand. "Are you sure you haven't done this before?"

"Well, I was seeing another prophet before I met you," she said slyly. "But that's over. His beard was way too scratchy."

"Well, I shaved this morning," Peter said invitingly.

Touching his face, she gave an impressed little whistle. Feeling her touch was too much, and he moved in closer for a kiss, forgetting all about falling stars.

"Wait," she said, abruptly distancing herself from his advances.

"What?" he asked, wondering what he'd done wrong and how quickly he could make it right.

"What are you going to do about it?"

"About what?" Peter asked, perplexed.

"About your dream?" she asked with genuine concern on her face.

"Oh, I don't know," he said, trying to refocus. Sitting back, he thought about his options for the first time. "I've made some announcements in churches, but I think I may have worn out my welcome there."

"Maybe you should skip the churches," Marian said. "I mean, you can get an interview with almost anyone."

"Yeah, I've had lots of offers," he said, recognizing a tinge of pride in his voice. "A producer from *Good Morning America* offered to fly me and a guest to New York." As he said it, he wondered how he would break the news to his mom that she was no longer his plus-one.

"Really?" Marian said, impressed.

Whisking his girlfriend off to New York or LA for a nationally televised interview sounded pretty exciting. As first-class tickets and five-star hotels flashed in his head, another picture began to take shape. It was the portrait of a battered and bruised Jeremiah enduring extreme hardship to get the word of God out to his people.

He was no Jeremiah, but he also knew he could do better than pimping out his prophecies to the highest bidder. With a concerted effort, he wiped away the glamour and grandiosity and got back to thinking in practical terms about his next step.

"The thing is," he finally said, "I probably need to do something fast because sometimes these things happen within a day or two."

"That makes sense," Marian agreed.

"I also think these people might be more local."

"Why do you say that?"

"The office building was definitely in downtown Nashville. I don't know about the radio tower; most radio is local, isn't it?"

"I guess," she said, even though she frowned, unsure.

Undeterred, Peter continued to make his case. "And the Capitol building might have been in DC, but it felt closer to home, somehow."

"So you go with someone local who will get it on the air fast," she summarized.

"Yeah," Peter said. "It could be television, or maybe just the local paper." The latter was particularly appealing if it meant he wouldn't have to watch awkward videos of himself on TV and the internet. Not having to answer hard questions from reporters or angry protestors was a bonus. "*The Tennessean* would print it. All I'd have to do is type it up and mail it in—end of story."

"People want to see you," she challenged him. "You have a nice, sincere face." Reaching out, she stroked his cheek again. "Smooth, too."

Trying hard to ignore her half-kidding caress, Peter confessed, "I get nervous being on camera."

"You have to get over that," Marian said firmly. "You're a prophet now."

CHAPTER 19

Lots of local reporters had left multiple messages since Peter was heralded as the so-called prophet. Only one, however, had left a message every single day since the stock market crashed. Cindy Sizemore's dogged persistence had caused Peter to go through a range of emotions: attraction, annoyance, anger, astonishment, and—even though he had a girlfriend now—back to semi-attraction.

They had spoken briefly after she'd followed him to Kingston to cover the coal plant disaster, and he had called to let her, along with almost every other reporter in the city, know about the "Understanding Islam" service. What he would now be proposing was something he had not offered to anyone else—an exclusive interview.

All humility aside, he knew how much a one-on-one interview would mean to a local beat reporter hungry for the greener pastures of bigger media markets. When his call went into her voicemail, he left a brief message and waited by the phone. He knew it wouldn't take long, and it didn't.

"Hi, is this Peter Quell?" she chirped.

"Yeah, hi, Cindy," Peter said. "Thanks for calling back."

"Of course," Cindy said, obviously trying not to sound overly excited. "What can I do for you?"

"I had another dream, and I want to get it out as soon as possible."

"Are you having a press conference?" she asked.

"No," he said, "I want to do something small, so it's just you."

There was a slight pause on the other line. "On camera, right?"

"Yes," Peter confirmed.

"Where?"

Now he hesitated, not having even considered the location.

"I could come to you," Cindy offered quickly.

"No!" Peter blurted out. His mother's house was the last place he wanted to be interviewed. The fact that he lived at home with his mom had already been more than adequately documented.

"You could come here to the studio," Cindy tried. "Do you know where Channel Seven is?"

"No," he said to both her suggestion and following question. For some reason, he didn't like the idea of giving her home-field advantage. Glancing out the window, he noticed the sun was shining; it was a beautiful day. "How about Centennial Park?"

"Sure," she agreed. Peter guessed she was willing to do it anywhere as long as he didn't change his mind. "One hour?"

"I can do that," he said, like he was taking a dare.

"I'll meet you in front of the Parthenon."

Driving up Hillsboro Road, Peter tried in vain to ignore the nervous tension coursing through his body. As he cut westward through the Warner Brother's Parks, he prayed for peace; all the while his mind kept rehearsing what he wanted to say and questioning whether he should have worn a different shirt.

The mellow midday classical music, courtesy of Nashville Public Radio, synced up nicely with Belle Meade's blue-blooded boulevard, providing Peter with a tranquil respite. On Harding Road, he rejoined the grind jockeying for position in West End traffic. This gave him time to worry over the interpretation of his dream and whether he was rushing the interview.

Once in Centennial Park, it was hard to miss the Parthenon—it being the only one this side of Greece. The giant replica was left over from a World Fair and was now supposed to symbolize that Nashville was the "Athens of the South." It made Peter think of the Oracles of Delphi. Did those girls ever get nervous before making a proclamation, or were they too stoned to care?

As he got closer to the city's beloved pagan temple, he spotted the Action 7 News van parked in the turn-around. From a distance, it looked like they were preparing to simulcast a world event. Crew members busied themselves with cameras and cables and monitors, stringing the insides of the van to a nearby picnic table.

Getting out of his car, Peter was hit by a fresh wave of anxiety, and yet he kept walking closer like a bug drawn to a bright, buzzing light.

Approaching the hive of activity, he suddenly heard, "Hi, Peter!" as Cindy stepped around the van in a black business suit, her nails reaching out to clutch his hand. "I appreciate you doing this."

"No problem," Peter said, noticing an older woman sitting in the news van who seemed to be supervising the production. Cindy steered him toward the picnic table that was being transformed into a mini-studio set.

"Now, I know you probably have a lot to say, so we're planning on making this at least a two-parter," Peter heard Cindy saying.

Peter nodded, then stopped. "Wait. What does that mean?"

"Oh, just that we'll air some of the interview tonight, and some tomorrow night," she said cheerfully. "If we can, we'd like to stretch it out three nights."

"No way," Peter said. "It all has to air tonight."

"This way is better," Cindy countered as she nodded positively, inviting him to join her in agreement. "This will build suspense and audience share."

Peter knew they wanted to save the big reveal of the latest dream for the grand finale. Ratings-wise, that might be the way to go, but this story had an expiration date, even if Peter didn't know exactly when it was.

"This is time-sensitive information, Cindy," Peter said firmly. "I have to have your assurance it will all run tonight, or the deal is off."

While the ultimatum seemed to vex the reporter, she stayed professional. "Excuse me for a moment," she said, pirouetting in a semi-circle and clipping her heels over to the woman in the van.

Peter watched the brief conversation take place between the reporter and what Peter assumed was the producer or executive. The woman, in turn, whipped out her cell phone and had another short, somewhat intense, conversation with someone else. After a minute, the woman said something to Cindy, who almost skipped back to the picnic table.

"I have great news," she said, letting a smile spread across her face. "We've gotten the go ahead to go live!"

"Live?" Peter asked, his heart doing a little flip.

"It's a big deal to break in, but corporate thinks this is worth it," Cindy said, beaming with excitement. "So, all your information will be out there in just a few minutes."

Now his heart seemed to be attempting a double backflip with a twist. "It will still be on the five o' clock news, right?" Peter stammered.

"Oh, they'll replay it at five, six, and ten," Cindy assured him as she directed him to the bench on one side of the picnic table.

As he took his seat, an audio tech materialized from under the table like a magical elf, clipping a tiny mike to his collar while the camera operator facing him began tweaking buttons on his video camera.

Peter started to apologize for his shirt choice before becoming distracted by the satellite dish on top of the truck. Soon, it would be transmitting pictures of himself, and his shirt, into outer space, or wherever they went.

Cindy took a seat on her bench across from Peter, facing her own camera. As she reviewed her notes, a young girl came over and patted her face with powder. Tilting her head, the reporter allowed the make-up girl to do her job, all the while keeping her eyes glued to her pages.

The girl turned to Peter when she was finished with the talent. "This will just take a second."

Peter closed his eyes as she brushed his face for an annoying second or two. "That's good," he said anxiously, waving her away.

The make-up girl shrugged and walked off, leaving him with a twinge of guilt for dismissing her so rudely. But he needed to think of anything else he should say to Cindy before the shooting started and it was too late.

"The only reason I'm doing this is to announce the dream," he reminded her. "If you try any 'gotcha questions,' I will walk out."

"What do you consider 'gotcha questions'?" Cindy asked, looking up.

"Anything that makes me look like an idiot."

"The only way you'll look like an idiot is if you walk off in the middle of a *live* interview."

"If I walk out, we'll both look like idiots," Peter reminded her.

"No. I'll look like an idiot if I don't ask you some real questions," she said. "I have to ask about your other prophecies."

He considered the request and couldn't really see the harm. "I'll answer a couple of questions about my other dreams."

"And don't you want a chance to answer your critics?"

"What critics?" Peter asked innocently. "Ed Pressman?"

"Don't you watch the news at all?" she asked, astonished by Peter's apparent naïveté.

"Not really," he said. "For the most part, I try to avoid it."

"Well, you have some critics," she assured him.

"One question," he relented, not wanting to seem unreasonable. He thought about it for a few more seconds. "And no questions about Jordan Stone. I barely know her, and there's nothing going on, so don't even bring her up."

Cindy nodded, crossing a line off her pad.

As final adjustments were made, Peter noticed all the media activity had drawn a small crowd of park-goers who were taking a break from their leisurely strolls and duck-feeding to form a loose circle around them. Toward the back of the onlookers, Peter spied an older black man wearing a baseball cap pulled over graying hair and an unkempt beard. *Jesse? The homeless prophet from the Ryman alleyway?*

Just as Peter started to call out to the old man, a ray of sunlight bounced off a silver reflective screen, momentarily blinding him. The production assistant lowered the reflector while Peter blinked and waited for his vision to clear. As soon as he was able, he scanned the small audience for Jesse, or his look-alike, but whoever he was had disappeared.

"You okay?" Cindy asked.

Had he imagined him, or had the man just disappeared in the twinkling of an eye?

"We're ready here," a cameraman announced.

"Peter?" Cindy tried again.

Looking over, Peter nodded, trying to visually and mentally focus on the reporter across from him.

"Okay," Cindy said warningly, pressing an earpiece he hadn't noticed before. "We're going live in just a sec."

The way she said *live* sounded ominous. But in spite of his qualms, he gave her a second nod.

Almost instantly, she launched into her introduction with a professional ferocity that startled him. "Thank you for doing this, Peter!"

She looked like she had been plugged into an electrical outlet—her eyes and smile had widened, and her voice had become more animated.

"So many people here in Nashville, as well as around the nation, are fascinated with what you have been able to foresee, and we are all very anxious to hear about your latest dream!"

Suddenly, Cindy became more serious, and Peter tensed, sensing trouble was lurking around the corner. "There have been allegations swirling around you, and I first wanted to give you the opportunity to tell your side of the story."

Resenting that Cindy was making it sound as if it was his idea to defend his record, Peter recalled Jesse's challenge to be fearless.

"As I just told you off camera," Peter cut in, "I'll answer your questions, but the only reason I'm here is to talk about the new dream."

Clearly caught off guard by this response, Cindy cleared her throat. "Well, some say this has all been an elaborate hoax to fool the public. How do you respond?"

"How would I go about rigging the stock market?" Peter asked.

"Your critics say the stock market prediction was luck, or they question the validity of the audio tapes."

"There was a church full of people there," Peter said. "Why don't you interview them?"

"Actually, I have interviewed quite a few of them," she said. "And everyone I've talked to backs up your claims."

"Okay," Peter said. "Then that leaves luck. And, trust me, I'm not that lucky."

"But there have been lingering questions about what actually caused the coal ash spill," Cindy said, as if she was auditioning for *Sixty Minutes*. "In fact, some reports have linked you to an eco-terrorist organization that was behind the levee breaking."

"Some reports?" Peter said mockingly, angered by the allegations. "Where are these reports?"

Cindy hesitated, glancing at her notes.

"What evidence is there to support any of this?"

Again, Cindy was slow to respond.

"There isn't any," Peter answered for her. "And I would expect a journalist to check out *reports* before giving them credence by blindly repeating them."

"Is there any truth to the report that you were questioned by the TBI?" Cindy shot back.

Wondering how she knew about that, Peter went ahead and said, "Yes. A TBI agent questioned me, and I told him what I'll tell you. I don't know any eco-terrorists."

"What about Victor Birdsong?" Cindy chirped.

"I met Victor the day after the ash spill, just before the press conference we did together. As far as I know, he is concerned about the environment. I don't think that makes him a terrorist—and to characterize him that way is slander."

Cindy opened her mouth, but Peter wasn't through.

"The day I was in Kingston, the spokesman *for the coal plant* said the dam broke due to normal erosion. I don't know of any evidence to suggest it was anything other than that. If someone has *evidence* of any explosives, they should come forward with it. Otherwise, you should stop repeating conspiracy theories like its news."

Again, Cindy cleared her throat, which Peter realized was a nervous tell. Still, to her credit, she kept her cool and went on with the next question.

"There have been some doubts about whether the mosque fire was an actual prophecy since you didn't announce it in advance."

"I didn't *publicly* announce it," Peter corrected her. "But several in the Muslim community have publicly said that I did talk to them about it before it happened."

"Why didn't you make a public announcement regarding the mosque fire?" Cindy asked, one neatly plucked eyebrow arched inquisitively high.

"This isn't a game where I'm trying to score publicity points," Peter said. "I've had a few dreams with messages to specific people, and I hadn't felt the need to announce those to the general public either." He stopped and thought about it. "I guess I also didn't want to be responsible for putting an idea like that in a crazy person's head.

"Each dream is unique and needs to be handled differently," Peter went on as he noticed Cindy glancing back down at her notes, giving him an opening. "For example, in this latest dream, I don't know who to warn or tell, so I'm just—"

The reporter snapped to attention as she realized her interviewee was attempting to segue away from her line of questions. "I want to get to that in just a second!" she assured him and her audience. "But what do you say to critics like Mark Shelton, the pastor at Victory Church?"

"What does he say?" Peter asked as he recalled the fiery Trinity church substitute-pastor/poacher.

"He says you are a false prophet and accuses you of using the occult to obtain your prophecies."

"Wow," Peter mustered. The "false prophet" moniker rang hauntingly familiar, and he wondered if he'd finally found the original source of the hate-filled callers and hecklers. "If I made a deal with the devil, you would think I'd try and get a little more out of it. I mean, I'm broke and living at home."

Cindy nodded thoughtfully.

"So, no, I haven't sold my soul—and I'm not dabbling in the occult or using a Ouija Board to get my information," Peter said dryly.

Seemingly satisfied, Cindy moved on. "Well, I understand that you have a new dream you would like to share with us?"

"Yes," Peter said, relieved. "A couple of nights ago, I had a dream there was a constellation of stars in the sky, and it made the shape of a cross. From this cross, three stars fell to earth. One hit a radio tower, one hit a capitol building, and one ran into an office building in downtown Nashville."

Leaning forward, a concerned Cindy asked, "And what do you think that means?"

"I think three prominent, local Christian 'stars,' if you will, are going to take a fall. I don't know who or how, but they will be exposed, and their reputations will come crashing down." Taking a breath, he added, "I think one will be someone on the radio, one will be a business leader of some kind, and another will be a government official, like a politician."

"And they will all be Christians?"

"That's right," Peter said, resisting the urge to insert disclaimers like *I think so* or *That is what I understood it to mean*. "Well-known Christians," he repeated, feeling the limb he was climbing out on begin to bend.

"When can we expect this to happen?" Cindy asked, ready to schedule it on her day timer.

"I don't know," Peter said. "Based on previous dreams, I would say pretty soon."

"Why do you think God is sending this message at this time?"

"Well, I'm not sure about that either," Peter said. "If I had to guess, I would say He is sick of hypocrisy. Maybe He wants to weed out leaders who are hiding behind Christian façades, or even using Christianity for their own agenda."

Another thought came to mind. He would be going off script, which was always dangerous, especially while cameras were rolling and satellite dishes were beaming signals into space. Still, the thought persisted, and the pause lingered. Thinking of Jesse and Victor and Abbas, and even his archenemy, Peter went for it.

"You know, I heard Mark Shelton once say that you can boil a frog by turning up the heat so slowly it doesn't even realize it's being cooked alive. His point was that we can get so used to bad things around us that we don't even notice them anymore. And I agree with him about some of those things. But there are other things that I think some Christians are missing, too.

"The events I've dreamed happen all the time. There are hate crimes and environmental disasters, and poor and sick people keep falling through the cracks. I believe God is calling our attention to these events because He wants us to sit up and notice them, too. I think God expects more from Christians, because we, of all people, should know better."

Surprised by the veracity in his own voice, Peter turned slightly away from Cindy's gaze to look directly into his camera. "You know, sometimes Christians are the last ones to act on these issues, and I think God wants that to change. I think He wants Christians to lead—and to show the world there is another way, a better way." He nodded at his audience. "That's all I wanted to say."

CHAPTER 20

After he finished the interview, Peter called his mom at work to warn her about what he had done and apologize for not giving her more warning. Neither of them wanted to go home and face the inevitable tidal wave of calls. Instead, Ms. Quell made arrangements to go to her sister's place, and Peter called Uncle John.

Phil, the local anchor, opened with the same sense of phonetic urgency reserved for announcing the passing of the Pope, a president, or the Nashville equivalent—a country music star. "Another pronouncement from our hometown prophet, Peter Quell," he exuded with Channel-7 pride, "and our own Cindy Sizemore has the exclusive interview! Cindy."

Now in the studio and sitting so close to Phil's anchor chair she could reach out and touch it, Cindy swiveled to face camera one.

"She's cute," Uncle John commented from a leather chair in his library, which doubled as a living room.

"Yeah, like a Pitbull," Peter commented.

"Thanks, Phil," Cindy said. "Yes, I'm very pleased to offer only Channel-Seven viewers this exclusive interview with Peter Quell. which we aired *live* a little earlier today.

"This was the first one-on-one interview he has allowed with anyone in the media." After pausing to let the significance sink in, she went on, "Peter and I sat down today at Centennial Park to discuss the past, present, *and the future*."

As much as he hated listening to his nasally voice on a recording, watching himself in high definition was a hundred times worse with all of the visual imperfections on display: thinning hair, watery, squinty eyes, pale skin with red blotches. He really should have let the make-up person do her job.

Why did I wear that shirt? Peter asked himself.

Worse than his wardrobe was the way he was beginning to sound like a prophet, ornery and annoyed with the rest of the world. And he couldn't believe it when he heard himself saying, "I mean, I'm broke and live at home," when responding to the accusation of making a deal with the devil.

"Even I have to bring up that I live at home?" Peter yelled at the TV. "And now everyone knows I'm broke, too! They should start calling me the Loser Prophet."

Uncle John gave him a smile as Peter squirmed, watching his evil TV twin pontificate on possible purposes for the dreams. He hoped Marian wasn't watching even though he knew she'd see it eventually. Finally, it ended with a triumphant Cindy back in the studio sending the newscast to a commercial.

"That was good," Uncle John said, providing the first rather tepid review.

"I don't think so," Peter groaned. "Obviously God got the wrong person for this job."

"I would say you're doing pretty well," Uncle John said,

turning the volume down on a commercial. "It's a lot to handle."

Peter nodded in agreement, grateful to have someone appreciate the pressure he was under.

"It's just so weird because I don't even know where these dreams come from. I mean, I believe they come from God. But I don't know how or why. They just come with no explanation."

"It's an amazing gift," John said as he got up and strode over to his kitchen. "Ever since Adam and Eve, we've been trying to hear from God again."

Peter was a little unsure whether he thought it was a gift or not.

When John came back from the kitchen, he carried a couple of beers. "You know, there is a theory that we could all hear God's voice at a much earlier time in our existence, before we filled our heads with our own stuff."

Taking a beer from his uncle, Peter looked up, interested.

"This professor postulated that ancient man wasn't conscious in the same way we are today." John went back to his easy chair, taking a seat and a sip. "It's like one side of their brain could talk to another part."

"So they were never lonely," Peter said, trying to be funny.

"Maybe," John said seriously. "It might have been similar to what schizophrenics experience, except it wasn't a mental disorder."

"So they actually heard audible voices?"

"That's the theory. They were able to hear a voice that told them what to do," John said. "It's right there in ancient Greek literature. In the *Odyssey*, the humans are interacting with the gods left and right. And then much later, the Greeks can't hear them anymore, and they need to use go-betweens, like the Oracles of Delphi, to communicate with them."

"The Oracles of Delphi," Peter repeated, thinking of Marian and making a note to call her later.

"The transformation is in the Bible, too," John continued, now getting into his professorial role. "In the beginning, God is walking and talking with Adam and Eve like He's their next-door neighbor. And then there's 'the fall,' and there's a break in our connection with God."

"Okay, but God still talks to His people throughout the Bible," Peter said, thinking about all the Biblical encounters with the Almighty.

"Yeah, God still talks to a select few: Noah and Abraham and Moses," John said, stroking his beard. "But it keeps getting less frequent and harder to do. I mean, Moses is climbing up a mountain to get reception."

After taking a long drink, Peter settled back and asked, "So why did we stop hearing the voices?"

"The theory was that when we developed language, we became self-aware, and that kind of drove out the need for this other voice, the one we think of as God."

Peter thought about this for a while. "Well, I'm not hearing a voice. I'm having dreams."

"Maybe the voice and the dreams come from the same place," John said.

"Inside my brain?" Peter asked skeptically.

"No," John said with a firm shake of his head. "They have to originate from another source. Somehow, you are getting revealed knowledge. And that is a gift."

Peter took another swig of beer, still unconvinced.

"You don't have to understand or even like something to appreciate it." John held his beer aloft until Peter hoisted his up, too. This was no celebratory toast, just a somber acknowledgement of a blessing that bore great responsibility.

Glancing at the television, Peter saw that they were replaying a segment of the interview. Before he could get caught up critiquing his own distorted image again, the picture suddenly went black.

Uncle John put the remote down and stood up. "What do you say we grill outside tonight?"

When Peter pulled into the driveway at home the next day, he was relieved there were no signs of reporters, arsonists, or even his mom. Ms. Quell had opted to stay over at her sister's, which pleased Peter. Not only was he a little worried about his mom's safety, but he figured it might be nice to have the place to himself for a little while.

Entering through the back door, he was greeted with the familiar sound of a ringing phone. With a heavy sigh, he checked the answering machine, where he found the usual slew of messages waiting for him.

The other three news channels had made the obligatory phone call asking for a few minutes of his time, or at least a comment. They almost sounded hurt, like he had cheated on them with Channel 7 and now he owed them something.

Mad as hell, Jordan Stone shouted, "You all but outed me! A radio star? Please! I just announced I'm getting a divorce, and now I've got to announce...my condition. At least now I know how you do your little trick. Well, thanks a lot, Peter. I trusted you!"

"Hey, man, it's Tom McAllister!" his new best friend said. "You should call me—" Peter erased it.

"You are such a liar," the next venomous voice spat. "You think you speak for God? You're the one that's going down—like Satan falling from the sky—" Next.

The following voice was as warm as butter and inviting as honey—an antidote to all the misplaced hate and phoniness that had proceeded it.

"Hey, I just saw the news and thought you were great," Marian said. "Maybe you can come over tomorrow night? I'd like to see you."

Peter nodded to himself. The feeling was mutual.

That night, Peter was outside on Marian's back deck, staring up at the disarray of stars. Imagining constellations seemed like a feeble attempt to overlay order on a chaotic canvas.

With Jacob already tucked away in bed, the couple was free to huddle up on a lounge chair on this chilly evening. Under a blanket, Marian's body spooned his; her head nuzzled up to his neck.

"Are you making a wish?" Marian asked.

"Don't I have to spot a falling star first?"

"Everyone is looking for a falling star, thanks to you," she said. "On my drive to work this morning, people were calling in to the radio show with all sorts of theories on the identities of the falling stars. Everyone knows someone who deserves a good smiting. It's open season on born-again celebrities."

"I went to the library again today and checked out this website about me," Peter confessed. "It's gotten pretty elaborate since the last time I saw it. It has these chat rooms with these long discussion threads."

"I'll have to check that out," she said, giving him a nudge.

"Yeah, well, all the latest threads were just names of celebrities that someone supposedly has some dirt on. There were pages of them. I mean, it's like an echo chamber for gossip. It really made me nervous that I had started this…virtual rumor mill."

After a moment, Marian said, "You know, Bill is taking Jacob for the weekend. I thought, maybe, we could get out of town for a night or two?"

He could use a place to stay for a couple of nights, and it would be nice to avoid the whole three-star media circus. Was she also letting him know she was ready to take their relationship to the next level?

Ostensibly, they had not "gone all the way" due to Jacob's presence in the house. What if he walked in on them? So, because of Marian's child, as well as her Christian values, Peter assumed Marian viewed sex as a serious step that should not be taken casually. He felt the same way, too.

"That sounds good," Peter said thoughtfully.

"Yeah?" Marian said, sparking to her idea. "Where would you want to go?"

"Oh, I don't know," Peter said, suddenly remembering the balance of his checking account. "It would have to be some place close, driving distance, which isn't far in my car."

"Gatlinburg?" Marian suggested. "It'll be beautiful this time of year."

"I don't know if my car would even make it that far," Peter grumbled. Having a girlfriend made him all the more aware of his bankrupt state. "Besides, this isn't a good time. I need to get a job first."

"You have a job," she said, snuggling up to him supportively. "You're doing God's work."

There was no profit in the prophecy business—at least not in his type of soothsaying. The televangelists and *propheteers* who were quick to explain a disaster after it happened seemed to be doing just fine. "Yeah, well, I need to talk to my boss about a pay raise."

"I'm sure you'll get a real job when things settle down," Marian said pleasantly.

"I don't know," Peter said, his mood suddenly darkening. "Even before I started having dreams, I wasn't working. And subbing doesn't count. I've never been able to hold onto a normal job. You should know that about me."

"Who wants normal?" Marian asked, trying hard to keep it light.

Without warning, Peter stood up, almost knocking Marian off the chaise. "Don't say you haven't been warned," he growled as he left her house in a foul huff.

Congressman Bragg stood before the unblinking cameras, putting what was left of his best face forward. "Well, first, I want to apologize to my family." He smoothed his red silk tie and sniffed a little, forging on in his raspy Southern voice.

"And I want to apologize to my constituents who believed in me and all the volunteers and donors." He wiped at a dry eye, perhaps deciding not to specifically mention his biggest donor, the pharmaceutical industry.

"I want to apologize to the hardest working staff on Capitol

Hill." Hanging his neatly combed silver head of hair, he acted like he needed a moment to recompose. "I'm sorry, this is tough."

He seemed to think that if he acted sad enough, surely the people would rise up in one voice and forgive all of his misdeeds. When no one tried to stop him, he soldiered on.

"As I'm sure all of you have heard, I was involved romantically with a woman who was not my wife. Because I need to spend some time working on my marriage, I have decided not to seek reelection."

Watching him on TV, Peter thought the congressman looked most authentically pained when talking about cutting his campaign short.

"There have been a lot of lies and half-truths about this affair, and I want to set the record straight. So, I will entertain questions, and after that, I will not be speaking on this matter again. As I've always said, I'm all about moving forward, not dwelling on the past."

A reporter asked, "How did you first meet Ms. Wallace?"

"She was working as a lobbyist," Congressman Bragg said matter-of-factly. "We got to know each other while we were crafting important legislation together."

Quickly following up, the reporter asked, "Do you have a comment about the sex tape that has been widely played on the internet?"

The congressman grimaced. "It's unfortunate that the media has become so preoccupied with that tape. I also deeply regret that children in this country have access to that kind of material on the Google."

After a moment of further reflection, he added, "Some of my comments on that video were taken completely out of context." His Adam's apple bobbled in his throat. "We were engaged in a role-playing exercise that involved some coarse language I would normally never use."

Peter made a mental note to check out the video the next time he had a chance.

"The costumes were not my idea either." Clearing his throat,

Congressman Bragg raised a defiant finger. "Rest assured, the American taxpayer did not pay one dime for anything in that video."

The only thing Peter knew about the congressman was that he prided himself on being an "unapologetic tax cutter." His commercials touted his courage in consistently voting against welfare, healthcare, and basically any government program. His opponent's commercials said the congressman blocked legislation that would have helped the DEA crack down on the opioid crisis.

"Ms. Wallace says you used your position to force her to engage in those acts," a reporter that sounded a lot like Cindy Sizemore said.

"I didn't make her do anything!" Bragg blustered. "If anything, it was quid pro quo!"

"Then why did Ms. Wallace come forward with the tape?" Definitely Cindy.

"She is obviously trying to hurt me," Bragg responded, his face almost the color of his power tie, which seemed to be choking him. "She became upset when I tried to end our relationship. Now if you'll excuse me."

One down, Peter thought as the congressman made his hasty exit. *Two to go.*

CHAPTER 21

Peter had learned to ignore the incessant ringing of the telephone at his mom's house. A honking car horn, however, still got his attention. Sneaking a peek from his bedroom window, he recognized the silver Nissan in the driveway. Throwing on some sweatpants and running shoes, he hurried downstairs and out the front door.

The driver's side window slid down, revealing his infinitely patient, incredibly cool girlfriend. "Hurry up and pack a bag," Marian said.

"Where are we going?" he asked as he approached the car.

"It's a surprise," she said, a smile playing on her lips. "Just grab enough stuff for a couple of nights."

With a shake of his head, he stubbornly said, "I told you, I can't afford to go."

"You can't afford not to go," she replied.

She was right, and he knew it. Reporters would be sniffing around soon, looking for a comment on Congressman Bragg and wanting to know if he had any new information on the identities of the other two falling stars.

The prospect of spending another weekend hiding inside his mother's house was debilitating. On the other hand, he wasn't sure he was ready for a serious relationship, and the confusion left him standing like a frozen statue in the driveway. Feeling a warm touch on his arm, he looked down at the kind face in the car.

"Don't overthink it," Marian said.

Gazing into her trusting eyes, his fears momentarily melted away. "Give me a minute," he said as he jogged back up the sidewalk and into the house.

Seeming determined to keep their destination a secret for as long as possible, Marian drove southeast on I-24. Before getting to Chattanooga, she pulled off the interstate and began winding along the Cumberland Plateau, following signs to the picturesque town of Monteagle.

With the cat out of the bag, Marian said, "I figured this would be a nice change of scenery."

"I may never leave," Peter said, his gaze transfixed on the oranges and reds in the trees through the window.

They stopped in town for dinner, which Peter insisted on buying, his widow's mite of a contribution to the weekend. By the time they came out of the restaurant, the sun had disappeared behind the mountains, making the final series of twists and turns all the more exciting.

At the end of a long desolate street, they stopped by a quant house with a German-sounding name on the mailbox.

"Here we are," Marian announced as she pulled into the driveway. "There's supposed to be a waterfall behind it."

"Great," Peter said, touched by her thoughtfulness.

After they brought in their bags and an ice chest Marian had packed, they ran around like little kids exploring all the rooms. It wasn't a big house, so it didn't take long to settle on the king-sized bed in the master suite. Just as Marian had said, they could hear the rush of water beyond their window.

"You like it?" she asked hopefully.

"I love it," Peter said.

They turned to kiss, slowly at first, then picking up the pace as their bodies wrapped around each other and moved together. Quickened by desire, clothes cascaded off the mattress to the hardwood floors below.

Scrambling to slip under the warmth of the covers, Peter felt the tide of desire mixing with hidden insecurities rising up inside of him. Abruptly, he turned away, isolating himself on his side of the bed.

"What's the matter?" Marian asked softly.

"I guess I'm a little nervous," he muttered. "It's been a while."

"Yeah, for me, too," she said.

He was pretty sure she was more experienced than him. Still, it was endearing to hear her try to empathize. Turning back around, he faced her and once again found solace in those dark eyes. Instinctively, he moved into her arms and, holding her close, let nature take its course.

It was mid-morning, and Peter sat on the screened-in back porch with a cup of coffee; the soothing sound of water on rock was in sharp contrast to the legalistic voices from his past. *He had been with a woman, a divorced woman. God would punish him. He certainly wasn't worthy of being a messenger of God. There could be no more dreams.*

But now there was another voice, and it had gotten stronger. It reminded him that God loved him despite his sins and mistakes. It also felt like Marian was a gift from God, too; a gift that moved him with gratefulness.

"Come in here!" Marian yelled from inside the house.

Setting his coffee down, Peter slowly got to his feet.

"Come on!" she called again.

Hurrying into the living room, he found Marian at the breakfast table with her open laptop.

"Isn't this your girlfriend?" she asked.

Jordan Stone adorned the screen. Her straightened blonde hair hung like a curtain over dewy eyes as she spoke to a sympathetic-looking television hostess.

"This was just one of those things that happened," the songstress was trying to explain. "I'm very happy to be expecting my third child. Obviously, it didn't happen exactly the way I planned. You know, you can't control everything. Sometimes, God has a different plan."

"Isn't she getting a divorce?" Marian asked.

Before Peter could answer, the hostess was asking the next obvious question, "And the father is not your soon-to-be ex-husband?"

"No," Jordan said through a patently obvious fake smile. "I'd like to keep the father's identity private, at least for right now."

"Ohh," the hostess cooed with a gleam in her eye. "You have to give us a hint."

"He has to be ready for that," Jordan explained, shaking her hair. "We both do."

"I see," the hostess said respectfully. "Is he in the Christian music business, too?

"I just don't want to say any more than I already have," Jordan politely countered. "We need a little more time before we make any announcements." The Christian superstar forced another fake smile that made Peter feel sorry for her. "I just wanted to go ahead and get this out of the way before any more rumors got started."

"Does she think this is going to stop the rumors?" Marian asked incredulously.

"Well, this is exciting news," the hostess said smoothly. "Congratulations on the baby."

The video stopped, and Marian muted the sound. Turning to Peter, she asked him, "Did you know anything about this?" He hesitated for a moment too long. "You're not the father?"

"No!" Peter exclaimed, almost choking on the single syllable.

Marian seemed to accept the emphatic response. "But you knew she was pregnant?"

"I had a dream, and I told her about it," Peter acknowledged. "That's it."

"What else have you been holding back from me?" Marian asked.

"Nothing," Peter said truthfully.

"So, do you know who the father is?" she asked curiously.

"Only that it's not me," Peter said with a laugh.

The woods were on fire with the colors of autumn, and the crispness in the air actually made Peter feel more alive than he had in a long time. He was following along behind Marian on a trail that was supposed to lead them to a large scenic rock formation. At every rock they came to, Peter took childish delight in asking, "Is this it?"

"You'll know when we get there," Marian assured him as if she was speaking to her seven-year-old son. "Besides, it's about the journey, not the destination."

"I don't care where we're going," Peter exclaimed, as they delved deeper into the woods. "It's just good to be away from everything back home!"

"I knew you needed to get away," Marian said over her shoulder.

"I'm not kidding about not wanting to go back." Then, just to see how it sounded, he added, "I hope I don't have any more dreams, either."

"Do you really want them to stop?" Marian asked, slowing to walk closer beside him.

"I don't know. I dread all the stress and grief that comes with each one," he said, pausing to think about it. "On the other hand, I know it's going to stop one day, and I think I'll miss them, too."

As they scrambled up a steeper incline, Marian helped him over an outcropping of rock.

"I can see that," Marian said. "But it's not just about you. It affects a lot of other people."

"As long as I don't screw it up," Peter said, still catching his breath.

"If you mess things up, I'm sure God can find someone else," Marian said as she turned her back to walk ahead of him. "Any ass will do."

"I am going to assume you're talking about Balaam's donkey," Peter said.

Marian let out one of her light laughs that Peter loved. He jogged to catch up.

"You're not screwing it up," Marian said, more seriously. "You are doing important work."

A breeze swept passed them, blowing a few more leaves off the trees' limbs, sending them languidly drifting to the ground around them. The leaves crunched under their shoes as they walked in silence for another minute or two.

"Can I ask you a question?" Peter finally asked.

"Sure," Marian said.

"Is that why you were interested in me?" he asked. "Because of my dreams?"

With a shrug, Marian conveyed a modicum of guilt. "I was intrigued when I started hearing about this 'Peter Prophet.' When I saw a photo, I remembered the nice man I'd met at Grace Church and realized who you were. So, yeah, I was curious."

Detecting a cloud of doubt pass behind his eyes, she quickly added, "I never would have invited you over if I didn't like you. And didn't trust you with Jacob." After a pause, she continued, "I mean, it didn't hurt that you seemed to be on speaking terms with God."

Peter shook his head, dismissing the last reference.

Marian clasped his hand hanging by her side. "As I got to know you, I liked you more and more because you're a good man who is trying to do the right thing."

That compliment, he could accept. The way he figured it, you were always attracted to someone for some reason, whether it was their looks or their job or the fact that they didn't live at home with their mother. If she had initially been interested in him because he had prophetic dreams, well, he could think of worse things.

As they walked in silence, Peter noticed the fading sunlight shining through the skimpily clad trees and dappling her face.

She suddenly stopped to look up at him. "Oh, I almost forgot the most important reason I like you," she added. "You happen to be a terrific kisser."

"I knew that was the real reason," he said as he slipped his arms around her waist.

Brushing away her own windblown hair, Marian tilted her head back and closed her eyes. Peter leaned forward, enjoying this part of the journey.

By Sunday afternoon, the couple was reluctantly packing up and saying good-bye to their weekend waterfall house. Peter volunteered to drive, freeing Marian to talk to Jacob on her cell phone, flip through a magazine, and go on a never-ending search for adult contemporary music on the radio, not an easy task in East Tennessee.

As she scanned the dial, a vaguely familiar sound crackled through the speakers. "Hold it for a second," Peter said, trying to place the voice.

The man had the practiced authority of a preacher, although the fire-and-brimstone sermon he was brandishing was mostly against the evils of socialism.

"They want to take away every last freedom you and I enjoy. First, they'll take your guns so you can't defend yourself. Then they're going to brainwash your children with state-run education. Then their death panels will decide if you live or die. It's like Nazi concentration camps, only for God-fearing white people."

"Oh my God," Marian gasped. "This guy is totally nuts."

"Yeah," Peter said, a pained half-smile of astonishment on his face as Ed Pressman's rant broke free from the limits of sanity. "I think this is bad, even for him."

Marian started to turn the channel.

"Wait," Peter insisted. "I have to hear this."

"The white man has become the endangered species," Ed

bellowed. "And he's under attack from all sides! You have spics coming up and taking our jobs. You got ragheads using their oil money to blow up our buildings. The chinks making knockoffs of our inventions and selling them back to us. And you got the coons sucking the country dry with their government hand-outs."

With her mouth literally hanging open, Marian stared over at Peter, who was just trying to keep his eyes on the road.

"Oh, I'm sure the FCC will fine me for telling the truth, but to hell with them and their government control," Ed said, his tongue thick and heavy. "Good Christians everywhere need to arm themselves for the Armageddon that is upon us. It's already here, people!"

"This is what our f-foundin' fathers fought an' died for," he continued, a slur creeping across his words. "Their blood's on our hands if we don' take up arms'n fight again' this tide of Godless Communism."

"What is he talking about?" Marian whispered.

Peter couldn't respond, mesmerized by the bizarre stream of hate speech.

"If you don' fight these Commies, they'll destroy this country and our God f-fearin' way of life!" Ed yelled, his voice scratchy. "Kill a liberal, and save your eternal soul!"

The station abruptly went to a commercial. As Gold Buyers of America began to state their case for buying bullion in uncertain times, Peter finally turned the radio down.

After a long exhalation, all he managed to get out was, "Wow."

"Did that just happen?" Marian asked.

"I think so," Peter said.

"You can't say those racist things on the radio," she stated.

"He just said out loud what a lot of these radio guys insinuate all day long."

"Yeah, but he went too far," Marian persisted. "You can't call for violence, can you?"

"I don't know," Peter admitted. "I don't think so."

They sat in silence for a mile or two before Peter turned the radio back up. The station was coming out of commercial break with a taped "money and investment" show instead of the regularly scheduled *Ed Pressman Patriot Radio Hour*.

"You know, that might just have been your radio star," Marian pointed out.

"I was thinking the same thing."

"What about Jordan Stone?" she asked. "I thought she was your radio star."

"No, *she* thought she was the radio star," Peter corrected her. "Maybe she got ahead of herself."

He glanced over at Marian, and they exchanged mildly amused looks.

"If your girlfriend came out for nothing, she sure is going to be mad."

"She's already mad," Peter said. "Not as mad as Ed Pressman…."

"He's f-freakin' mad," Marian said, finally picking up a station coming out of Music City. Sitting back, they tried to let the sweet sounds wash the bad taste out of their minds and leave the voices of the old South behind.

CHAPTER 22

In an ironic twist of fate, Ed's on-the-air meltdown proved to be the most listened to audio clip of his career. Radio stations around the country were inundated with irate callers who heard the broadcast when it first aired. The story then bounced around the blogosphere for a couple of hours before it was picked up by cable news, who immediately inserted the racist rant into their news cycle.

Just as he predicted, Ed did catch the attention of the FCC, as well as the advocacy groups representing the groups of people he had slandered. They went on the offensive, mounting a campaign against the man who had been offending all of them for years. As a result, the groundswell of public opinion turned hard and fast against the self-proclaimed Super Patriot.

In his defense, Mr. Pressman issued a statement explaining he suffered from physical ailments and had been under the influence of prescribed medication. Further investigation revealed the radio provocateur was obtaining a potent mix of pain killers from three different doctors and a pharmacist who was already under criminal investigation.

With his excuse only exacerbating his problems, stations across the country began reluctantly dropping their ratings star. Faced with dwindling subscribers and the prospect of heavy fines, the syndicator pulled the plug on the show. The whole episode, from drug-induced diatribe to dismissal, took a little over one week. Uncharacteristically quiet, Ed retreated to his multi-million-dollar estate.

Just a few miles away, Peter was also trying to avoid the media that had become entrenched around his mom's house. An often-reported angle on the Pressman story was the prediction of a "radio star's fall." Only now, interest in Peter was expanding beyond the city limits and garnering national attention.

A small group began showing up outside the Quell house, gathering under a banner that read, "PETER PROPHET." Over their everyday clothes they wore white bathrobes, apparently to make themselves look more like prophets. Peter thought they came closer to resembling escaped mental patients, which was also a possibility.

As a counterbalance, there were almost always a couple of protesters from the anti-Peter contingency to hoist the predictable "FALSE PROPHET" sign. Occasionally, they would shout something witty and urbane, like "False prophet!" at the house or at the pro-Peter people.

During the day, at least one or two members from each group maintained a vigil at the house, their ranks swelling to a half-dozen or more after work hours. Not too surprisingly, the anti- and pro-Peter factions often faced off in verbal shouting matches, especially when cameras were rolling.

There was also a mixture of curious onlookers who came by foot, car, and even the occasional tourist bus. The result was a carnival-like atmosphere with a little tent revival thrown in. The mayhem necessitated an almost-constant police presence that added an element of stability, as well as drama, to the spectacle.

Police repeatedly informed visitors they were not allowed to step on private property, although that seldom stopped them. And, of course, inside the house, the phone never seemed to stop ringing, bombarding the answering machine with the usual litany of requests and threats.

Peter would have simply unplugged the phone, except he didn't want to miss the occasional call from someone he actually wanted to talk to, such as Marian or maybe Uncle John or even his dad. It was late in the week when Peter heard a distinctive laid-back voice leaving a message, "Yeah, I'm calling for *Peter the Prophet*?"

Peter snatched up the phone, "Chris? Is that you?"

"Don't you know?" his college friend in California asked. "I thought you were supposed to know everything before it happens."

After they shared a laugh, Chris asked, "Is it true what they're saying about you?"

"Yeah, I've had a few dreams that came true."

"I just found out the other day, and when I looked you up on the internet, I couldn't believe it," Chris said. "How are you doing it?"

"I don't know," Peter confessed. "It just happened. It's really a God thing."

"Well, if it was going to happen to anyone, it would be you," Chris said. "You were always a freak. I mean, we tried to treat you normal, but you know you were a weirdo."

"Thanks," Peter said, almost missing the brutality of male bonding.

"Yeah, I found out when some dude called out of the blue and asked if I knew you," Chris explained. "When I admitted I did, he started asking me all these *really* personal questions: who you hung out with, names of ex-girlfriends, any stories or dirt I had on you. It was creepy, and I didn't tell him anything. I don't even know how he got my name. But I thought I should let you know."

"Yeah, thanks," Peter said, thinking immediately of the creepy "reporter" who had seemed to materialize at the ash coal spill. "Was it a reporter?"

"Yeah, that's what he said," Chris said. "It just seemed off somehow."

After Peter finished catching up with his buddy and hung up, the thought of someone digging into his past continued to linger. It could be the TBI, although Agent Myers didn't seem like he'd be so clandestine. Once again, Peter's thoughts came back to the shadowy figure at the press conference he'd held with Victor Birdsong.

That night, his oldest friend, Roger, who was now living in Florida, called to tell Peter he'd also received a suspicious call from a reporter; Chad in Atlanta had a similar story. And how many friends had been contacted and hadn't bothered to let Peter know? What about those who Peter didn't consider friends? What about ex-girlfriends?

The thought gave him a cold shiver.

As the garage door automatically rose, Ms. Quell braced herself for what was awaiting her at the end of the driveway.

It was 7:45 a.m., the same time she left for work every morning, and as usual, she eased out, careful not to hit a blood-sucking reporter or one of the robe-wearing zealots. By the mailbox, she feigned a smile and waved through the windshield at a couple of photographers, then shot a harsh look at one of her son's ever-present protestors.

"I should run you all down," she hissed to herself through gritted teeth.

Her economy car dawdled down the street; then she signaled a left-hand turn out of the neighborhood. As soon as she was on the main road, Ms. Quell took a sudden right, gunning all four cylinders to the end of a deserted cul-de-sac.

Pulling to the side of the road, she put her car in park and carefully checked her rearview mirror before springing the latch on the trunk.

Rising like a zombie from a shallow, cramped grave, Peter

swung a leg over the back bumper and crawled out of the tight trunk space.

"Move it!" his mom yelled from her open window.

Peter jogged around to let himself inside the car. Even before he got the passenger door shut, his mom hit the gas, fishtailing out of the dead end. Back at the main road, she turned south, away from her usual route to work.

"I think we got away clean," Ms. Quell said, clearly caught up in the caper. "Do we have a tail?"

"I don't think so," Peter said, checking the side mirror. "Unless they're using a school bus."

His mom nodded coolly, the wind rippling her graying hair as she blew past a speed limit sign. *All she needs is a cigarette hanging off her bottom lip,* Peter thought.

At a four-way stop, his mom cranked the wheel hard, making a turn that would take them farther into the country. They had lost the school bus, and yet Ms. Quell continued to drive like the cops were in hot pursuit and she wasn't going to let them take her alive.

"I think you can slow down now," Peter said, buckling his seat belt. Either his mom didn't hear, or she chose to disregard him. "Whose house are we going to again?"

"I told you, it's just a vacant house," she said vaguely. "It belongs to someone who goes to Trinity."

"How do you know about it?" Peter persisted.

"Dan set it up," she said.

"Oh, Mom," Peter muttered disagreeably.

"He is very sorry how things ended with you and him," she said quickly. "Anyway, he wants to talk to you."

"I don't want to talk to him," Peter said stubbornly.

"Well, you can tell him that when you see him," she said. "He's meeting us there." Before Peter could protest further, she tossed a piece of paper at him. "Now help me find this place."

Less than thirty minutes away, Leiper's Fork looked like the

192

tiny town that time forgot. A mile past Puckett's Restaurant, Ms. Quell and Peter turned down a country road, leaving what was left of civilization behind.

After a couple of passes, they found the unmarked gravel driveway that threaded through the woods before opening up to a clearing that revealed an elegant Victorian house. Ms. Quell parked their getaway car in front of the grand old lady—right next to Dan's sedan.

Still pouting over the plan he had not been privy to, Peter tramped to the back of the car to retrieve the suitcases he had shared trunk space with a little earlier. At the top of the front steps of the manor, the door swung open, and his pastor stood in the entryway.

"Come on in," Dan announced magnanimously.

"Thank you for doing this," his mom said gratefully. "We appreciate it so much!"

Peter grunted as he walked past his pastor and into the big house with their bags.

"I'm glad I could help," Dan said. "This belongs to a member of the church that is out of town for a couple of months. She said she would be happy for you to use it. Hopefully, it will give you a little peace and quiet for a change."

With an open floor plan, the family room flowed into a big renovated country kitchen with hardwood floors and granite galore. Decorated in Southern chic, the house possessed a rustic charm that didn't come cheap. Sporting a fourteen-point rack, an imperial stag beamed down on them.

"Oh, it's wonderful," Ms. Quell gushed, turning around to take it all in. "Isn't it, Peter?"

Peter had already ventured down the hallway, dropping his mom's bag by the master bedroom and searching for a second bedroom to call his own.

Upstairs, he found a room with a small desk under a window, the view partially shielded by an overgrown evergreen. The super

193

soft bed sealed the deal, and he planted his bag by the dresser to claim it.

By the time he came back into the living room, Dan was waiting for him alone.

"Peter, can I have a minute?" Dan asked, sitting in an easy chair and gesturing toward the couch. "I just want to say I'm sorry about not standing with you on the Muslim thing."

"Yeah, I am, too."

"You are challenging me on some things, and sometimes an old man needs a little time to change," Dan explained. "I'm trying to make it up to you now."

Peter looked around. "Where's Mom?"

"I asked her to give us a few minutes," he said, motioning again to the couch where Peter reluctantly sat. "This last dream you had is really getting a lot of attention. Did you know some people want to start a church around you?"

"What?" Peter exclaimed; then he recalled the white-robed clan outside their house. "That's just crazy."

"It's also making some people pretty mad," Dan said sternly. "You have people like Mark Shelton railing even harder against you."

"Yeah, what's his problem with me anyway?"

"Mark considers himself a student of 'End Times' theology," Dan said. "He believes the world is heading toward Armageddon and sides are being drawn up on either side of Israel. That makes Muslims Enemy Number One."

"So by making Muslims his enemy, he's trying to expedite Armageddon?"

"I'm sure he would see it as aligning with God's side," Dan said graciously. "All I'm saying is—you have a lot of people who want a piece of you. Some of them want to worship you, and some of them despise you, and I'm not sure which is more dangerous. That's why I insisted to your mom that we get you both out of her house, at least until things settle down."

Realizing his pastor was probably right, Peter stayed silent and listened.

"I know we don't see eye to eye on everything, Peter," Dan continued, "but I do care for you. I've known you and your mom, for—What? Fifteen years now?"

Actually, it had been closer to twenty years since a devastated divorced woman and her gawky adolescent boy had shown up at Trinity, looking for acceptance. Dan had welcomed them with open arms, and he had been there for them ever since.

"I know that, and I appreciate it," Peter said with genuine affection. "And I appreciate the place to stay." Looking around at his temporary new home, he added, "I just hope it will stay a secret for a little while."

His eyes stopped on the buck who seemed to say, *Your secret is safe with me.*

Peter was glued to the news when his mom came home from work carrying bags of groceries. Without offering a helping hand or even a word of greeting, he urgently waved her over into the living room. Setting the bags down, Ms. Quell idled closer to the TV, her hand over her open mouth.

"Phillip Drake, a prominent businessman in Nashville Tennessee, surrendered to federal law enforcement agents today," the network anchorwoman read. "He is accused of defrauding investors and is being charged with multiple counts of wire fraud, securities fraud, and money laundering. Let's go to our reporter in Nashville, Trevor Johnson, for more on the story."

"Thanks, Donna," Trevor said, standing in front of a high-rise office building. "Authorities are saying that Mr. Drake was running what amounted to a Ponzi scheme by using new investors' money to pay off any withdrawals."

A video of a middle-aged man in a suit leaving a courthouse played over the commentary.

"When the stock market crashed, Mr. Drake could no longer meet the redemption requests, and the scam was exposed."

Next, the screen showed a photo of a smiling Mr. Drake receiving a framed certificate.

"This comes as a tremendous shock to the local business community, who only two years ago honored Phillip Drake as their businessperson of the year."

Donna, the news anchor, cut in. "Trevor, the other part of this story is the prediction, or so-called 'prophecy,' that was recently made."

"That's right, Donna," Trevor said. "A local man named Peter Quell has been getting a lot of attention for some predictions he has been making. His latest 'prophecy' was made less than two weeks ago to a reporter at our own affiliate station here in town."

The scene cut to the video of Peter being interviewed by Cindy in the park.

"I think three prominent, local Christian 'stars,' if you will, are going to take a fall," Peter was saying. "I don't know who or how, but I think they will be exposed, and their reputations will come crashing down. I think one will be on the radio, one will be a business leader of some kind, and another will be a government official, like a politician."

Trevor appeared back on camera. "Just a few days later, Congressman Bragg was coasting to an easy re-election when a scandalous sex video was made public. Then Ed Pressman's career came crashing down after a drug-induced racial rant. And now we seem to have the third 'falling star' with the arrest of Phillip Drake."

"Quite a trifecta," Donna commented.

"Yes, and these are not the first predictions that Peter Quell has made," Trevor continued. "He first came to notoriety when he apparently called the stock market crash back in August, as well as a disaster at a coal-burning plant in East Tennessee."

"Yes, I remember that story," Donna noted.

"The Muslim community has also claimed that Mr. Quell gave them advance information regarding an arson attack on one of their local mosques."

"That's remarkable," Donna threw in.

"Of course, he is not without his critics," Trevor said, compelled to present both sides of the story. "Some religious leaders have questioned his legitimacy, pointing to the mosque prophecy as proof he is not speaking for Christianity. One prominent local pastor has gone so far as to accuse Mr. Quell of being a 'false prophet.'"

"Has Mr. Quell made any comments regarding the arrest of Mr. Drake?"

"Peter Quell is a very hard man to get a hold of these days," Trevor admitted. "We tried to contact him several times; we're not even sure where he is at the moment. Since all this started, he has only granted that one interview, and that was to announce this prophecy, a prophecy that was fulfilled today."

"Fascinating report, thank you, Trevor," Donna said, turning back to face the nation through her looking glass. "We will have to keep a close eye on what else Mr. Quell has to say."

There was a short pause as the anchorwoman listened to the voice in her head. "And if you would like to see more of that interview of his latest prediction, just log on to our website and click 'Peter Quell.'" With the sincerest of smiles, Donna cooed, "We'll be right back."

Peter turned off the TV two seconds into a commercial for erectile dysfunction.

"Good job, honey," his mom said, patting him on the shoulder.

Peter nodded, accepting that another dream had once again proved true.

CHAPTER 23

As autumn gave way to winter, it remained the general consensus that Peter should stay sequestered at the farm, out of reach of the media and his more devout devotees and detractors. That was just fine with Peter, even if it sometimes felt like time had slowed to a stop.

In the mornings, Peter had taken to reading the Bible, often finding peace and solace in the psalms and proverbs. Most afternoons, he went for a jog on a rough, ankle-spraining horse trail that looped the wooded two-hundred-plus acres that surrounded the house. At night, he watched TV and read and talked with Marian on the phone after she put Jacob to bed.

On Saturdays, he made the drive into Franklin for their weekly rendezvous. Their relationship settled into the easy familiarity that couples have, albeit one with the unique challenges of managing the needs of a seven-year-old child and a thirty-one-year-old reclusive prophet.

Before Peter drifted off to sleep every night, he would half-dread, half-hope for another divine visitation. Almost a month since his last dream, he assumed that God was probably finished with him, and maybe that was for the best.

Peter had finished a brisk run and was trotting back up the long driveway when he noticed a strange car parked in front of the house. Slowing to a walk, he took note of the government plates along with the two figures who were still seated inside the sedan.

Whoever they were had spotted him too, because the front doors opened, and two pairs of polished black cap toe shoes stepped out from each side of the vehicle. Peter prepared to sprint back into the woods if he saw white robes or heard the words "false prophet."

The passenger stretched, straightening his business suit and adjusting his sunglasses in Peter's direction. While the passenger didn't look familiar, the driver's face came into focus like a bad dream.

"Agent Myers," Peter said as he came closer.

"Hello, Peter," the TBI agent said, a constipated expression clamped on his face.

"How did you find me?" Peter asked, truly curious.

"Why are you hiding from me?" Agent Myers countered.

"I'm not hiding from *you*," Peter answered. "I'm hiding from everyone."

Agent Myers gestured to his companion, who had come around the car. "This is Agent Bryant with the *Federal* Bureau of Investigation."

Federal Agent Bryant may or may not have nodded before saying, "You mind if we go inside? We have a few questions."

Not wanting to get off on the wrong shoe with the FBI, Peter motioned for them to follow him up the front porch steps. Once they did so, he opened the door and let them go inside first.

"Nice house you have here," Myers commented as he entered living room and began casing the place. "Who owns it?"

"Someone at Trinity Church," Peter said, figuring they already knew more about it than he did. "Our pastor, Dan Cox, said my mom and I could stay here for a while."

Going over to the kitchen, Peter called out, "You want any water to drink?"

"No, thanks," said Myers, who had drifted into the kitchen with him.

The fact that the agent was sticking so close and keeping an eye on his every move made Peter nervous. Grabbing a bottle of water from the refrigerator, he scurried back to the living room, passing by Myers.

"Hey, those water bottles aren't good for the environment, are they?" Myers cracked from behind.

Ignoring him, Peter went back into the living room where Agent Bryant had removed his sunglasses and was taking inventory of the homeowner's books. Trying to play it cool, Peter took a seat on the couch and had a swig of water, waiting for them to make the first move. After a moment, Agent Bryant took a seat in one of the two chairs, Myers following his lead.

"You've been on quite a roll since I saw you," Myers said, taking out his handheld recorder and clicking it on. "Let's see, there was the mosque fire. Then the fall of three prominent men." His tone dripped in disbelief, which Peter chose to disregard. "I asked you to inform me if you had any more dreams, did I not?"

"Yeah, sorry about that," Peter mumbled. "These situations tend to develop quickly."

"You're sorry?" Agent Myers said, shaking his head.

Before Myers could say anything else, the federal officer leaned forward. "How do you do it?" he simply asked. "How do you know what's going to happen?"

"I dream it," Peter said, matter-of-factly. "Sometimes I have to figure out what the dreams mean. The answer usually comes to me one way or another."

The agents shared a look that Peter couldn't interpret, but it bothered him nonetheless. He had been glad the FBI man was there to keep Myers in check. Now, he wished someone else, even his mom, was in the room.

"What prior knowledge did you have of any of these men?" Bryant asked. "Congressman Bragg, Ed Pressman, and Phillip Drake?"

"I'd heard Ed Pressman on the radio a couple of times," Peter said, thinking back. "I barely knew of Congressman Bragg. I mean, I'd seen the campaigns commercials. That's about it. And I'd never heard of Drake."

"Are you sure no one told you anything about any of them?" Bryant asked, emphasizing each word.

"Think carefully, Peter," Myers cautioned. "Because if you try to hide something from us, and we can establish any connection between you and one of these men, or even someone you know and one of these men, then you are in serious trouble."

"Well, just like with Victor Birdsong, I don't know if someone I know might have some connection with one of these guys," Peter said. "As far as I know, no one I know knows any one of them." Peter took a swig of water. "That's a lot of 'knows.'"

"Do you think this is funny?" Agent Bryant asked in a stern tone.

"No," Peter said, feeling about six years old.

Reaching down inside of him, he tried to find some of the bravado he had exhibited at the end of his interview with Agent Myers back in Kingston. While he came up short, he went ahead and bluffed.

"What is it you think I did here? I mean, do you think I drugged Ed Pressman and made him say racist things on the air? You think I forced the Congressman to have sex with a lobbyist?"

"Your predictions were pretty vague, so it was probably just a coincidence," Agent Bryant said. When Peter didn't try to defend himself, the federal agent continued, "I was sent here to find out exactly what is going on, and that's what I intend to do."

"I already told you," Peter said. "I have these dreams—"

"Come on," Myers cut in, angrily. "You know how that sounds?"

"It went on all the time in the Old Testament, and people don't seem to have a problem believing that," Peter said, before adding, "but in this day and age, it sounds crazy. I get it."

The agents exchanged more glances, again sharing some secret Peter didn't have the clearance for.

"Can I ask you a question?" Peter asked his guests. Neither man responded, so he went ahead. "Are you contacting people I know and asking a bunch of personal questions about me?"

"Why do you ask?" Agent Bryant asked.

"Because someone is," Peter responded. "They say they're a reporter for some publication no one has ever heard of, like 'The Daily Times'—something generic. It's all very sketchy."

"I guess that's the price of being a celebrity," Agent Myers said.

"If we contact anyone, we will identify ourselves as federal agents conducting an investigation," Agent Bryant said in such a straightforward manner that Peter was inclined to believe him.

Finished answering questions, Bryant took back control of the interrogation. "Have you had any dreams since the one about the 'three stars falling'?"

"No, sir," Peter said, deciding not to try to explain the difference between regular dreams and *prophetic dreams* to the federal officer.

"If you have any other dreams going forward, you need to contact me immediately," Agent Bryant said slowly and deliberately. "Do you understand?"

Peter nodded that he did in fact understand, which did not necessarily mean he would do it.

Suddenly getting up and towering over him, Agent Bryant reached inside his coat, his hand hovering over a bulge below his breast-coat pocket. After giving Peter a moment of abject fear, the agent pulled out a business card and handed it to him.

"If I find out you have a dream and tell anyone before Agent Myers or myself, you *will* be taken to a federal facility and detained, and it will *not* be pleasant. Do you read me, Quell?"

"Loud and clear," Peter said into the cold eyes of Uncle Sam's G-Man.

As soon as the agents left, Peter began pacing around the house, punching the air, trying to expunge the nervous energy and anger that had been slowly building during the course of the interview.

They were no different than the drunks in the Ryman alley, or the two workers at the coal-burning plant who'd beaten him up, or the two racist rednecks who'd tried to burn down the mosque. Okay, maybe that was going too far. But at the moment, they just seemed like bullies with badges and business cards.

While huffing through the house, he noticed the answering machine light was blinking, which meant someone had called during his jog. Very few people had Peter and his mom's new phone number, so the machine blinked a lot less often, and when there was a message, Peter checked it.

It was from Dan. "Someone from the TBI was asking if I know your whereabouts. I gave them the address, so you'll probably be getting a visit." *Thanks for the heads up,* Peter thought. "You might also want to watch the news tonight. I hear something is going down. I'll call you when it's over."

It was only three o' clock in the afternoon, giving Peter two hours to ponder what was going to happen. He didn't have any outstanding dreams that needed to be fulfilled, so that couldn't be it. While Dan's message was vague, there was something in his voice that hinted this was not going to be good news.

Surfing the cable news channels for a preview of coming attractions, Peter couldn't find anything pertaining to him or his previous prophecies. In fact, it was a little humbling to realize the twenty-four-hour news cycle had long-since spun past him. It seemed like he needed to have a prophetic dream every night or two just to stay relevant.

In need of a friendly ear, Peter called Marian at work to tell her about the agents and see if she had heard any news about him. Too busy making a living, she gently informed Peter he would have to wait it out on his own.

After watching some mindless TV until 5:00 p.m., Peter finally flipped over to the local news where the answer to the mystery was immediate and impossible to miss.

All three channels led with Mark Shelton, the pastor of Victory Church, standing in front of a bevy of microphones. His carefully sculpted beard seemed designed to project wisdom and strength.

"The other night, I was looking up into the night sky, deep in prayer, when my sight became hazy." He rubbed his eyes. "When I looked again, the stars had aligned into the shape of a cross."

Looking upward, he seemed to be experiencing the vision in real time. "As I watched, one of the stars fell from its lofty position." Now he pointed out its descent. "This flaming star fell all the way to earth, landing in front of me with a tremendous crash!"

The preacher-turned-prophet continued to pantomime his reactions. "I went over to this smoking hole in the ground and stood over it. As the smoke cleared, I could see a figure in the bottom of this deep pit."

As he strained his eyes into the imaginary hole, Shelton's voice warbled with dramatic inflection. "As I peered down through the heat and smoke, I could make out a face. A face I recognized." With a slight pause, he finally revealed, "The face of Peter Quell!"

The actual face of Peter Quell looked pretty shocked.

"What do you believe it means?" a reporter asked.

Mark seemed surprised by the question. "I think Peter Quell's true nature will be revealed. You know, in second *Peter,* the second chapter, it warns of false prophets. It says they will secretly introduce destructive heresies and false stories, and they'll bring swift destruction on themselves as well."

"And when will this happen?" a reporter who sounded like Cindy asked.

"Swiftly," Mark said, as he looked into the camera, seemingly directly at Peter.

Peter felt numb. It was truly a stunning experience to be so publicly and viciously trashed. For several minutes, his mind simply spun in place without forming any coherent thoughts. When he finally found some traction, he went in reverse by second-guessing himself.

Was it possible he really was a false prophet? While he'd thought he tried to do the right thing, maybe he'd been duped. That put everything in doubt.

Just then, the phone rang, and anxious for any diversion, Peter snapped it up.

"Did you see it?" Dan asked.

"Yeah," Peter said, his head pounding.

"What do you think they're planning?"

"I have no idea," Peter said. "I was going to ask you the same thing."

There was a pause as they both searched for an answer that seemed beyond them. Feeling more vulnerable and scared than he ever had before, Peter asked, "Can you come over?"

"It's ridiculous," Ms. Quell said to Dan as she offered him a plate of cheese and crackers. She had arrived just in time to watch a repeat performance of Shelton's press conference on the six o' clock news and still manage to throw together some appetizers before her pastor made it to the house.

"It's just like my dream!" Peter said, passing on the plate of hors d'oeuvres. "He can't even make up anything original, so he uses my dream and tacks me on the end of it. I could sue him for copyright infringement."

"Just ridiculous," his mom repeated as she nibbled at a cracker.

"Yes," agreed Dan, who'd already been a recipient of his own Shelton sneak attack. "I'm sure it doesn't help that Mark knew all the men whom you predicted would go down in flames."

"Really?" Peter asked, surprised by that revelation.

"Well, Nashville is a small town, and it gets even smaller when your religion and politics overlap," Dan observed. "Ed Pressman endorsed Steve Bragg and gave him friendly interviews. I'd bet Ed and Drake contributed to Bragg's campaigns and Mark's new church. In return, Mark helped turn out the vote for Bragg, and probably directed his wealthier parishioners to invest with Drake."

"I had no idea they were so connected," Peter said. "It's like they all had a reason to come after me."

"Shelton is probably feeling some heat right now, and my guess is he'd like to redirect some of it to you." Dan popped a cube of cheese in his mouth. "But I don't think it's a conspiracy or anything."

"There is obviously an attempt to smear me, and it's coming from him!" Peter retorted, pointing to the TV, now showing a muted sitcom. "I had the FBI paying me a visit today, so don't tell me I'm paranoid either!"

"The FBI was here?" his mom exclaimed, choking on a cracker

"I was going to tell you," Peter said, realizing his mistake too late.

"What did they want?" Mom asked, glancing around nervously.

"Just asking questions about how I knew what was going to happen," Peter said, now trying to play it off as no big deal. "It was standard stuff. I'm not in trouble."

"Oh, dear," his mom muttered, reverting to a frightened little girl. "Do you think Mark's vision about Peter could mean he's going to be arrested?" she asked Dan, her voice almost quivering.

"He didn't have a vision, Mom. He's making it all up—and I'm not going to get arrested. I didn't do anything wrong," Peter said, looking at Dan for confirmation.

"That didn't keep them from arresting Paul," his mom said, her voice high and tight. "Or stoning Stephen!"

"Yes, well, I'm assuming that Mark didn't have any sort of legitimate vision," Dan said, trying to get the conversation back on track. "That said, the fact that he would make such a bold statement tells me he has something in the works."

"Like what?" Mom asked, still hovering just below hysterics.

Dan turned to Peter. "Is there anything he could use against you?"

Peter was already thinking along the same lines. Prior to his current relationship, he had been woefully inexperienced sexually, almost virginally so. But that didn't seem like something a fundamentalist could use against him. "Not really," he said. "I've pretty much been living like a hermit since I got home."

"Well, except for Marian," his mom pointed out.

"I have been seeing someone for about a month," Peter informed Dan. "She's divorced and has a young son."

"Have you slept with her?" Dan asked point-blank.

Bristling at the personal intrusion (in front of his mother, no less) Peter thought about not answering before noticing his mom was already nodding in the affirmative.

"Yes," Peter confirmed.

Dan seemed to be doing some moral arithmetic in his head before concluding, "Well, if that's all he has, it's pretty thin."

"That's all I can think of," Peter said. "I mean, besides the fact that I've been living at home and don't have a job. But I think everyone in the greater metropolitan area already knows that."

Sitting back in his chair, Dan rubbed his chin. "I guess we'll find out soon enough," he stated in an ominous tone that Peter didn't like one bit.

CHAPTER 24

"The secret is to fry the taco shells," Peter explained as he attempted to flip a flour tortilla floating in a skillet of cooking oil. With a pop, the pan spat grease on his spatula hand. "Ahh!" he yelped, jumping back in the large country kitchen.

"I didn't realize this was going to be so exciting," Marian said as she sipped her glass of red wine and watched with amusement.

It was the day after Thanksgiving and the first time in a while the couple had a chance to spend some time together without one of their chaperones present. Peter's mom was on a road trip to visit an ailing relative in West Tennessee while Marian's ex had whisked Jacob away to go skiing.

Wanting to impress his girlfriend, Peter insisted she come over so he could make her the only dish he had in his culinary repertoire: his "World Famous Tacos."

Another drop of hot oil landed on Peter's forearm, singeing his hair and sending him once again dancing away from the skillet. "It's trying to kill me!"

"Turn it down," Marian instructed gleefully.

In a flurry, Peter turned off all the burners and began spooning taco meat, replete with habanero chili peppers, onto the least burnt of the tortillas. As a side, he plopped a couple of sizzling scoops of re-refried beans on each plate. Scurrying the food over to the table, Peter quickly blessed the steaming mess.

While the cook watched, Marian bravely took her first bite from the greasy taco.

"What do you think?" he asked.

As she chewed, she picked the napkin out of her lap and, very ladylike, removed the food from her mouth.

"It's not that bad!" Peter declared.

"I'm going to order a pizza," she said, leaving the table with a kind smile.

As Marian went to the phone, Peter shook his head with disappointment. "Apparently, some people just can't appreciate a world-class meal."

Hoisting his flimsy taco, he took a big bite, sending half the slick meat sliding out one end of the shell. What managed to make it into his mouth began a chain reaction that went from a warm sensation to a full-blown firestorm. Not bothering with his napkin, Peter spit the concoction from hell on his plate and drained his glass of water.

"Make it an extra-large!" Peter yelled to Marian.

It was the kind of disaster that might have derailed Peter in the past; however, Marian's calm countenance counterbalanced his tendency to overreact. He still couldn't shake the feeling he was living under Mark Shelton's curse, and he feared bigger disasters than bad tacos were looming around the corner.

"Do you think there could be some truth to what Shelton said about me?" Peter blurted out over a Supreme pizza the size of a tire.

"What are you talking about?" Marian asked, mid-chew.

"His prediction," Peter said. "I mean, I don't know for sure where my dreams are coming from. What if I am being used by a demon or something for evil purposes?"

"Are you serious?" Marian asked, waggling her slice in his direction. "Your dreams have stood up for the environment and a different religion. Oh, and they've exposed a racist, a thief, and an adulterer—all of whom were total hypocrites with their 'patriotism' and 'ethical investing' and 'family values.'"

Peter started to say something, but Marian was fired up—and maybe a little tipsy.

"In my Bible, God is usually on the side of the poor and oppressed—not the rich and powerful." She turned to fully face Peter. "Help me understand how Christians can be so against helping the poor?"

"I don't think they're against helping the poor," Peter said. "I just don't think they want the *government* helping, at least not too much."

"Don't they keep talking about how they want us to be a 'Christian nation?'" she exclaimed. "Well, read your Bibles, people, especially the Jesus parts."

"Yeah, well, I know I'm not perfect either," Peter said. "I worry that I'm failing everyone."

"That's just dumb," she said, picking up her wine glass and taking a sip. "Doesn't the Bible say that if a prophet is from God, what he says will come true?"

"Yeah, I think it does," Peter said. "Somewhere."

"There you go," she said. "I mean there have been a lot of so-called prophets, from Nostradamus to…what's his name? Edgar Cayce. And we're still waiting for some of their predictions to come true."

Marian pointed at him. "You say something is going to happen, and blam! It happens! That's because you're the real deal."

Smiling at his cute girlfriend, Peter pulled her closer, leaning in for a kiss.

Marian kisses him back, careful not to get any red wine on their host's cushions.

It was mid-morning when the phone rang, waking Peter, who crawled out of bed and stumbled down the stairs. The answering machine was going to beat him to the call, and not really wanting to talk to anyone anyway, he let it win.

"Hey, it's Dan," he heard his pastor say. "I got a call from that reporter at Channel Seven, Cindy Sizemore. She wanted to talk to you. When I told her that wasn't going to happen, she asked me to pass on a message."

Peter thought about picking up the phone, but Dan seemed to be doing a fine job on his own, so he let him continue unabated.

"She said someone was shopping a story about you to the local news stations. She didn't go into details; she just said it wasn't really news, whatever that means, and no one took it, at least no one local.

"Apparently, some show called *GossipTV* is running it. Cindy didn't know any more than that, just that it's supposed to be on tonight at six. So, I guess we'll talk afterwards."

As Dan hung up, the machine started to blink like a red distress beacon.

"What was that?" Peter heard Marian ask from behind him.

"It sounds like whatever Mark predicted is happening tonight."

She came up behind him, wrapping her arms around his chest. "Is there anything we can do about it?"

"Not really," Peter said.

"Then let's not worry about it and go get some breakfast," she whispered in his ear.

Venturing into the thriving metropolis of Leiper's Fork, Marian and Peter filled up on eggs and bacon and biscuits and gravy at the Country Boy Diner. Even with his cap pulled low,

211

a couple of other patrons whispered and stole glances in his direction.

"Your meal has been paid for," their waitress told them as she topped off their coffee cups.

Looking over, Peter tipped the bill of his cap as one of his benefactors gave him an encouraging thumbs-up.

After breakfast, the couple wandered over to a contemporary art gallery, then to a cool antique store that looked like it could have furnished the house where he was staying. In a town with its share of celebrities, no one else seemed to spot Peter, or if they did, they didn't care.

Just out of town, on the Natchez Trace Parkway, they pulled into a parking lot where horses were being unloaded from trailers. Marian and Peter hoofed it up the trail for hikers that wound to the top of a ridge. At the peak, they were rewarded with a vista that overlooked a gently sloping valley stretching out before them.

"It's beautiful, isn't it?" Marian commented.

"Yeah, it is," he said, his thoughts a million miles away.

"What's the matter?" she asked, breaking away from the dreamlike setting.

"Oh, I don't know," he lied, then tried to come clean. "I guess I just wished I could see what's going to happen to me."

"Whatever it is, we'll get through it," Marian said, taking his hand and giving it a squeeze.

At that moment, a cool breeze blew over them like a breath of fresh air. Drinking it in, Peter gave silent thanks for the small hand that interlaced his own and prayed for the strength to weather the coming storm.

"I guess we need to turn on the TV," Peter said nervously as he glanced at a clock on the wall for about the one hundredth time.

Settled back on the couch, Marian let out a sigh. "Let's don't and say we did."

As he sat down, his girlfriend cuddled up next to him,

wrapping him up so tightly he couldn't take hold of the remote. With a laugh, she did her best to distract him, which worked for a minute or two.

"Sorry," Peter said, finally taking the remote and pulling away. "I have to know."

"I know," she said, giving up with a pout.

Working the controls, he found *GossipTV* and quickly surmised the most honest thing about the program was its name. As the title implied, the fast-paced tabloid show was mostly comprised of celebrity rumors, although they were happy to humiliate anyone with any name recognition whatsoever.

After the first commercial break, the buxom blond hostess reappeared with a picture of Peter over her shoulder, causing him to tense in anticipation.

"The prophet from Nashville, Peter Quell, has called some major predictions lately, including the downfall of three prominent members of his own community. We wonder if he foresaw this story coming," the blond exuded with a sly smile.

"Our own Dirk Shanahan sat down with one person who may know the prophet better than anyone else—in this juicy scoop you'll only see on *G-TV.*"

A reporter with frosty tipped hair, presumably Dirk, sat across from the former member of Peter's youth group and one of his frequent callers, Tom McAllister.

"What's Tom doing there?" Peter asked the TV.

"You know that guy?" Marian asked.

"Sort of," Peter said.

"I have known Peter Quell for over fifteen years," Tom replied in response to something Dirk had said. "We have been good friends, so it gives me no pleasure to do this." He was speaking fast, as if trying to get it all out in as few breaths as possible.

"The only reason I am coming forward is because Peter is representing himself to be a man of God. And I don't believe a man of God would be a homosexual."

"What?" Marian yelped; Peter was left too stunned to utter anything.

"How do you know about his sexual orientation?" Dirk asked earnestly.

"He made advances at me," Tom said. "He told me he was attracted to me—that kind of thing."

With a gulp, Peter felt like an anvil had just landed in his gut.

"But there have been rumors Peter Quell has been involved with women," the reporter stated. "There has even been speculation that he is the father of Jordan Stone's lovechild."

"For crying out loud!" Peter shouted.

"And more recently," the reporter went on, "there are reports that he broke up the marriage of someone who attends his church."

"Oh my God," Marian exclaimed, clutching at her throat.

"There is no truth to the Jordan Stone story," Tom said definitively, the first true statement to come out of his mouth. "I would guess the relationship he's in now is a sham. I don't believe Peter has had a real girlfriend. He told me he was interested in men and, ah, me. Of course, I told him I wasn't into that, and we haven't spoken since."

"You lying sack of shit," Marian hissed.

"Even though I don't approve of his lifestyle, I'd still like to be his friend," Tom said with utmost sincerity. "I pray for him every day."

The video ended, and the show cut back to the *GossipTV* hostess.

"This bombshell comes just after a Nashville pastor, Mark Shelton, predicted that Peter Quell's reputation would take a hit. While we at *GossipTV* certainly don't have a problem with alternative lifestyles, this news may not go over so well with Mr. Quell's followers in the Christian community."

Rotating, the hostess re-aimed her chest at a photo of a haggard, middle-aged man. "Do you recognize this former child star? We'll tell you who he is and why he's back in rehab—when we come back!"

"I'll tell them how gay you are!" Marian threatened.

As Peter turned off the TV, the phone beside him rang. Putting down the remote, he wearily picked up the receiver with a low moan.

"Did you see it?" Dan asked.

"Yeah," Peter managed.

"Do you know Tom McAllister?"

"We were in youth group at Trinity together," Peter said. "We were never really friends."

"Obviously," Dan stated. "Have you spent any time with him since you've been home?"

"I saw him once at Trinity," Peter said. "It was nothing. He seemed happy to hear I was unemployed and living at home." As an afterthought, he added, "He has called the house a bunch of times, but I never called him back."

"Do you still have those messages?"

"They've all been deleted," Peter said, sinking into despair. "How many people even watch that show?"

"It doesn't matter," Dan said. "It will get picked up by the blogs and newspapers. Pretty soon it will be news." He paused, as if not wanting to tell him something, then obviously decided to forge ahead. "I'm told there is already a mass email going around."

"What do you mean?" Peter asked, looking at Marian, who was trying to listen in.

"A few people have gotten emails over the last couple of days that basically say you are gay," Dan said, sounding annoyed. "These emails are like a virus. People just blindly forward them without any idea if they are true or not. I need to do a sermon on what the Bible says about spreading false rumors."

"What do the emails say?" Peter asked desperately. "Just that I'm gay?"

"Yeah," Dan said slowly, "and something about you being a

regular at gay clubs in Atlanta. I think there's a photo of you arm-and-arm with a couple of guys."

Seeing the stunned expression on Peter's face, Marian returned it with a quizzical look that begged for answers.

"Well, that's kind of true," Peter admitted. "I had a couple of gay friends in Atlanta, and we went to clubs sometimes. I danced a lot, but nothing happened."

"That's what they do," Dan said. "Mix in a little truth to make the lie go further."

"You know who's behind all this," Marian said, loud enough for Dan to hear through Peter's skull. "The one who 'prophesized' you would take a fall."

"It is suspicious timing," Dan said, responding to Marian's accusation. "I even heard Mark will be preaching on the sin of homosexuality tomorrow."

"I feel like I should do something in my defense," Peter said into the receiver as he stared at Marian, who was clearly ready to go to war. "Marian will back me up."

She nodded back vigorously.

"Are there any other women that would come forward?" Dan asked tentatively.

"Maybe," Peter said. There were a couple of old girlfriends, if he could track them down. Even if he could get them to go public, he hated to drag anyone into such an ugly fight. "I don't know if I want to go that route."

"Yeah," Dan said, understandingly. "Why don't we pray on it tonight, and let's talk tomorrow?"

"Will you call my mom on her cell phone for me?" Peter asked before hanging up. "Tell her what's going on before she hears about it from someone else."

Dan assured him he would.

As soon as Peter put the phone down, a furious Marian asked, "What are we going to do?"

"I don't know," Peter said as he got up and started to pace. "Pray."

"I'll pray for a good attorney so you can sue him," Marian said as she watched him pace around the room, his mind a million miles away. "Are you okay?"

"I don't know," he said weakly. His stomach hurt worse than if he had actually eaten one of his own tacos; his heart and head ached, too. What would his family and friends think? Most would probably wonder why it had taken him so long to come out of the closet.

"I've been 'outed,' and I wasn't even in," he groaned.

"We'll fight this together," she said.

"It's not your fight," Peter said firmly. Suddenly tired, he turned toward the stairs. "I'm going to lie down," he announced as he trudged upward.

Getting to her feet, Marian followed him up the staircase and into his bedroom. She found him lying on the bed, curled up in a semi-fetal position. Without a word, she lay down beside him, arranging her body next to his and placing an arm over his side.

As the minutes ticked by, the lie kept running through Peter's mind, refusing to give him any peace. Marian's breathing had become soft and rhythmic, so he gently raised her arm and slid back off the bed. She stirred without waking as he slunk out of the bedroom.

Creaking over the hardwood, he made his way back downstairs to the living room. Once in the large family room, he stood still for a while, not knowing what to do next. All he knew for sure was that he did not want to watch TV.

Slowly surveying the room, his eyes fell on a big family Bible the homeowners had left on the shelf. He walked over, picked up the hefty, leather-bound book, and brought it to the couch.

When he set it down on the coffee table, the book fell open before him. Reading the ancient text, the words seemed ordained from up above. As if the text was an elixir, it felt as if God was speaking directly to him through the priestly passages. It would not be easy, but at least now, he knew what he had to do.

CHAPTER 25

From the parking lot, Peter thought of Marian. She was probably rolling over in the big, luxurious feather bed. At first, she would wonder where he was, calling out his name. Then she would go downstairs to look for him, and she would find the note he had left for her.

Marian, I went to church. And then, after some deliberation, he had added, *Love, Peter.*

By the time she figured out where he was going, it would be too late. It had to be this way because she would try to talk him out of it. And she would probably have succeeded if given the chance because he did not want to do this.

Peter watched as a few hundred people made their way to the former arena that served as a temporary church. Until Victory built their own church, they were renting this mega-structure, which they managed to fill every Sunday morning.

On the ten-foot elevated platform stage, along with the music leader, sat Tom McAllister. From his highly visible seat of honor, Tom was listening raptly to Mark Shelton read to his flock.

"'If a man lies with a man as with a woman, both of them have done what is detestable. They must be put to death; their blood will be on their own heads.' Leviticus 20:13."

Mark Shelton lifted his bristly cheeks from the Bible. "You see? These aren't Mark Shelton's rules. These are God's rules. Now, people will say, surely it doesn't really mean that. Do you know what I say? I say let's let the Bible speak for itself."

"Amen!" a supporter cried in agreement.

"Does it sound harsh?" Mark asked. "Well, maybe it does, and I am not advocating murder because that's clearly forbidden in the Bible, too. But I have to be honest about what this Book says, even if it's unpopular."

Another round of "Amens" rose up from the crowd.

"You see, I didn't sign on to preach just the warm, fuzzy parts of this Book, the parts that are *socially acceptable* or *politically correct*," Mark said, giving the last two expressions a distinctly effeminate flavor. "I am called to preach it all, even the hard parts—the parts that make people squirm."

Turning around to generously include his stage-mate, he said, "Tom McAllister showed that kind of courage when he stepped forward on national TV to call sin out."

As a smattering of applause rippled throughout the auditorium, Tom gave a slight nod of acknowledgment.

"You see, we need to have more men and women willing to fight for our values, or else our way of life will be washed away by the world." He paused to cast his gaze above the crowd, staring like a disappointed father at a wayward child.

"Do you think the world cares if homosexuality runs rampant and men marry men? What about men becoming women? Do you think it cares about the murder of unborn babies? I'll give you a hint. The answer is no!" Mark paused to allow the applause and "Amens" of agreement to subside.

"But I'll tell you who does care." The answers came as quick as lightning strikes. "God cares, and I care, and my brother Tom cares—because we stand with God! How about you? Where do you stand?"

Shouts of "Amen!" and "Praise God!" rose up as the righteous crowd clapped and stomped and cheered as one. Every member of the audience made some sort of noise of support—all except one lone parishioner sitting in the back row. Head bowed, Peter was fervently praying for strength.

Having slipped in late, Peter had kept his head down until now. As the bluster from the crowd died out, he raised his head, swallowed hard, and shouted in a loud voice, "Leviticus 19:16!"

Heads snapped toward the scripture shouter. With a large leather Bible open in his hands, Peter took his stand and, in a voice that seemed to reverberate through the huge hall, read, "'Do not go about spreading slander among your people.'"

Immediately, it was clear Mark knew something was amiss. While the congregation could hoot and holler to their hearts' content, they never spoke out individual thoughts. The voice sounded familiar, and even from a distance, he managed to place the face.

"Is that who I think it is?" he asked over the PA system. Busy whispering among themselves, most of the crowd hadn't quite caught on yet.

"Leviticus 20:10," Peter yelled out, taking a few steps from his seat. "'If a man commits adultery with another man's wife—both the adulterer and the adulteress must be put to death.'"

Whispers rumbled through the whole auditorium, some unsure of what was happening, others beginning to realize the identity of the outspoken intruder. All the while, Peter moved down the aisle, carrying the big family Bible out in front of him like a shield.

From the stage, Mark craned to see the stranger moving toward him. "You have a lot of nerve coming into a house of God," he boomed from the stage.

"Leviticus 19: 13," Peter cried. "'Do not defraud your neighbor or rob him.'"

The congregation was openly talking amongst themselves now, throwing out "Boos" and shouts of "False prophet!" and even a lone "Foul spirit!" as the young man dared to make his way closer to the stage.

"Why don't you ever preach on these scriptures?" Peter shouted out to Mark. "Your friends have broken these commands, and you never said a word about them."

"How dare you?" Mark answered indignantly. "I have preached against adultery and theft," he bellowed, although no one in the congregation could remember exactly when.

"Leviticus 19:34," Peter said, stopping fifty feet from the front. "'The alien living among you must be treated as one of your native born. Love him as yourself for you were aliens in Egypt.'"

A snort came from the microphone, as if the pastor found this passage ridiculous.

"How many sermons have you preached about treating aliens as equals?" Peter asked, trying very hard to keep his voice from getting lost in the vast room.

"That scripture is talking about someone passing through a country," Mark said, "not an invasion."

Recognizing one of Ed Pressman's buzz words, Peter simply repeated the preacher's words back to him. "Let the Bible speak for itself."

With a plastered smile of rage, Mark began nodding vigorously, as if the fight was now on. He scanned the page of his open Bible and called out accusingly, "Leviticus 19:26—'Do not practice divination or sorcery.'"

"I don't!" Peter answered, automatically turning back to his Bible to find the verse Mark had read. The next verse jumped out at him. "But look at the verse 27. It says, 'Do not cut the hair at the sides of your head or clip off the edges of your beard.'"

Mark snorted derisively again, his eyes darting around the page as he subconsciously stroked his neatly trimmed beard.

"Leviticus 19:19," Peter called out before Mark could find

another suitable verse. "'Do not wear clothing woven of two kinds of materials.'" Looking up, he asked, "Is that suit a poly-blend?"

"You are making a mockery of the word of God!" Mark cried.

"No, you are," Peter yelled back, loud enough to be heard above the rustle of the crowd. "You are picking and choosing verses from the Old Testament that support your prejudices, and stir up anger, and cause division."

"You are on dangerous ground," Mark shouted, his voice crackling so loudly through the speakers it was painful to the ears. "Everyone, turn with me to Deuteronomy," he announced as he frantically flipped the thin paper.

Something told Peter to stay with him, and he turned, too. As he passed Numbers, he heard Mark say, "Here it is. Chapter 18:20— 'A prophet who presumes to speak in my name anything I have not commanded him to say, or a prophet who speaks in the name *of other gods*, must be put to death!'"

There was a chill in the air, and for a moment, the harsh verdict quieted the restless congregation who waited for the interpretation. Peter arrived at the verse and quickly read as his prosecutor began to weave the case for the death penalty against him.

"This so-called prophet claims to speak for Allah, who is a foreign god, which is all we need to know about him."

Before Mark could go on, Peter called out, "What's the next verse? Read verses 21 and 22, please!"

The crowd quieted down a bit, going back to their own Bibles to read for themselves. Mark glanced down at his page, not immediately answering.

Peter projected slowly and distinctly in his clearest voice, "'How can we know when a message has not been spoken by the Lord? If what a prophet proclaims in the name of the Lord does *not* take place or come true, that is a message the Lord has *not* spoken. That prophet has spoken presumptuously. Do not be afraid of him.'"

Shutting his own Bible, he faced the stage and opened his arms. "Tell me, Mark, what have I said that has not come true?"

The crowd seemed to turn in unison toward their leader, whose face reddened under his blasphemous beard. Even from fifty feet away, Peter thought he detected a flash of panic. Not answering, Mark dove back into the Good Book, almost ripping the pages as he turned them, like he was trying to dismantle a bomb in the final seconds of a countdown.

"Here," Mark said, his finger stabbing the verse. "Jeremiah 23, verse 14. It says, and I quote, 'Among the prophets of Jerusalem I have seen something horrible: They commit adultery and live a lie. They strengthen the hands of the evildoers, so that no one turns from his wickedness. They are all like Sodom to me; the people of Jerusalem are like Gomorrah.'"

Although the reading was rushed and, even with the aid of the microphone, barely decipherable, there were yells of encouragement from his faithful followers. Peter tried to respond, but Mark's amplified voice overpowered him.

"And make no mistake, you are committing adultery," the pastor said, looking directly at him.

Peter wasn't sure if Mark was referring to his relationship with Marian. Mark probably knew about that, but of course, that wasn't sensational enough, so he had publicly played the homosexual card.

"What were they doing in Sodom and Gomorrah?" Mark asked the congregation. "What was so offensive to God? They burned with lust. Men burned for other men!" Pointing his finger of judgment at Peter, he proclaimed, "You are sexually immoral in the eyes of God!"

"I am a sinner!" Peter declared in a full-throated cry. Even Mark became quiet, giving Peter a chance to confess his sin.

"Jesus said if you have lust in your heart for *anyone*, you've committed adultery. Jesus said if you have *anger* in your heart, you are a murderer." Finding a reservoir of power in his voice, Peter pivoted around to address the people. "We all fall short. That's why we all need Christ. So, who are you to judge me or anyone else?"

"I judge you with God's own word!" Mark yelled down at

him. With his Bible held high in the air, the pastor cut a glance somewhere behind Peter, sending a silent signal.

Hearing "Boos," Peter hoped the crowd might be taking his side; the accompanying shouts of "False prophet!" discouraged this overly optimistic thought.

Peter then spotted a couple of ushers from the rear moving steadily toward him and decided it was time to make his escape. Turning back to the front, Peter saw a linebacker squeezed into a blazer blitzing up the aisle.

Knowing time was short, he tried to yell above the din of noise and confusion, "You all are like Pharisees that pretend to love God, but you don't even know Him." The voices seemed to get even louder around him. "If you loved God, you would repent of your own sins."

Just then, a heavy hand fell on Peter's shoulder while another grabbed his arm. Looking up at the stage, he caught a fleeting glimpse of his old "friend," Tom, who was staring in horrified disbelief at the scene.

Leviticus 19:11, Peter managed to mouth at him before the crowd closed in.

The big usher/bouncer made a firm grip around his shoulder and started dragging him up the aisle. Closing his eyes, Peter found it easier not to fight and simply allow himself to be carried along. A few prods and jabs came in from the aisles as he was pulled through the back doors.

In the outer lobby, the hisses and boos softened while the grip on him tightened and the pace quickened. He noticed his feet were not even touching the floor and found he was suspended in the middle of a huddle of jumbled suits hustling him down a hallway.

Metallic doors clanked open, and he was transported outside into the light of day. The welcome sight of freedom was cut short when he was abruptly released by the scrum. Unable to set his legs underneath him, he went straight down, his head hitting the pavement. A sharp thud spun his world upside down as he fell into a hole of darkness.

When he woke, he made out the maniacal sounds of children's laughter mixed with taunts. As Peter struggled to get to his feet, a pain ignited and pulsed in his head. His awkward stagger apparently brought more levity to the situation as evidenced by a fresh round of cackles.

Raising his aching head, Peter discovered a handful of truant Sunday-school boys and girls laughing at the bum in the alley. Knowing he had to get away, he picked a direction and stumbled along, leaving the little demons to howl after him.

Emerging from the alleyway, he found himself in a vast parking lot full of shining cars and, thankfully, devoid of people. Getting his bearings, he hurried in the direction he hoped he'd parked.

The thought of facing Victory's exiting horde, hungry and anxious to get to lunch, was truly terrifying. In a daze, he miraculously managed to run right into the side of his ride. With shaky hands, he fumbled with his keys, unlocking the door. After getting behind the wheel, he began to weave out of the enemy camp.

At the exit, Peter hesitated, trying to remember the right way to turn—*Was it left?* His momentary delay agitated the rent-a-cop who had stopped traffic for him. Peter pulled out onto the highway, not caring if it was in the right direction, just wanting to get away.

On the long drive back to the house, he thanked God for delivering him and hoped he'd find Marian waiting for him. Instead, he found the note he'd left for her. Below, she had added, *I've gone to church to look for you. Love you too, M.*

Not wanting her to worry, he had been purposefully vague on his plans. Now she was needlessly searching Grace or Trinity Church. He felt bad for sending her on a wild goose chase. Still, it was better than the truth. If she had known he'd thrown himself into the lion's den, she would have rightfully worried. Unlike Daniel, Peter felt like he'd been sampled by the pride.

After leaving a reassuring message on her cell phone, Peter unplugged the home phone and went up to his room with the intention of sleeping for the rest of the year.

CHAPTER 26

I'm lying on the ground—unconscious. It begins to drizzle. As the rain comes down, I'm aware there are other people around. The rain steadily gets harder. People are trying to wake me up, but they can't. The water starts to rise around me. A moment later, I'm floating on top of the flood—as it overtakes everything.

After putting his pen down in his red journal, Peter took a moment to grasp at the wispiest of strands that connected him to the scene he had just left behind. When nothing else came, he lay back down.

It was Sunday evening, and he'd been asleep for roughly five hours. Other than a headache, he actually felt better than he had the day before, like a tremendous weight had been lifted. Not only had he faced his fear and confronted his accuser, he'd survived to tell the tale.

Getting into the shower, he let the warm water wash over him, and his water-themed dream streamed back to him. Was it literal or symbolic—or both? It seemed more muddled than his other ultra-lucid visions. Could that be the result of the hit on his head?

As he dried off, voices from inside the house turned his attention away from his own thoughts. Putting on some comfortable clothes, he hurried downstairs toward the distinct voice of a child, which confused him all the more.

Rounding the corner into the living room, he found his mom, Dan, and Marian sitting around, watching Jacob play with a robot in the middle of the floor.

Dan saw Peter first. "There he is," he announced triumphantly. "Lazarus has risen!"

Marian jumped up and ran over to give him a huge hug. Pulling back, she looked at him. "Are you insane? Showing up at Mark Shelton's church?"

"You heard, huh?" Peter said shyly, his voice raw and raspy from his earlier shouting match.

"The story is making the rounds," Dan commented.

"What are they saying?" Peter wanted to know as he came further into the room.

"That you and Mark were yelling Bible verses at each other," Dan said with a bemused smile.

"That sounds about right," Peter said. Looking at the bookshelves, Peter noticed the gap his host family's Bible had previously filled. "I think I lost their Bible in the scuffle."

"At least it went to a good cause," Dan said, absolving him.

No longer able to contain herself, Ms. Quell spoke up. "What got into you?" she asked harshly.

After all he'd been through, her severe tone annoyed him until he saw the consternation etched on her face, her brow a shadowy patch of worried hatch marks.

"When I saw that story last night, I felt like I had to do something. I just didn't know what," Peter explained, glancing from Dan to his mom to Marian. "I got out the Bible and opened to the verse in Leviticus about men being with men. I knew

Mark was probably going to bring that up when he preached on homosexuality."

Dan nodded.

"Anyway, it's in a section with a long list of laws that say all sorts of things. Some are still relevant, and some sound pretty crazy today."

In spite of his hoarse voice, Peter swallowed and carried on. "I realized Mark was using verses out of context to stir up dissent. I guess I felt like I needed to call attention to that."

Everyone seemed to be listening to him except Jacob, who had turned his robot into a truck and was rolling it on the floor while he made engine sounds.

"I don't think I convinced anyone at Victory," Peter said with a weak smile, then winced at a passing pain in his brain.

"What's the matter?" his mom demanded, looking suspiciously at her son.

"Oh, when they threw me outside, I hit my head," he said. "I'll be okay."

"They threw you outside?" Dan repeated.

"Do you have a headache?" Marian asked, concerned.

"Yeah," Peter admitted. "A little bit."

"We really should sue them," Marian said, ready to make the call.

"It's all right," Peter said, brushing off any legal action. "I went into their house and disrupted a service."

"They still can't throw you out on your head," Dan said, indignant.

"Well, I know one thing," his mom added with utmost conviction. "You are going to the doctor to get your head examined."

"I've been telling him he should do that for weeks," Marian said, trying to lighten the mood.

Dan chuckled, but Ms. Quell, for whom the joke was primarily intended, was not amused. "You should do what your mother says," she quickly added.

"Yeah! Do what your mother says," Jacob chipped in.

This got a round of chuckles, though Ms. Quell only went so far as to break a smile. As the laughter dissipated, the adults were left to watch Jacob roll his truck over the carpet and up Marian's leg.

"I had another dream," Peter announced.

The room got quiet; even the truck noises stopped in their tracks mid-calf.

"At least, I think I had a dream," he cautioned before filling them in on the scant details of what had made it into his journal.

"So, there's going to be a flood?" his mom asked when he was finished.

"I think so," Peter said.

"Sometimes, these things are symbolic, like the money or the stars from the sky," Dan reminded them. "Do you think the rain could mean something else?"

"I guess it could," Peter said. "I just don't know what it would be."

"Well, we knew coins weren't going to be falling, so we had to look for another explanation." Dan thought out loud. "Water, on the other hand, is entirely possible. There are enough rivers and streams that a lot of rain could flood areas around town."

"It seemed like it was a flood that would affect a lot of people," Peter said, trying to immerse himself in the remnants of the memory. For an instant, the expansive lake spread out around him. "The whole city."

There was a pause as everyone let the implications of such a prophecy sink in.

"Is it going to rain?" Jacob asked, tiring of his transforming truck toy.

"We don't know," Marian answered. "Maybe."

"Rain, rain, rain!" Jacob sang as he danced around.

"There's not even rain in the forecast," his mom said nervously.

"My concern is you seem a little more unsure about this one," Dan observed.

"I guess I am," Peter admitted. As he coughed, his scratchy voice got worse. "It's a little fuzzy. I don't know if getting bounced on my head caused me to have the dream. Or it could be making me have a harder time remembering it."

They all sat in silence for a moment before Jacob asked his mom, "How much longer are we going to be here?"

"I'm not sure, honey," Marian said. "Why don't you look at your picture book?"

Jacob didn't seem thrilled with that idea, opting instead to bury his face in the sofa cushion.

Dan picked up where he had left off. "Well, I wish you were clearer about this one, especially since the stakes are so high."

"What do you mean?" Ms. Quell asked, as if picking up on the "stakes" and wanting to know how high they went.

"Well, it's not a matter of warning an old man about his heart, or even a few Muslims about a mosque," Dan explained. "This is the kind of thing that needs to be announced to the city. And, if you're wrong in any way, Shelton will jump all over you."

"What more can Shelton do?" Marian asked, her defenses welling up. "He's already called him a 'false prophet.'"

"And gay," his mom reminded everyone.

"I guess it could be worse," Peter proffered. "He could be calling me the anti-Christ."

"Are you?" Marian asked him, covering her open shocked mouth.

Peter made a silly devil face, making Jacob laugh.

"You think it's funny," Dan jumped in with a somber tone, "but we are talking about getting God's prophecies right, people."

That gave everyone pause. After a moment, Jacob went back to trying to do a headstand on the sofa.

"I wish I felt a little more confident about this one," Peter repeated, both to himself and everyone else.

With his head wedged in the couch cushions, Jacob waved his legs around like broken helicopter blades. *Burying one's head seems like a pretty good option,* Peter thought to himself.

"Well, you could tell just a few people about it," Dan suggested. "Maybe someone in local government that could help prepare the city for a potential disaster. The Core of Engineers. Who's in charge of FEMA?"

"Yes, that's a good idea," his mom said, ever trusting of her pastor's sage advice.

Peter nodded thoughtfully as he watched Jacob bicycle his legs mid-air. At least the plan sounded safe. If it turned out he was wrong, fewer people would know about it, so it wouldn't be as big a deal, right?

The semi-promise he'd been forced into making with Agents Myers and Bryant also crossed his mind. Feeling the need for total disclosure, he went ahead and confessed, "When those agents were here, they told me they wanted to know about any dreams I had before anyone else."

"Well, you have to call them," his mom said automatically, just as he'd known she would.

"What are they going to do about a flood?" Peter asked.

"It doesn't matter," his mom insisted. "This is the *FBI* you're talking about. They don't mess around."

"I just don't see how it's any of their business," Peter muttered, more to himself than anyone else.

Switching to a violent flutter kick, Jacob's socked feet were coming dangerously close to Marian's face.

"So, we call the FBI and a few people in government," Dan said matter-of-factly. "That way your bases are covered."

"Yeah, maybe I should keep it small, especially since I'm not one hundred percent about this one," Peter said, and his mom nodded in agreement.

A pall settled in the living room; the stag's head with its crown of tines stared down at them.

"Well, you may be sorry you invited me," Marian said, as she pushed Jacob's dirty socks away and sharply scolded him. "Be still!"

For the moment, Jacob complied; even Peter stopped fidgeting.

Marian's looked to Peter. "Like Dan said, this affects the whole city. So it seems to me, the whole city should know about it."

Ms. Quell frowned, clearly displaying her disapproval. The lack of any positive response from Dan made his position plain. Jacob's feet slowly began to churn, causing Marian to snap her fingers and point at her son to stop.

Peter thought about the more than half a million people in the city, and especially the most vulnerable ones who didn't have refuge from rising rivers that snaked through the city.

And that made his mind skip to Jesse, who had set him on the hard, often lonely path of becoming a stronger, more faithful messenger.

"Not too long ago, I met another prophet," Peter said to the surprise of his small audience, including Jacob, who turned right-side-up to listen.

"He told me I couldn't be afraid to go all the way with my dreams. If I stepped out in faith, God would take care of the rest. So that's what I intend to do."

As he said the words, he felt the disapproval from two-thirds of his inner circle, and that would have to be all right. Whether they liked it or not, his circle was about to get a lot bigger.

Not wanting to wait until he could change his mind, Peter made the call that night. He gave Cindy directions to where they were staying on the promise that their location would remain confidential.

Cindy Sizemore was more than willing to come over that night to conduct an interview, but Peter insisted it could wait until morning. He hoped a good night's sleep would clear his head. Instead, the anticipation of being on camera kept him up most of the night.

By the next morning, the dull headache was lingering, and it didn't help that his mom was still sulking about his decision to go public. Whenever he tried to broach the subject, she would say something like, "Do whatever you think. I just hope you and your girlfriend are right."

Peter wasn't sure if she was upset about his decision to announce the dream or because he'd chosen Marian's plan over Dan's. Whatever her reasons, she didn't say much as she got ready and hurried out the door to work.

Not too long after his mom left, Cindy showed up at the front door. Clasping her Venti cup of coffee, the reporter bustled in with her two-man crew carrying cases of equipment. She was wearing more make-up and mascara than usual, and Peter wondered if she was trying to cover her own set of tired eyes.

"Nice place," she said, taking a look around, her eyes scaling the walls to the impressive rack.

"It's not ours," Peter was quick to point out before reminding her, "and you can't even hint at where we're staying."

"Of course," Cindy assured him as she walked over to the two chairs in the living room. "Do you want to do it here?"

"This is fine," Peter said. "Let's just keep it short and sweet."

While the camera and audio guys set up their lights and checked their levels, Cindy and Peter took their seats and quietly sipped their coffees. Despite his third cup, Peter's head was still in a fog. All he wanted to do was repeat his dream and go back to sleep, or maybe give in to his mom's demand to see a doctor.

As soon as she got the sign from her cameraman, Cindy set her cup on the table just out of frame. "You ready to go?"

"Yeah," Peter said. "Let's do it."

After a beat, Cindy started up in her coast-to-coast professional voice. "Thank you, Peter, for granting this second exclusive interview. There are several reports that you confronted Mark Shelton at his church during their service on Sunday. Can you confirm that?"

"Ah, yes, that would be true, Cindy," Peter said, wishing he'd remembered to set some parameters on the interview. What was he thinking? Trying to get back on script, he added, "The real reason I wanted to talk to you was about this new dream."

"Yes, we all want to hear about that, but if I can go back to the church service for just a second," Cindy said, not waiting for an answer. "I've talked to several people who were in attendance. They said you and Mark Shelton were quoting scriptures to each other." She glanced down at her notes. "Mostly from Leviticus."

Resigned to answering a couple of her questions, Peter said, "I heard he was going to be preaching a sermon about homosexuality being against God's law, and I was just pointing out some other things that were against God's law. A lot of them don't get the same amount of attention that homosexuality gets."

"Why do you think that is?" Cindy asked, seemingly interested.

"Mostly because it's easier to target minorities, like gays or immigrants, whenever you need a sacrificial scapegoat," Peter said.

"Speaking of homosexuality," Cindy said without missing a beat. "There have been accusations that you are gay. Care to comment?"

As much as he hated the question, he hated the ease of his answer. Easy answers seemed, well, too easy at this stage. And just like that, he knew what he had to do.

"Yes," Peter declared. "I am gay!"

Surprised by the revelation, Cindy arched her eyebrows as she waited for him to expound.

It was so quiet Peter could hear the camera lens adjusting and feel the eye pushing in for a close-up. After the declaration hung in the air for a long beat, he added matter-of-factly, "And I'm Muslim."

Somewhere in the distance, he could hear Mark Shelton yelling, "I knew it!" at the TV. Cindy just seemed confused.

Into the stunned silence, Peter continued on. "And I am homeless and hungry. And I'm sick and in need of a doctor." The words came easily now; Peter said them without even thinking. "And I'm an immigrant trying to feed my family. And I'm the whole planet that is being abused and not able to sustain the human race much longer."

Cindy didn't seem to know quite how to respond, so after an awkward silence, Peter helped her out. "Can I tell you about my dream now?"

"Yes, please," Cindy said, gratefully.

Peter reached down to the table and calmly took a sip of his coffee. Setting it back down, he felt an eerie calm, like a spirit of peace passing through him.

"I saw myself lying on the ground, and it was raining. The water started to rise. It happened fast in my dream. The water got higher and higher until it swelled up over everything—people, buildings, everything."

Peter's hands spread out, as if coving the Mid-Cumberland Basin.

Cindy waited to make sure he was finished. "And what do you think this means?"

"There's going to be a flood."

"Right here in Nashville?" Cindy asked, growing more concerned.

"Yes," Peter said, anxious for the interview to be over. His head hurt as he squinted into the bright rack of lights. Later, this would cause viewers to speculate he was in the midst of receiving another vision.

"Is there anything else we should know?" Cindy implored.

"I don't know," Peter said, his eyes drifting up the mantle to the majestic deer head. "Get to high ground."

CHAPTER 27

As soon as Cindy and her crew left the house, Peter drove himself to the county hospital. His insurance allowed him to see a doctor, who listened to his symptoms, shone a light in his pupils, and ordered a CT scan, all of which verified a grade 1 concussion. Treatment consisted of getting lots of rest and trying not to slip into a coma.

The drive back to the house was exhausting. The sunlight not only hurt his eyes, it seemed to scream a reminder that there wasn't a cloud in the sky. As was often the case, he began to second guess the way he'd put the prophecy out there in no uncertain terms. Of course, that was water under the bridge now, so to speak.

When he got back to the house, there was a moment of relief when he discovered his mom wasn't home yet. She would want to know all about the doctor's visit, as well as give him the rainless weather report. He thought about calling Marian before realizing she was probably trying to finish up at work so she could hurry home to make dinner for Jacob.

Listening to the quietude only the country could provide,

Peter made a sandwich and ate it slowly at the kitchen table. By the time he finished, he realized he was bone-tired and wrote a note for his mom: *Went to doc...I'm OK. Need sleep.*

Not taking the time to watch his own interview on the news, he went upstairs to his room and closed the door. Lying in bed, he silently prayed for forgiveness for any mistakes or sins he might have made during the day.

Up above, a fast-moving front was rolling in from the West. Warm, wet air collided with the colder, heavier atmosphere, the pressure systems mixing and mingling before settling into the Middle Tennessee basin.

Without a warning peel of thunder or flash of lighting, a soft, silent rain began to fall all around Peter as he drifted off to sleep.

Before leaving for work the next day, his mom woke Peter up just long enough to make sure he was still alive. "Peter?" she cooed. "How is your head?"

"Still there," he said, annoyed and groggy. "What is it?"

"Nothing," she said, backing away. "I was just going to tell you it's raining."

"Really?" Peter said, waking up a bit.

"Don't get too excited," she said. "It's not a hard one. Not enough to flood or anything."

Turning over, he pulled the blankets over his head.

"I'm going to work," Ms. Quell announced, backing out of the bedroom door. "Enjoy your beauty rest."

Around the city, people were waking up to read the front-page story in *The Tennessean* about the latest Peter Quell prophecy. Or they were checking out their local morning TV or radio shows, all of which had pounced on the prediction, along with the "breaking news" that it was, in fact, raining.

Despite Peter's accuracy in the past, no one seemed to be taking the prophecy terribly seriously. The local meteorologists were confident that the front would push out by the afternoon and cheerily reassured folks that this system would not cause much, if any, damage.

As the gray day wore on and the rain stubbornly refused to stop falling, the prophecy began to garner more sober attention. Nashville TV weather reporters interrupted their regular daytime soaps and talk shows with updates, sometimes mentioning Peter's gloomy forecast.

On the radio, a popular DJ only played songs related to rain and kept referring to "Peter's wet dream." Callers to a radio sports show wanted to discuss Peter's record more than the Titans or Predators.

All the while, Peter's flood prophecy began to leak out beyond Nashville. Cable news networks, already familiar with Peter Quell, inserted the story into their regular rotation. A cell phone video recording of the shouting match between the prophet and the pastor at Trinity was putting up big numbers on YouTube.

And, of course, news feeds and tweets kept the prophecy popping. The net result was that "Peter Quell" was the most searched name that day. Not only was Peter back in the news, he was the news—and all the while, Peter remained in a state of torpor, oblivious to all.

By later in the afternoon, the stubborn rainmaker still wasn't going anywhere. Reports that creeks and rivers were inching upward sent people flocking to the windows of their offices and homes to watch what seemed like an attack from above. What would normally be nothing more than an innocuous soaking rain now turned menacing in the wake of Peter's prediction.

With the rainfall measuring seven inches, the Army Corp of Engineers released water from the dams to siphon off the rising lakes. That deluge inflamed the rivers and creeks that snaked through the downtown and suburban neighborhoods.

Drainage ditches filled to the brim; water pooled in low-lying fields and roads; cars slowed to a crawl to traverse the fast-flowing tributaries that were springing up all around them.

While the city was on the verge of panic, Peter slept like a baby to the soothing lullaby pattering above his head. Peacefully floating on a lake of tranquility, he felt so light that he began to rise. The ascension was slow and steady, reminiscent of a hot air balloon without the burst of fire every ten seconds.

Fifty, one hundred, two hundred feet in the air...

The lake I'm drifting on is covering my hometown. There are a few outcroppings of high rises that stand out from the water world, including the Bellsouth "Batman" building.

The apocalyptic vision made Peter aware he was dreaming. As the veil of illusion dropped, he focused on every little sight and sound.

Little dots have taken refuge on the roofs of the scattered buildings and surrounding hilltops. Some of the people are lifting and carrying others above the water line.

Through the steady drumbeat of rain, I think I hear something else, distant and melodic.... Music....

Connecting the dots with the sounds, I realize people are singing a song, a beautiful song.

Sun!

A harsh clacking penetrated his somnambulistic state, threatening to break him out of his fragile dream world. Pushing the annoyance into the background, Peter stayed high above the water, taking in the choir of voices.

A few precious moments later, Peter woke up with a start, succumbing to what he recognized as a loud rap from the front of the house. Scrambling for his journal and a pen, he wrote quickly.

The persistent pounding broke his attention away again. Satisfied he had summed up his vision, he hurried downstairs and through the living room. Swinging the front door open, he looked out into the rain.

Under a yellow rain slicker flashed the fiery eyes of Cindy Sizemore. "I've been out here for twenty minutes!" She turned to motion behind her. "In case you haven't noticed, it's raining!"

"I'm glad you're here. Come on in. We need to talk," Peter said, opening the door wider. Looking down, he added, "Let me put some pants on first."

"You want some coffee?" Peter asked, fully clothed, although still not showered.

"Sure," Cindy said, still shivering from the wet and cold.

"Why are you here?" he asked as he puttered around the kitchen.

"The flood," Cindy said, seated in the high-back chair from which she had conducted their recent interview. "You know, the one you prophesied."

"I knew it was raining," Peter said, glancing toward a window over the sink. "It's really flooding?"

With a sigh, Cindy patiently watched as the impossibly out-of-touch man came over to the living room with their coffees.

"Yes, it's flooding," the reporter said, taking her cup. "People want to hear from you. I didn't know if you had a comment or had anything to add...?"

When he didn't respond, she went on, "Since I'm the only reporter that knows where you are, I thought it was my journalistic duty to follow-up. I tried calling, but all I got was a busy signal."

"Yeah, I unplugged the house phone," Peter said absently.

"Of course, you did," Cindy said, taking a sip and singeing her lips.

"Actually, I think I do," Peter said.

"You do what?" she asked, dabbing at her irritated mouth.

"I think I do want to add something."

This seemed to surprise the reporter. Putting her cup down, she reached into her coat and pulled out a handheld camera. "I'm ready when you are."

Peter sat down on the couch with his mom, who was thankful to have survived the trip home. While preparing their frozen microwaved dinners, she regaled him with harrowing tales of driving through swamped country roads.

Taking their dinners to the sofa, they turned on the TV, curious to see if his interview would make it in time for the local news. Peter was pretty confident it would, knowing if Cindy had to, she would swim to the station.

The weather woman was standing in front of a map with so many whirls and swirls of multi-colored activity it resembled a Vincent Van Gogh painting. While she was giving a never-ending rundown of "flash flood" areas, the resolute voice of Phil the Anchorman broke in.

"I'm sorry to interrupt, Heather," he said, commandeering the camera. "We'll continue to run those flood areas at the bottom of your screen. Right now, Cindy Sizemore has breaking news exclusive only to Channel Seven!"

The shot widened to include their ace reporter, still dripping wet.

"Cindy, I understand you have just gotten back from talking to Peter Quell?"

"That's right," Cindy said, wiping away a streak of eyeliner running down her face. "He had another dream he wanted me to pass along immediately. So let's go ahead and roll that please." The screen filled with a close-up of the hometown prophet.

"Oh, Lord," Ms. Quell muttered at the sight of her son on TV. "I should have stayed home today."

Even Peter was jarred by his own image. Sporting three days of stubble and a potentially terminal case of bedhead, he did not look like the most reliable source of insight and wisdom.

"Okay," Peter said from the TV. "So, I just had a dream. Maybe it was the second half of the earlier dream I had, or maybe the first one got interrupted or something."

After considering that for a moment, he continued. "In this one, the city was still flooding, but I noticed people were on the top of buildings and on hilltops. They were helping each get to higher ground. And they were singing—singing to God."

For a moment, he drifted back to the music, seeming to draw inspiration from the memory. "As everyone sang, the clouds parted, and the sun broke through, and the waters started to go down."

Tossing up his hand, he signaled that was it.

"What do you think the message means, exactly?" Cindy asked off-screen.

"Just that we need to help each other. And turn to God," Peter said, rubbing his head, "especially when things look their worst."

"Talk about looking your worst," Peter heard his mother mumble at her son's rough appearance.

"How do you suggest we turn to God?" Cindy's disembodied voice asked.

"Well, everyone has to work that out," Peter said, his hand having moved down to give his beard stubble a scratch.

"Okay, most of us say we believe in God, and I'm sure most of us do. I'm just saying, we could all live like we really do have faith. For one thing, I don't think God wants us to live in fear of each other.

"We could also show more compassion, especially to those who are struggling to just tread water. You know, the less fortunate." He thought for a moment. "And those who are fortunate, too. I don't think God wants us to hold back. We all need each other more than we know.

"Sometimes we make it so complicated, but Jesus said it comes down to loving our neighbors as ourselves and loving God with all of our hearts.

"The test comes when bad things happen. But even when the storms come, it doesn't mean God doesn't love us. It's an opportunity to find out who we are and to make changes for the better."

243

Suddenly aware that he'd gone on a bit, he smiled shyly. "None of that was in my dream exactly. You just asked me what I thought."

The camera abruptly switched to the anchor desk in the studio.

"That was all he wanted to say," Cindy said, her face cleaned up and her wet hair pulled back.

For once, Phil the Anchorman didn't have a quick retort.

Fortunately, Cindy was there to fill in. "If I can add a personal note?"

"Of course," Phil said gratefully.

"I have followed this story closely from the beginning, and I was skeptical about someone being able to actually see the future," Cindy said. "But I have seen Peter Quell predict the future time and time again."

For a moment, Peter saw the reporter's mask slip.

"What if God is behind it?" Cindy asked her audience, her clipped patter slowing and softening as she talked. "I mean, that's the only way I can explain it. And if it really is God, well, that's a pretty big deal. That's about as big as it gets. Maybe we should listen."

Phil touched his earpiece, waiting for his producer to tell him what to say next. When all he got was deafening silence, he nodded slowly and opened his mouth. "Yes, that's truly something."

Both anchor and reporter sat in an awkward silence before they cut to commercial.

Peter turned off the TV and looked at his mom. "What do you think? Did I go too far?"

"I wish you had taken a shower or at least combed your hair," his mom answered. "But I am proud of you."

"Really?" Peter asked, a little surprised.

"When you first moved home, you were like a whipped puppy with his tail between his legs," she said. "I was proud of you when you started subbing because I knew it was hard for you."

Gesturing to the TV, she said, "And now, my goodness, you don't even bother to take a shower before you talk to the whole city." Shaking her head in disbelief, she added, "You don't see how far you've come, but I do."

"Thanks," Peter said, getting up off the couch. He walked over to his mother and kissed the top of her graying head. After gathering up their plastic dinner containers, he headed to the kitchen to throw them away. "I think I'm going to my room for a while."

"Okay," his mom said, picking up the remote and turning the news back on. When her son came out of the kitchen, she called after him, "So, are we all going to drown, or what?"

"I have no idea," he called back on the way up to his bedroom. "I'm just glad I'm on the second floor."

In his adopted bedroom, he lay down and listened to the steady drumbeat overhead. It seemed like the past few months had been one long, surreal dream. How had he gone from total obscurity to a phenomenon? How had he gone from whispering in Dan's ear to having a scripture smackdown in front of an auditorium of evangelicals who wanted to tear him limb from limb?

His mom was right; he had come a long way.

The phone rang twice and then stopped. He waited, hoping it wasn't for him. Unless…

"It's Marian," his mom called up.

From his bed, Peter anxiously picked up the phone. "Hey! I'm glad it's you!" he said as he heard his mom hang up.

"Hey," Marian said. "Jacob wants to know when it's going to stop raining."

"I wish I knew," Peter said.

"We just saw the newscast," Marian said. "You had *another* dream?"

"Yeah," Peter said. "I woke up this afternoon, and there was Cindy at the door. It was kind of weird."

"Should I be jealous?" Marian asked, half-kidding.

"The minute I stop being a story is the minute she loses all interest in me," Peter said.

"Then I should be pretty jealous, because you and the flood

245

are all that's on TV," Marian said. "Channel Seven is almost looping the latest interview you did, and the cable channels are practically doing a Peter Quell marathon. They even have a video of you and Mark Shelton going at it at his church."

"Great," Peter said, continually in awe of the speed and omnipresence of the internet.

"I'm telling you, you're everywhere," Marian assured him.

"Yeah, well, don't get used to it," Peter said. "Trust me, in a couple of days, I'll be yesterday's news again."

"You act like you'll never have another dream."

"I don't know," Peter said as he stretched out over the length of his bed. "I feel empty." He paused. "Like I'm all dreamed out. And I'm okay with that."

"Okay," she said acceptingly.

"What about you?" he asked.

"What about me?"

"Will you still love me if I never have another dream?"

"I already told you, I was fascinated with a guy who could see the future," she said with a chuckle. "But honestly, being in a relationship with a prophet is not all it's cracked up to be. So, yes, I'll love you even if you never have another dream."

After they said their good nights, Peter listened to the sound of falling rain. Spontaneously, he began to pray for those who were caught in the rising waters, that God would have mercy on them all. And he prayed that his dreams would make a difference, even a tiny difference, to the people who had heard them.

As his thoughts became as diffused and colorful as fireworks bursting in the night, he knew sleep was coming fast and bringing dreams with it. Something told him these would not be dreams of things to come. These were of the here and now.

For one night only, he would be allowed to see through the eyes of God…

CHAPTER 28

As night fell, waters rose. Ankle-deep creeks morphed into raging rivers; rivers eclipsed their banks and sprawled into lakes; lakes reached out to form indoor swimming pools. Low-lying areas were filled first, then the flood seeped into basements and crawl spaces before beginning the steady ascent to the main floors of homes and businesses around the city.

Community centers and homeless shelters were the first line of defense, actively going out and bringing in those with nowhere to go. Trinity, Grace, and Victory were just three of the many churches that opened their doors to souls seeking a dry sanctuary. Doors were opened at the mosque in Columbia to any neighbors needing refuge from the rain.

Neighborhoods banded together, gathering in homes for moral support and to make plans to evacuate if needed. Some checked on family members and elderly neighbors; others took the opportunity to reflect on their lives and how they would do better if the rain ever stopped.

Having fled the TV station, Cindy Sizemore plowed through swamped city streets to her downtown apartment. As she navigated past abandoned cars, her head swam with her on-the-air, off-the-cuff comments. For some reason, she had jettisoned her planned remarks and editorialized way past the point of professional journalism.

Pulling her car into the damp underground parking garage, she punched in her security code and took the elevator up to the twelfth floor, wondering how much longer she would even be living there. Stations in Miami and Houston had already contacted her about jobs. Hopefully, she hadn't blown it with her outburst.

Entering her meticulously clean one-bedroom apartment, she gravitated toward her favorite feature—the view from the wall of windows. With her head almost in the dark clouds, she stared at the grotesquely engorged Cumberland River, all the while trying to find perspective on the Peter Quell story.

From the very beginning, she had asked to cover the holy roller who had supposedly predicted the stock market crash. Once she had the assignment, she had chased it down with everything she had, wanting to expose "the prophet" as the fraud he surely was.

But Peter had confounded her. He seemed clueless, even as prophecy after prophecy came true. And she began to ask herself, *What if he's real?* That question begged the ultimate follow-up, *What if God is real?*

She wasn't sure what acknowledging God would mean exactly, although she had a sneaking suspicion it might be inconvenient to her career plans. There was an aggressive schedule in place, and she didn't want anything, including God, detouring her.

And yet, she couldn't escape the fundamental question of her reason for being. It had always been there, lurking in the background, nipping at her heels, wanting an answer.

As lightning flashed in the distance, she caught her own reflection in the plate glass window. Instantly, she had her answer.

It had been waiting on her all along, and it was so obvious it took her breath away.

She had not been chasing the story; the story had been chasing her. More accurately, God had been chasing her. God knew her name, and He wanted her. That night, on the twelfth floor, Cindy Sizemore let herself be found.

Sending a splash pluming into the air, a BMW roared away from a "SoBro" watering hole, one of the only places Ed Pressman could still find a few ears willing to listen to his rants, especially when he was buying the rounds. Fueled by alcohol, he savored the angry power that coursed through his veins, even if it was a faint echo of the feeling he used to get when thousands had hung on his every word.

Punching the programmed radio stations, he stumbled across a replay of the "prophet's" latest soft-headed pronouncement; the sappy speech about "God" and "love" almost made him puke. Was the nutcase actually suggesting everyone should just hold hands and sing "Kumbaya" until the rain stopped?

The world has lost its freaking mind, Ed thought as he swerved past a timid subcompact cautiously inching its way through a water-covered street. People needed a strong, unvarnished voice that told them how it was, even if the truth was harsh and ugly.

With his blood boiling hot, he hit the gas and surged into an intersection with a blinking yellow light overhead. This time, the water did not spray; it just swirled in thick currents around him as the sheer volume sucked him deeper into the channel.

The torrents running past his windows took his breath away. Feeling his high-performance tires lose their touch with the asphalt, his anxiety spiked. Grappling to suppress complete panic, he looked around.

From a safe distance behind him, the subcompact had stopped to watch him float away. Buildings and lights slowly twirled as his car languidly spun in the water's unassailable grip.

Totally at the mercy of the dark rapids, Ed actually felt a wave of relief when he slammed against a retaining wall underneath an overpass. At least he had stopped moving.

Assessing his situation, he realized the driver's door was pinned against a slab of concrete while the passenger side was being pounded by a constant rush of water. All at once, Ed knew he needed help.

While he talked a lot about God on his radio show—mostly with phrases like "God-given rights" or "God-fearing Americans"—he hadn't really given the Big Man a whole lot of thought. After all, Ed had been "the big man"—an invisible voice who commanded others what to think and who to hate. Now his legions of listeners had vanished, and he was utterly alone.

For the first time, God had Ed's undivided attention. The shock jock's first thought was to make some kind of a deal; however, this idea was immediately rebuffed with a cold slap of water that had found its way into his car. Realizing God was in no mood to bargain, Ed got real and prayed like his life depended on it.

Phillip Drake cursed the rain. He had spent most of the afternoon with his attorney, and if that wasn't bad enough, he was struggling to get home to spend what precious little of his freedom he had left with his wife.

For the moment, he was out on bail, although his lawyer assured him it was just a temporary reprieve. No matter what kind of deal he cut, he was going to do time.

Contrary to public opinion, he hadn't started out with a master plan to deceive anyone. He had made some poor investment decisions, and rather than humble himself and come clean, he had papered over the losses with increasingly elaborate deceptions. When the market crashed, his time to make things right ran out.

With a heavy sigh, the once pillar of the community glanced over at a building where one of his former clients worked. Just below the portico, he made out a poor schmuck trying to find shelter. As the man turned, his face was illuminated by a streetlamp, and for a split second, Drake thought it might actually be his old investor.

The sad truth was, it was not entirely impossible, since he had squandered most of the man's money. Many of his customers had lost their retirement funds, kid's college savings, and even their homes. Whenever he dwelled on the havoc he had wreaked, it drove him to despair. Sometimes, he wasn't sure he could live with the overwhelming sense of guilt.

Pulling over, Drake surprised himself by getting out of the car and hurrying over to the hunched-over man. As he approached, he could plainly see this was not his ex-client and couldn't understand how he had ever been mistaken in the first place. This black man was grizzled and gnarled from years of living on the streets.

"Are you all right?" he asked the man who was clearly not.

"It's pretty bad out here," the homeless man understated.

"At least God promised not to destroy the world with a flood again, right?" Drake said in an awkward attempt at humor.

"He didn't say nothing about Nashville, though," the man retorted.

"That's true," Drake admitted, watching water spew out of the holes in a manhole cover like mini geysers. "Do you have a place to go tonight?"

The man shrugged, as if this was it.

"Well, you can't stay here," Phillip Drake heard himself say.

A soggy nametag hung by a thread to the man's jacket, the name almost indecipherably smeared and faded. Taking the man by the arm, Phillip led him toward his warm, dry car.

"Come on," Phillip gently urged, straining to read the name tag. "You're coming home with me tonight, Jesse."

The water was coming for Tom McAllister. Already lapping under his doorway and finding its way through the walls of his apartment, it was a sure sign, if ever there was one, that God was out to get him.

251

All Tom had ever wanted was acceptance, and he had found it at Victory Church. One of the first to enlist in Mark Shelton's army of Christian warriors, he had felt strong, aligning himself behind someone as unyielding and virtuous as Shelton. It was also easier to take a stand against the evils of the world within a cocoon-like platoon.

When Mark began to preach against Peter, Tom had quickly joined in the prophet bashing. Since they had been in the same youth group, Tom could bring a more personal touch to his insults—*Even back then, he thought he was better than everyone else.*

When Mark Shelton heard that one of his parishioners personally knew the "prophet," he asked him to try and get closer to Peter. Wanting to please his pastor, Tom continued to leave messages, none of which were ever returned. The snub further enraged Tom, proving that Peter was truly a tool of the Prince of Darkness.

When all else failed, Mark summoned Tom to his office for a private meeting. There, he told him he had launched an investigation and knew for a fact that Peter was gay; he just couldn't find anyone brave enough to step forward with firsthand testimony. The pastor then proceeded to guide Tom through a hypothetical "conversation" that could have taken place.

Before Tom knew what was happening, Mark had set up a meeting with a television producer, forcing him to go through with the charade. Tom wasn't comfortable with what he was being asked to do, but Mark reassured him he was serving a greater good by speaking out.

There were lots of pats on the backs and hugs of support from around church that helped shore up his difficult decision. It wasn't until Peter had come to Victory and mouthed the words "Leviticus 11:19"—*Do not lie*—that Tom fully recognized what he had done.

He had betrayed a prophet, and it felt like the flood wasn't going to stop until it swallowed him whole. Trapped and afraid, Tom just wanted out from under the crushing weight of his sin.

Lifting up his voice, he cried aloud, pleading for Father in Heaven to have mercy on his soul.

With water sloshing around him, Ed Pressman desperately scanned the receding faux woodgrain dashboard for an ejection seat or a panic button to push. Water was pouring into the car, transforming his luxury sedan into a roomy, soon-to-be-submerged casket.

In his moment of desperation, a loud crash landed on his sarcophagus lid. Thinking the bridge had collapsed on top of him, Ed yelped and jumped up, hitting his head on the tinted glass above him. Looking up through his moon roof, he could make out a shadowy figure standing directly over him.

The stranger bent down and rapped hard on the tempered glass. Pushing a button on his console, Ed was surprised the electrical system still worked well enough to even open the roof. As soon as the glass slid back, an open hand reached down into the interior.

Instinctually, Ed grabbed hold, allowing the strong arm to wench his wet, heavy body upward. Placing his shoes on the car seat, he managed to stand up through the opening. The man on the roof took hold under Ed's armpits and pulled Ed's torso out, leaving Ed to squirm the rest of the way.

Crouched on top of his rapidly filling car, Ed breathlessly looked up into the dark eyes and deeply-lined face of the Hispanic man standing next to him. With the cold water flowing around them, it felt like they were just two men marooned on a tiny island in the middle of a monsoon.

The man motioned for Ed to follow as he leapt with surprising agility to the inclined retaining wall. Reaching back, he offered Ed his leather mitt of a hand, and once again, Ed latched on. Anchored in place, the Hispanic man swung Ed to the relative safety of the concrete slab.

From there, they both scrambled up the embankment to the

overpass. At the guardrail beside the second-story street, the man waited on Ed to catch up. Bent over and breathing hard from the exertion, Ed reached the railing and grabbed hold to steady himself.

"Thanks," he muttered between gasps of air.

"You okay?" the man asked in a Spanish accent.

Ed nodded, glancing down at the river of water ten feet below them. It was overtaking his car and draining like a whirlpool into the moon roof. When he looked back up, the man was rambling across the bridge.

"Wait!" Ed called after him. Digging into his soaked pockets, he fished out some bills. Not bothering to look at the denominations, he shoved the money outward. "Here!"

Turning, the man seemed surprised, if not confused by the gesture. "No, no, it's okay," he insisted in broken English, offering up a smile in return. "Vaya con Dios," he said, before disappearing into the night.

Already on edge about the weather, Sandra Drake was worried about her husband. She knew Phillip was prone to bouts of depression these days and wondered if he might allow himself to be swept away in the waters. There were moments when she half-wished he would disappear, along with all the shame he had caused them.

When she heard the front door open, she gave thanks to God and asked for forgiveness for her terrible thoughts. As she rounded the corner, she saw a ragged black man standing in her foyer, dripping on her travertine floors with her husband at his side.

"This is Jesse," Phillip Drake announced. "Jesse, this is my wife Sandra."

The man was not there to kill them, at least not immediately, and her alarm was replaced with general confusion and concern.

Ever the Southern hostess, Sandra tried to feign a smile as if this was all perfectly normal. She had tried to remain gracious when her husband lost their money, their status, their friends, and now, apparently, his mind. She would even be gracious when she left him.

Jesse stared at Ms. Drake for a moment before returning to admiring the impressive house with cathedral ceilings and gothic columns in the entryway. "You got a nice place here."

"Thank you," she said amiably.

"Let's put him in the main guest room downstairs," Phillip suggested.

"Oh, is Jesse staying the night?" Sandra asked over a lump in her throat.

"We can't let him stay out there," he said as he motioned to the water slapping against their arched, double-pained windows.

Turning to his new houseguest, Phillip asked, "Are you hungry?" Jesse nodded. "Okay, why don't I make you something to eat in the kitchen while Sandra shows you to your room?"

Resigned to the fact this was actually happening, Sandra walked down the hallway with her house guest. "We'll put you in the first room on the right."

"You don't have to worry," Jesse said, turning into the bedroom. "I'm not going to steal your good china."

"Oh, no, of course not," Sandra said, faking a laugh as she stood at the doorway, clutching her throat.

"It's a good thing your husband is doing," Jesse said reassuringly.

"Yeah," she managed.

"You know," Jesse said softly, "everyone deserves a second chance."

"Yes, well," she said, trying to find the right thing to say in this uncharted social situation. "I'm sure you'll get back on your feet."

"I'm not talking about me," Jesse said.

Sandra blinked, not sure if she had heard the man right. "I'll be back in a minute," she stammered before hurrying back down the hall.

Bustling into the kitchen, she found her husband foraging through the refrigerator. "What are you doing?" she cried.

"I'm making a sandwich," he said innocently.

"You know what I mean," Sandra hissed over the granite island. "This is crazy!"

Phillip turned around, a loaf of bread in his hand. "It feels right," he said with real compassion for the strain he was putting on his wife. "The court will probably take the house next month. But tonight, we have six bedrooms, five that we never use. I mean, what is crazier...for us to let Jesse use one of our rooms, or to let him sleep in the rain?"

"We don't know him," Sandra reminded him. While her husband didn't have an answer to that, he didn't seem bothered by it either. "Did you tell him about your charges?"

"No," Phillip said. "Why?"

Sandra shook her head, privately wondering about the mysterious stranger down the hall.

Putting the bread down, Phillip came around the counter and reached out to draw his wife to him. "Let me do this one good thing," he said into her hair.

As he clutched her tight, she closed her eyes and, in a whisper, repeated, "Everyone deserves a second chance."

Living on high ground, Jordan Stone wasn't particularly worried about the flood, and yet, she felt nervous all the same. As she patted her growing belly, she knew that Peter Quell was for real. Actually, she had known that for a while; she just hadn't fully accepted it because that would mean God was watching her.

She was not proud that she had been unfaithful to her husband. Because she'd been too scared to tell her "boyfriend" about the pregnancy, he had learned about it when she announced it on national TV. Just as she feared, he wanted nothing to do with her or the baby. For the first time in her life, Jordan Stone felt alone.

Asking for forgiveness from God, she had found some relief, although that hadn't solved all her problems. No longer able to play Little Miss Perfect, she wasn't sure where she would go from here. To her surprise, part of her was actually relieved to be free of her old persona.

Acting on a moment of inspiration, she got out her guitar and, after spending several minutes getting it back in tune, put a few angry power chords together. She hadn't written an original song in years, and the feeling was so old it was new again.

Already feeling judged and found guilty, she put together her lyrical defense. A far cry from the usual fare of sentimental songs typically selected for her albums, this was raw and personal. Maybe it was terrible, too, but she didn't care what anyone else thought. She was writing this one for herself.

Drop the Rock

I'm not the girl you thought you knew
If I fool you twice, shame on you
You say I'm a girl with bad behavior
But I'm just a sinner in search of a Savior
I don't need the cheers of my so-called fans
Just the forgiveness from one good man
Cause when the world said they wanted me dead
He knelt down and wrote in the sand
He said...
Drop the rock if you've ever sinned
Drop the rock you have in your hand
Drop the rock and make my day
Drop the rock and walk away
What you do to others, you do to me,
So, drop the rock and set yourself free

EPILOGUE

By the following morning, the rain had stopped, and dabs of sunlight managed to filter though the thinning clouds. It was a welcome sight, met with cheers of joy and tears of relief from a weary city.

But even as the rivers were retreating, they were leaving broken dreams and heartache in their wake. Ruined flooring, wet dry wall, and warped furniture began to pile up in front of mud-plastered homes.

Subdivisions that had never been considered in a floodplain were declared federal disaster zones. Local and federal officials were on the scene, offering assistance to thousands of displaced citizens. Businesses, large and small, were closed, many never to reopen.

Without any instructions, Nashvillians spontaneously congregated in the hardest hit areas, selflessly pitching in to help each other out. From contractors to musicians, everyone was a neighbor, regardless of what they did or where they lived.

Mark Shelton grabbed the first available microphone to announce, "The flood never got as high as Peter Quell described, clearly making him a false prophet. Furthermore, no one changed as a result of the flood. And I didn't hear any singing."

Mark's attacks abruptly stopped when Tom McAllister came forward to retract his earlier statement. "What I said about Peter Quell was not true," he told the newspaper. "I don't really know Peter Quell anymore, and I certainly don't know anything about his sexuality. As far as I know, he's the real deal, a prophet of God, and I hope and pray he'll find it in his heart to forgive me."

Tom did not find a great deal of forgiveness from his own church, which dwindled from an army for God to a small squadron of Mark's followers.

When Jordan approached her record label with her new collection of self-written songs, she was promptly dropped like a rock. So she produced the album herself and found an independent label to distribute it. Despite playing everywhere, from bars to coffeehouses, sales languished, and critics scoffed.

Everything changed when she appeared on a popular daytime talk show and gave an open interview about her struggles with her marriage. Many of her older fans gave her a second chance while a wider audience gave her new songs a first listen. Catapulted back on the charts, her album went double platinum.

Because of the press conference at the coal plant disaster, an up-and-coming filmmaker became aware of Victor Birdsong and featured him in a documentary that became a centerpiece of the environmental movement. Eventually, Birdsong was invited to speak before a congressional committee that forged a forward-thinking, comprehensive energy policy.

Abbas continued to speak for the Muslim community, trying to persuade others that the vast majority of people who shared his religion simply wanted to worship in peace. Hassin and his fellow mosque members in Columbia attempted to quietly exercise their religious freedom, all the while keeping one eye on Mecca and one eye on their neighbors.

After several years as a successful national reporter, Cindy

Sizemore became the host of *Modern Miracles*, a reality show that explored the supernatural events that take place all around us.

Ed Pressman eventually got a new radio gig and could regularly be heard bashing taxes, terrorists, unions, and liberals; although some said his views on "undocumented immigrants" had softened.

Congressman Bragg became a well-paid lobbyist for the pharmaceutical industry.

After Phillip Drake was released from prison, he and his wife started a homeless ministry that provided a place to stay for society's castaways while also giving them job training and assistance.

Dr. Dan Cox remained the pastor of Trinity Church for years to come, becoming a leading voice for reconciling denominational differences and even hosting an annual forum to promote interfaith understanding.

There was a whirlwind of interest about Peter Quell immediately following the flood. Some didn't see that anything had changed and wanted him to explain the error of his interpretation. Others still believed and eagerly wanted to hear the next pronouncement from the prophet.

When no new dreams surfaced, attention slowly began to fade. And, as they always do, new disasters and scandals came along to divert public attention. People remembered the prophecies, although somewhere along the way, Peter became more suburban legend than man.

For the real person, life settled into a comfortable routine. Much to his surprise, with some concerted effort, he found a decent job, and as soon as he was able, he rented a small house. Eventually, he started going to a small church near where he lived, often attending with Marian and Jacob.

The dreams left as suddenly as they had come, and he found himself missing them more than he had imagined. Truth be told, he even felt a nostalgic twinge for the attention they had brought him.

It was during those times he reminded himself of the enormous burden of responsibility that also came with them.

In place of his dreams, he tried to practice the art of contentment: appreciating a job well done, a home-cooked meal, time spent with a friend. He looked for the beauty in the little things that came his way, from a chance encounter with a stranger to a seemingly mundane chore.

Life was good, and he rarely complained, and yet, sometimes, it felt like something was missing.

Then one Sunday afternoon while he was enjoying the simple pleasure of a nap, the curtain of foggy sleep lifted to reveal a vivid, multi-colored stage. It was a *dream*, like the ones he used to have, and when he woke, he felt refreshed and excited.

Scrambling around, he searched for his old red journal, finally finding it buried in a desk drawer below a stack of computer paper and a cell phone charger. Flipping through what seemed like reams of forgotten dreams, he came to a blank page toward the end.

Taking a moment to collect the images and words in his head, he slowly began to write them out once again.

Sunday

I'm in a meadow, gazing up through trees limbs to a blue sky. Out of the glow of the sun, a hazy figure takes shape. The man looks familiar as he settles on the grass, and then I recognize him, looking better than the last time I saw him.

"Jesse!" I call out. "How have you been?"

"Me? Just living the dream," the older prophet says with a wink. He wears new clothes and has been to the barber. "How are you doing, young blood?"

"I'm okay," I say.

"Yes, I believe you are." Raising an eyebrow, he asks, "You still dreaming dreams?"

"Not for a while," I say. "Well, except now."

Jesse nods, seeming to already know this. "You know, you don't have to dream dreams to do the Big Man's bidding. There are always jobs to do—here, there, everywhere. Just keep your eyes open." Glancing upward, he adds, "He'll show you what to do."

"I already do that," I say, maybe a little defensively.

"Yeah?" Jesse says, a note of disbelief in his voice. "Don't be afraid to take some chances, make some mistakes. That's all a part of it."

I nod, suddenly recalling recent opportunities I had probably missed.

"Well, I got to be heading down the road," Jesse says, already fading away. "Oh, I was supposed to tell you," he says as he brightens back up a bit. "You did all right back there."

"Thanks," I say, knowing he's referring to the prophecies. "I don't feel like I made much of a difference."

"Most everyone feels that way," Jesse says with a nonchalant shrug. "You just do the best you can; let God work out the rest." He cocks his head as if listening to a private signal only he can hear. "You did more than you know."

Jesse's smile blends with the sunlight just before he dissolves into the background. For a moment, I stare through the trees, hoping he'll make another appearance yet knowing he won't. And I'm okay with that, because he has delivered the message I needed to hear...

Even if I never have another dream, my work isn't done.

In fact, I'm just getting started.

The End

AFTERWORD

Thank you for taking the time to read *Hometown Prophet*. If you enjoyed the book, I hope you'll leave a review on Amazon or your place of purchase. There is also a sequel coming.

Hometown Prophet is a work of fiction, but does include some events that have taken place in Tennessee. The US experienced a bear market from October 9, 2007 until March 9, 2009, with the S&P 500 losing 50% of its value.

The coal ash spill at the TVA Kingston Fossil Plant in Kingston, Tennessee, occurred on December 22, 2008. In February 2008, the Islamic Center in Columbia, Tennessee, was destroyed by arson. And on May 1, 2010, Nashville experienced a flood that has been described as the worst natural disaster in the city's history.

These were inspirations for some of the dreams. The events themselves were fictionalized, and the timeline between them was compressed for the sake of the story.

Any other similarities with actual events or real persons are purely coincidental.

The theory that Uncle John discusses in Chapter 20 is taken from ideas found in *The Origin of Consciousness in the Breakdown in the Bicameral Mind* (1976) by the late Princeton professor Julian Jaynes.

AMERICAN PROPHET

Ten years later, Peter once again begins to have dreams in *American Prophet*. Some of the same characters are back, and the stakes are even higher.

In an age of viral pandemics and social media posts, Peter's popularity soars to new heights. Along with the adulation, Peter is up against powerful adversaries, including the President himself. As his dreams take him on a spiritual journey through a divided country, his greatest challenge will be learning to love his enemies.

Please visit www.jefffulmer.com for updates, promos, and maybe even a prophetic word.

Made in the USA
Las Vegas, NV
13 April 2024

88617233R00157